Bryn's Virtues
Courage

TreVaughn Malik Roach-Carter

Winnipeg, Canada

Developmental editor: Sanford Larson
Proofreader: Francisco Feliciano

Published September 2025 by Dreamsphere Books, an imprint of Story Perfect Books.

Dreamsphere Books
PO Box 51053 Tyndall Park
Winnipeg, Manitoba R2X 3B0
Canada

Visit dreamspherebooks.com for more great reads.

To my mother,
who supports me in
everything that I do.

Bryn's Virtues
Courage

Chapter 1

Light danced in the air like a vibrating symphony. The gold-and-white tiled floor reflected sunlight and bathed the hall in warmth. There was a sense of quiet that I didn't expect. Just beyond the hall was a loud and bustling bullpen, overflowing with hard-working journalists. The sounds and energy of life didn't flow through the closed doors at the end of the hall, creating an illusion of quiet loneliness. I was never afraid of being left alone with my thoughts, but to be confronted by silence in this situation made my mind feel much too exposed.

"Nervous?" a soft voice asked.

"Is it that obvious?" I responded. The girl next to me had short black hair tucked neatly behind her ears.

"It's not uncommon," she said, releasing a sound that was a mixture between a giggle and a sigh. "This is intimidating. I'm sure most people never imagined they'd make it this far."

We were both candidates for the Executive Assistant position, to Elizabeth Stone, the head of Divinity Magazine. It was the most influential fashion magazine anyone could read, much less work for.

We sat in a waiting room located between Miss Stone's office and the bullpen. This room's floors and walls were gold and white. The furniture was purple. An empty glass desk sat by the office door: This was where the future Executive Assistant would work.

"I know what you mean," I told her. "This is the fourth place I've interviewed this week. All the others...dead ends." I had been searching for jobs in fashion for two years, and other than clothing stores, I hadn't been very lucky. Then I heard about this position opening up. I jumped at the chance to apply, even if I was almost guaranteed rejection.

"Oh wow, that sounds exhausting," the girl said with a drop of her jaw. "I can't even imagine. This is the only job I'm applying for. Elizabeth Stone is the best, and I need the best. I had my dad make some calls to get me an interview."

I didn't even want to ask what gave her father the power to make a call like that.

"That's nice of him," I said with a smile, ready to be rid of the conversation.

"I applaud you for trying out for this," she told me, her voice a hint heavier than before.

"What does that mean?" I asked. Her eggshell pantsuit was clearly worth more than a month's rent on my apartment. If anyone had an advantage, it was the girl in designer clothes. Definitely not the girl whose entire wardrobe was made up of thrift store finds and self-made ensembles. It went without saying.

"Don't get me wrong, I'm all for you putting yourself

out there. I support and respect you for that." She raised her shoulders and bared a small smile as if to hide what she was saying behind some form of innocence. "It's just that…this interview is just a formality for me. It doesn't seem fair to you."

It went without saying, but there she was: saying it.

"So, you think I should just give up?" I felt heat rumble just beneath my skin. I knew exactly what she meant, but I wanted to make her say it with her chest.

"I didn't mean anything bad at all!" she insisted. "I just hate watching people embarrass themselves."

"Embarrass myself? I should be embarrassed because I don't have a rich white daddy who can call and get me a job at a place where most people would kill to even have their application read," I scoffed. "You're right; my chances of getting this job are slim. But that shouldn't be because of the privilege you wield like a weapon. You, me, and everyone else applying should be on equal ground, separated by qualifications, not status. Don't act like you're doing me a favor by telling me to give up. Especially when you have no problem benefiting from the unfairness."

"I didn't mean to offend you," the girl huffed, crossing her arms. "I just—"

"Don't try to justify what you're saying. I'm not trying to hear any of it!"

"You're being so aggressive for no reason," she stammered as her pale cheeks and ears reddened. "I'm not saying anything bad!"

"Really? Because it sounds like you're trying to

intimidate me, which isn't *good*." My voice bounced off the walls of the empty lounge and echoed down the joining hallway. "I'm a person with experience, qualifications, and a personality. If I get this job or any other job, I shouldn't have to jump hurdles—that are simultaneously boosting you—to do so!"

"Excuse me," a low, regal voice said. The two of us looked up to see a tall woman wearing a smooth black double breasted blazer dress with gold embroidered lapels and a large golden belt buckle at the waist. She stood beside a younger blonde girl, in a flowing yellow high waisted maxi skirt and a salmon-colored lace blouse, holding a stack of papers.

The woman, who was most definitely Elizabeth Stone, looked at the two of us with an unamused glare. The blonde girl's eyes were widened and full of concern.

Elizabeth Stone had a strong and sturdy build. Her skin was dark, and her hair was a ball of curls. She was stunning, dripping with excellence.

"What are your names?" Miss Stone asked with no inflection.

"I'm Cassidy Johnsen!" The girl jumped up from her chair and stood in front of me.

Miss Stone put her hand out to the blonde girl, who handed her the top paper from the pile. "My first interview today. Your application looks quite impressive." She examined the papers and then looked Cassidy square in the face while she tore the application in half. "But what I heard here is not."

"You're not even going to meet with me?" Cassidy whined. "You've got the wrong idea!"

"I don't think I do. I absolutely don't want someone who acts like you just did working on my magazine, especially not directly under me. I've had to hurdle many obstacles to get where I am today. I'm not in the business of building more for those who come after me."

"That's not fair," Cassidy protested.

"Seems you're only concerned about fairness when it benefits you," she responded with swiftness. "You may go."

"My dad—"

"You may go." Miss Stone took the rest of the papers from the blonde. "Please escort her out of the building."

The girl approached Cassidy and gently guided her down the hall, remaining silent as Cassidy argued and complained.

"Thank you for that," I told Miss Stone. "I'm a very big fan of yours, so the fact that you've stood up for me here means the world to me. I just wanted to say that before I left. I'll see myself out." I turned to walk away but she stopped me with her voice.

"Why would you leave?"

"I just blew up on that girl. It wasn't very professional."

"You stood up for yourself. I value the strength that takes." She smiled. "Whoever taught you that professionalism is more important than your integrity was dead wrong."

"So, you're still going to interview me?" I asked her.

"What is your name?" she asked.

"Bryn Gonzalez-Ortiz," I answered, straightening my back and putting my interview face back on, trying my best to wipe away any embarrassment or surprise.

Miss Stone stopped flipping through the pages and looked at me. She narrowed her eyes for a moment. Her body shuddered and my mind wavered while I tried to determine what that reaction meant. She tore her eyes away from me and went back to the papers. She pulled a particularly thin application to the top of the pile and said, "Come on in."

Her office was bigger than my living room. A large redwood desk sat in front of a brown loveseat with two matching cushioned chairs on the opposite side. The walls were decorated with landscape paintings of nature. Images of lush green forests of flowers and trees, frolicking does, and naked women bathing in rivers and waterfalls. The entire wall behind the desk was a giant mural of vibrant colors. A beautiful island floating in an ocean of crystal blue waters. Prismatic colors made up the sky. Pearly white buildings were embedded into the mountains of the land. I felt like I could have walked directly through the painting and found myself on the sandy shores of the island it depicted. I didn't recognize it, but I could only imagine it was even more breathtaking in person.

"Do you like it?" Miss Stone said. "I had an artist friend paint it for me. It's a personification of paradise. Makes the office feel less…constricting."

"This isn't what I expected your workspace to look like," I told her.

"Why is that?" She sat down at her desk. I suddenly regretted speaking the thought out loud, but it was too late to take it back.

"I expected more fashion photography or prints of magazine covers," I told her, taking a seat in front of the desk. "Less nature and fantasy islands. Not that there is anything wrong with that!" I hoped she didn't think I was laying down judgment. I was just surprised.

"This is me," she said with a smile. "I feel like my personal space should reflect me. There is enough work out there with the staff."

"That's understandable," I said.

"Let's get into it," she said, laying my application on her desk. "This is an interview for a position as my personal assistant. You'd be replacing Mila, the young woman who was with me earlier. She isn't being fired, don't worry. She's moving up to other things, and I'm incredibly happy for her. How did you hear about the position?"

She spoke all at once as if she didn't have time for pauses and wouldn't allow for interruptions, as if to tell me I wouldn't speak until she decided it was my turn.

"It's kind of funny actually," I began. "I'm currently looking for a job and I've been applying at boutiques, looking into stylist positions, and even tailoring jobs. No offers were coming my way, and I needed money, so I started helping out my downstairs neighbor." I shifted in my seat as I became painfully aware of the eyes staring at me and the ears intently listening. "She runs a business from her apartment. She sells jewelry, art, and things. She needed someone to run some deliveries. While making my first delivery, I stopped at this little café and the man in front of me in line was on the phone talking about how Elizabeth Stone was looking for a new assistant. I don't know who he was, but I jumped at the opportunity. I mailed my application here the next day."

"How lucky," she said, looking at my forms on her desk. "And what got you into this line of work?"

"We tell a story with our appearance. Everything from our hair, to our clothes, to our accessories, to the color of our underwear." Miss Stone stifled a laugh. "We use these tools to express our inner selves, the person we want to be, or even messages that we want to tell anyone who looks at us. I think that's an amazing and powerful art form. So, studying and writing about that has always appealed to me." My answer felt very generic. Probably because I practiced saying that in the mirror too much. It felt like the exact thing that you would expect an interviewer to want to hear, so you say it. But it was still my truth. And I hoped she saw it for what it was.

She looked at me for a long moment. Was this a look of disappointment? I opened my mouth to speak, not knowing what to say next, but she spoke before I could. "So, you want to be a Fashion Journalist? You know that's not what this position is."

"Oh yeah! I get that," I assured her. "But I figured that this is the best place for me to break into this field. You're an icon in this industry. So being your assistant, working directly under you, and learning from you would be an amazing opportunity."

"Something you couldn't pass up," Miss Stone said softly.

"If I passed up the opportunity," I explained. "I'd never forgive myself."

"An opportunity you don't think you can get?" she asked, an eyebrow raised. Was she trying to insinuate that I was naive for applying?

"If I didn't think I had a chance, I wouldn't be here," I told her. "I'd be stupid to think I had a huge chance. But a small chance is better than no chance." I was an inexperienced college dropout, and my only reference was my high school Journalism teacher. There was nothing on paper that would make me stand out to this woman. But my parents always taught me to show my worth, beyond what is seen on the surface. I knew that if I was hired, she wouldn't regret it for a second. Even though I didn't have a lot of experience to show for it, I knew that I was a skilled writer with an eye for fashion. I just needed to get my foot in the door and I would soar.

"I like that mentality," Miss Stone said, leaning back into her chair. "I think that it will take you far in this industry. In life too."

"Thank you," I said, feeling a glowing warmth in my chest.

"One more question," she sighed heavily. "Tell me about an obstacle in your life and how you overcame it."

I hated these kinds of questions. I got them a lot. Too much. I always felt like people wanted me to talk about racism or transphobia. But I never wanted to. Not that these things didn't plague me. They definitely did. There was only one true answer to these types of questions, but I couldn't talk about it. Not fully.

"I'm adopted," I said firmly. Her facial expression responded for a brief moment, but I couldn't decipher what her mind was saying. "I have wonderful parents who love me and accept me. That's never been an obstacle."

"Then what was?" she asked me. The interview was verging into odd therapy territory.

It was risky, but subtlety was my best friend in these situations. "Not to get into specifics…"

"You don't have to say anything you're uncomfortable with," she told me. A sense of safety rested in her voice, and I felt a little bit better.

"The curiosity." I found the words that bridged truth and lie. "I never felt the need to know them. I didn't need my bio parents as parents. I needed them as puzzle pieces to understand me, I guess. And then of course, there is always that big question. Why did they give me up? I was angry for a while after I found out. But eventually, I reached a point where I realized that there was no way to know. I was abandoned as a newborn, with absolutely nothing connecting me to where or who I came from. That was the facts, and there was no going around that." I wasn't sure if this was the answer she was looking for, but I know my story is unique to me. If she was going to hire me, she should know this background is the foundation that built her future assistant.

"Plus, I have an amazing support system that helped me realize that no matter who I was or what my origins are, nothing would change my standing with them. I am a Queer Trans woman of color. I've found a lot of comfort from existing in my community. My community, my friends, and my family, they all taught me I didn't need to know my parents to understand who I am. And the wondering why, it lingers sometimes, but that's not important either. I'm the person that I am because of my family and chosen family. Anything in my past or in my genes is just…extra."

"Such a strong community." She sounded like she had a sense of pride in her voice.

"Honestly, with them behind me, I can do anything."

Miss Stone stood up from her desk and clapped her hands together. "Thank you, Bryn, I think I've heard enough."

"Wait, really?" I asked, standing up with her. "You don't want to ask more about my qualifications?" Even though I didn't have much to say in that department. I had four years of high school journalism and an associate degree in journalism from my two years of community college. I also had a million stories from my various clothing store jobs. I could tell her about all of it.

"I can read all of that in your application," she told me as she offered her hand. I gave her mine and her massively meaty palm covered it. I tried to give her my best firm handshake without crushing the bones of her fingers. I released that worry as soon as she let go of my hand.

She opened the door for me. Three other girls and one guy sat in the waiting room, all talking to Miss Stone's current assistant.

"I'll be in touch with my decision," Miss Stone said with a smile.

"Thank you for meeting with me," I said before leaving the waiting room. I was careful not to pay too much attention to any of the other applicants.

I made my way through the hall and exited through the door that rested at the end. I was immediately greeted by the clatter of voices tumbling over each other. The large open space was filled with lined up desks. People ran from desk to desk talking to occupants as they typed away at their computers. Some people stood at presentation boards against the far wall, discussing photos of clothes and models that were displayed.

I traversed the maze of workers, ultimately ignored. I approached the elevator and pushed the down button. I turned to look at the controlled chaos one last time as the doors dinged and opened.

I stepped into the silver box and as the doors began to close, I heard "Hold the door!" I quickly pressed the needed button on the panel and the doors jolted to a stop.

A young woman flew through the opened doors, nearly dropping the stack of manilla envelopes in her hands. "Thank you so much," she gasped. "I'm late enough as it is, and knowing this building, the wait for the next elevator would have killed me."

"No problem," I said to her, prepared to spend the rest of the elevator ride in still silence.

"Did you just interview to be Miss Stone's assistant?" she asked. Her emerald eyes sparkled with a glitz of excitement. Her almond-burnt skin had a soft glow to it. She wore a shoulderless black top with a white skirt that had black lace around the hem.

"I did," I told her. "We'll see if I get it."

"Good luck! She's the best." Before I could respond, she spat out more excited words. "I love your outfit! Where'd you get it?"

"I made it actually," I told her. "From hand-me-downs and thrift store finds." I was wearing one of my dad's old button-ups that I modified into a peplum top, 70s-style crosshatch pants that I hemmed into cigarette pants, and refurbished Oxfords.

"Wow, that's amazing. It's fun but not super exaggerated. You've got skills!" she said with a chipper tone. The elevator dinged and the doors opened. "It was nice to meet you! I hope you get the job!" She ran out onto the second floor as the silver doors shut behind her and took me to the building's lobby.

I passed businesspeople in suits and blazers and left the building, with my fate resting firmly inside. The sun peered through metal giants engulfing the streets flooded with people. A world booming with life and color.

I began my walk to the subway.

A sweet smell hit my face, joined with the savory smell of cooking meat. A small woman stood at her street cart, flinging a bacon-wrapped hotdog from her grill onto a toasted bun before piling on a rainbow of caramelized peppers and onion and slathering ribbons of condiments on top like a personal signature. I smiled at the street vendor as I passed, and she nodded at me as a bicyclist handed her some crumpled dollar bills.

A few blocks over, I reached into my pocket and grabbed the change left over from purchasing my breakfast bagel. I dropped the loose coins in the coffee cup of the bearded man that sat beside a shopping cart full of handcrafted trinkets and treasures made of another man's trash.

"Bless you, ma'am," he said kindly.

"Hope it helps," I told him as I continued on my way.

Closer to my destination, two young men carried boxes from a moving van into a building. "Don't get that one by yourself, dude," one of the boys said as he carried a stack of small boxes inside. "It's hella heavy." As I approached the van, the guy who was left behind made eye contact with me.

"Hey," he greeted me with a smile. He squatted down and grunted as he lifted a large box. He didn't take his eyes off of me until he lifted the box into the air, and it swiftly slipped from his hands. "Look out!" The box fell from the van and towards the sidewalk, right in my direction.

I acted fast, putting my hands out and bracing for impact. I wrapped my arms around the cardboard before it could hit the ground. Stopping its momentum, I held it while the boy in the van apologized profusely for dropping it in the first place.

"It's okay," I told him, nodding towards the box in my hands as a form of reassurance. I gingerly placed the box on the sidewalk.

"Dude, I told you to wait!" the other guy said as he rushed down the small steps of the building. "Are you okay, Miss? I'm sorry, my brother can be fucking dumb." He examined both me and the box for damages when he got close.

"Yeah! No harm done," I insisted.

"How did you catch that?" the brother in the van asked.

"I just have good reflexes," I responded. I began walking again without giving them an opportunity to continue the conversation.

"It took the two of us to get that thing in the van," I heard one say to the other as the distance between us grew bigger.

I spent the forty-minute subway ride kicking myself over the incident. My parents' voices in my head rang like an alarm. The walk to my apartment building from the subway stop had never felt quicker, my feet propelled by my worry. My fingers fumbled as I input the code into the keypad on the wall, prompting me to put the code in again, getting it correct the second time. The door clicked unlocked and I pulled it open, careful not to pull it from the threshold, and passed through. I headed past the elevator, straight towards the stairwell when a voice stopped me.

"Bryn!" A tall woman with long shiny black hair in a

thin red nightgown stood in the doorway of her opened apartment. She was in her mid-twenties, just a few years older than me. "I've got some more deliveries. They'll be ready to go out tomorrow morning if you're available."

"Yeah, Ceci," I said eagerly. I was happy to get work from her. Not only did she pay abnormally well for simple delivery jobs, but she was also by far one of our nicest neighbors. "Thank you so much for letting me help you."

"Of course!" she laughed. "Although, I should be the one thanking you. I couldn't possibly deliver on my own. Not as swiftly as you." Her voice was smokey and her face cool and unbothered.

"Have a good rest of your day," I said as I continued up the stairs. I stopped at the third floor and went to the end of the hall. I pulled my keys from my purse and unlocked the door. Two pairs of eyes shot up and looked at me.

"How did it go?" Lucinda and Macks asked in unison. They were both on the floor of our joint kitchen-dining room-living room, surrounded by poster boards, markers, scissors, and scraps of paper scattered across our floor and kitchen table.

Macks wore a neon yellow shirt with an abstract drawing of a cat on it, a personalized gift from an old artist friend. Their high-waisted blue jeans were splattered with remnants of dried paint. Gold and blue fishes dangled from their ears.

Lucinda had deep umber skin, dark and beautiful. She wore an oversize T-shirt with the words "plant mom" written out over sketches of various flora. Her head was wrapped in a silk piece of cloth decorated with a rainbow of geometric shapes.

"I have no idea," I told them as I fell on our lumpy gray sofa. Macks jumped up and sat on the arm of the couch by my feet while Lucinda sat on the floor by my head and caressed my arm. "It lasted all of two seconds and she barely asked me anything."

I decided not to complain about the incident that happened before the meeting. Lucinda was currently dealing with enough ugliness in the world, I didn't want to add my interaction onto her plate. I just know she'd make a crusade out of it, but she was in the middle of her own revolution.

Lucinda had worked at Cake'd, a popular bakery in the city, famous to tourists for their erotic-themed cakes and pastries, and a gem to locals for their delicious and expertly crafted treats. The owner had recently found himself in hot water due to complaints of racism and sexual harassment. Lucinda quit and was leading the charge against him. She was currently preparing for a protest right at the shop's front door.

"Even if you don't get the job, something else will come your way," Macks insisted.

"They're right," Lucinda piled on. "But if that woman doesn't hire you, she's not as much of a genius as you think she is."

The conviction in Lucinda's voice almost made me believe that Elizabeth Stone, top of her field, might actually be inferior.

"Something else happened today," I said. "On the way home."

"What?" Macks asked with a sense of worry and excitement in their voice.

"On my way home, I passed some guys who were moving into a building. Like the kind of guys that look like they go to the gym three times a day," I began.

"Oh no, did they mess with you?" Lucinda asked, growing tense.

"No, they seemed like nice guys," I insisted. "But one of them dropped a really heavy box, too heavy for either of them to carry alone, practically right on top of me."

"And you caught it?" Macks asked, their voice heavy with accusation.

"It was a reflex!" I defended myself.

"Did they notice?" Lucinda asked, shutting Macks' shock out of my brain.

"They definitely noticed but I doubt they'll find a need to search for an explanation," I said.

"You're sure?" Lucinda asked, peering into me with her brown eyes. "They won't be wondering why some perfectly average girl was able to outmuscle them?"

"They'll probably forget about it by next week," I reassured my housemates. "It was just a close call that got my head spinning a bit."

This was a constant fear I shared with not just my best friends but also my parents. The five of us have been in a constant state of fear, wondering what might happen if someone catches wind of my secret and starts asking questions.

Questions none of us really had the answers to. The only thing we knew was one simple yet unbelievable fact. I had superhuman strength.

Chapter 2

"So, what's the next move?" Lucinda asked me as we approached Ceci's door. "I don't want you to fall into this position of freelance delivery girl. It's not reliable work. No matter how well she pays you." She had decided to join me on my errands for Ceci so she could distribute fliers around the city. After I made the deliveries and she hung up and passed out a significant number of fliers, we stopped for lunch before heading back home.

"I'm still looking for a job," I told her as I knocked on the door.

"I'm worried," Lucinda said. "With both of us not working, things will get rough real fast. Macks' job isn't going to cover the rent."

"I know, but we'll both find something," I insisted. A small part of me was hopeful that my search would be over soon, but I had just been turned down for two positions and the only pending status was the assistant job for Miss Stone. "I know you're worried. And that is super valid. But try to have some faith too."

"Faith only gets you so far," she sighed, dragging her fingers through the ends of her light brown hair.

Lucinda was so focused on her activism that she feared what her employment status would look like in the near future. She didn't know if any bakery would rush to hire her after trying to destroy one of New York's prominent cake shops. Her former boss had a relationship with many bakeries in the city and any others would surely hear about her efforts from gossip or the media.

The door in front of us swung open. "Hello ladies," Ceci said with joy. "How'd the deliveries go?"

"Good," I told her. "Everyone always seems really happy to receive your stuff."

"I would hope so," she laughed. "Or else I wouldn't be very good at what I do." Ceci wore a silver-gray cardigan over a black jumpsuit. The form of her clothes accented her long legs.

"What is it that you do?" Lucinda asked her. "I'm just realizing I'm not sure what it is you're selling. From what Bryn tells me, it's all random stuff."

"I'm a craftswoman," she said proudly. "I truly do make random things. I grow herbs and make medicines and teas. I make jewelry. On occasion, I'll make charms meant to stimulate a specific aspect life or the mind."

"Like good luck charms?" Lucinda asked.

"Sometimes. But luck isn't the only thing people need. I can make charms for just about anything," Ceci explained.

"And people pay for it?" Lucinda asked, skeptical.

"Luce," I tried to rein her in before she said something rude to the only person paying me at the moment. She tended to be an uninhibited and impulsive person, and not everyone responded positively to her. Sometimes it seemed like Macks and I were the only people who understood that the things she would say on a whim were just free and harmless thoughts escaping her mind, not insults.

"Not just pay for it. They special order. I mostly work on commission." Ceci answered, seeming eager to explain herself. She narrowed her eyes on Lucinda. "Do you not believe in that sort of thing? You have always struck me as a person of…high spirituality."

"I don't know," she responded quickly, almost scoffing. "I think I'm more cautious than anything else." She shifted the bag of take-out we ordered for Macks, from one hand to another, dropping the few fliers left over from the day. I quickly leaned down to catch them while Ceci did the same. She handed me the papers that managed to make it to the floor.

"I heard about that," she said, looking at the Cake'd flier. "Such a shame. I think it's amazing how you are trying to hold this man accountable for his actions."

"He refuses to even acknowledge the allegations," Lucinda said, passion building in her voice. "He thinks if he pretends it's not happening and that he is above it all, it will just go away."

"It pisses me off that all it takes is white charm to disrupt and illegitimize claims of racism and sexual assault," I said, trying to hold in my rage. I had been reading articles where Lucinda's ex-boss was saying that the claims shocked him, seeing news interviews where he laughed it off, and even official statements on his social media accounts saying that he had always striven to make Cake'd a safe and comfortable business for both customers and employees. But not once did he ever address the allegations with an outward denial. Just pure deflection.

"We are holding a protest next week at the shop if you want to come," Lucinda told her.

"I would love to be there," Ceci said as Lucinda handed her a flier. "Anything I can do to help. He can't get away with this." She stared at the flier intensely for a few moments. Like she was lost on the page or perhaps within her own mind.

"Thank you," Lucinda said, breaking the silent trance. "I appreciate all the support we can get."

"Of course," she said. "Oh! I almost forgot what you came here for." She disappeared into her apartment and returned to hand me five twenty-dollar bills. I slipped the money into my pocket and thanked her for the work before saying our goodbyes.

Lucinda and I climbed the stairs to find two packages at our door. A large cardboard box topped with a smaller box wrapped in white paper. I picked them up and carried them in behind Lucinda. "We got mail," I called out. Macks appeared from their bedroom and joined us around our tiny dining room table.

"Another care package from your parents?" they asked as I ripped through the taped cardboard with one tug of my hand. The box was filled with canned food, boxes of rice, a bag of flour sealed in a large plastic bag, protein and granola bars, laundry detergent, dish soap, and a box of my dad's favorite cookies.

My parents sent us a care package once or twice a month. They worried about the three of us a lot. So, they would often send gifts, money, or just stop by for a week on occasion to make sure we were still alive and kicking. They moved away from the city a few years ago and I stayed behind and moved in with Lucinda and Macks. My heart was in this city, and I had dreams that could only be chased here, just like the two of them, so it only seemed natural. Plus, I wasn't quite ready to say goodbye to my best friends. Macks and I had known each other since elementary school and Lucinda came into our lives while we were in college.

"I love your parents," Macks said as they began unpacking. "Where would we be without them?"

"Oh my gosh," Lucinda said looking at the smaller package we received. "This one is from your mom." She handed the small parcel to Macks, and they hesitated before taking it.

"I haven't spoken to her in over a year," Macks said, examining the object. "She addressed it to Macks." They sounded surprised. This was understandable because getting their mom to call them by their name was a constant struggle. She only liked to use the name that she chose for them.

"Maybe she's coming around," Lucinda said with tempered hope.

"Maybe," Macks said as they tore the layers of white paper. They uncovered a small wooden box with pearl-colored carvings of dots and lines that almost looked floral. They lifted the lid and removed a folded piece of paper. Reading it aloud, they said, "This belonged to your grandfather. He gave it to me the day you were born. He wanted to give it to you himself when you came of age, but he was very sick. I think he knew he wouldn't live long enough to do so himself. I know we aren't speaking, but I must respect my father's wishes. Wear it well and with pride."

Macks pulled a chain of braided brown strings from the box. At the end of the necklace hung a chunky black beetle in a translucent emerald-colored casing, embroidered with brass filigree around its rounded rectangular shape.

"What is that?" Lucinda asked, examining the insect.

"It's this necklace my grandfather wore," Macks said. "He had it on in every picture I've seen of him."

"So, it's like, some kind of family heirloom?"

"Yeah, I'm pretty sure it was passed down through the generations," Macks told us. "This was the most important thing he carried with him from the Philippines. My grandma told stories about it. It's supposed to be this symbol of power and protection. But no one ever told me that my grandfather wanted me to have it."

"Maybe this could be a bridge between you and your mom. Couldn't you ask her more about it and your grandfather?" I asked.

"Doesn't sound like she's ready to talk," Macks responded as they crumpled up the letter. They looked at the pendant before hanging it around their neck.

This broke my heart. I had seen Macks' struggle with their family. I had been a shoulder to cry on, a support system in their darkest moments, even giving them a place to stay with my own family when theirs was too unbearable or otherwise unloving. My parents, bless their souls, gave them the love they needed. I only wished that it could come from their own parents. I know there is a piece of Macks missing, and only their parents could fill that hole.

I wanted them to know the warmth that can come from a parental relationship, and I'm glad my parents were able to offer the closest version of that, while Lucinda and I provided more love and support than they could possibly know what to do with. And while we were there for them, I continued to hold out hope that their parents would come around.

Instinctively, like a magnetic pull, Lucinda and I moved closer to Macks. Leaning into them in a wordless embrace that spoke volumes. As they gazed down at the pendant around their neck, no doubt seeing images of their mother playing in their head, I couldn't help but conjure my own.

My mother. A pillar of grace. More powerful than I could ever be, even with my strength. Everything seemed to come so easy to her. I wanted life to be as easy as she made it seem. In all of the world's problems, she was the solution. The horrors of the world, which should have terrified me, couldn't touch me as long as I was in her protective arms. We were soulmates, made perfectly for each other.

The universe gave her to me.

Out of all the orphaned children in the world, Marcela Gonzalez-Ortiz somehow found me. Chose me.

The child of immigrants who dreamt of the home her parents told stories of. An art teacher and pottery maker. A genius baker but somehow a terrible cook. A storyteller. A woman who holds everyone she meets in her heart. A maternal force of nature. She shaped the woman I was today by navigating my childhood with a sense of calculated confidence.

When my parents told me that I was adopted, it didn't occur to me that I was missing some piece of myself. I never saw it that way. I never imagined that I was abandoned as a newborn. The way I saw it, when they brought me home, they gave me everything I needed.

As a child, my mother would take me to work with her every Friday, and on the way home, we would go to the park. She worked at a private school in a white neighborhood. The park in the area was greener and cleaner with brand new equipment and sprinklers to cool you off on hot days. I was too young to understand why the park by our house was not given the same love and care. For one fleeting day of each week, she'd let me experience that love and care.

Eventually, kids in that neighborhood took notice of our routine appearances. A particular group of boys would wait for me at the top of the slide each week. Once we were face to face, they'd jeer about how my brown skin was actually a layer of dirt and how poor I must have been to not be able to afford bathwater.

After weeks of swallowing these comments, I went to my mother in tears. Appalled by what I told her, she rushed us home and I was sure that was the end of it. I was sure I would never go back to the nice park again. But sure enough, we went back the following week. I dreaded seeing the playground bullies again. But this time, the park was full of children and parents from our neighborhood. My mother had rallied the parents together to organize a massive playdate with playmates who looked more like me. A playdate that continued week after week while the park in our neighborhood went through a quiet rejuvenation. By the time summer came around, our neighborhood park was a beautiful wonderland of a different kind. To this day, I don't know how she made that happen, but we never needed to find joy in hostile parks again.

When my dad got injured at work and was unable to go back for the month and a half it took for his arm to heal, my mom began selling her pottery to help keep us afloat. Awake with the rising sun to mold clay, off to work during the day, and then back home to continue molding until midnight. Then every weekend she'd pack up her creations of the week and the three of us would set up shop at street fairs and farmers' markets. When my father healed and returned to work, my mother continued to sell her crafts, turning her passion into a third income.

When I told her that I was a girl, she embraced me. Her pregnant belly was warm against my tiny body, and I wished I could develop inside of her like my baby brother. To be birthed anew into the daughter I was meant to be.

When my strength first developed, I was afraid to touch anyone, worried that I might break them. She refused to let me fear myself. She went to the bodega and purchased three cartons of eggs. She told me that if I could grasp something delicate and keep it safe, I could hold my mother's hand.

She sat with me on the roof of our building, as I trained myself in control. She talked me through it. A perfectly normal mother, without the slightest idea what was happening to her child. Somehow, she knew exactly how to fix it. After seven eggs shattered at my touch, eggshells sprinkled at our feet and our matching sundresses were dirty and yolk-stained, she placed the eighth egg in my hand, and it did not break for a whole fourteen seconds.

She cheered and celebrated my restraint. I looked into her bright smile and knew that I could do this because she believed I could do it. Day after day, she stood by my side as I tried not to crush things. Eggs, oranges, baseballs, her favorite vases. Eventually, I held my mother's hand again.

Macks deserved a mother like this. Not a mother who refused their name and sent curt letters in the mail. And if they couldn't have a mother like mine, I was happy to share her with them.

Chapter 3

"I have to admit, you were kind of right," Macks said to Lucinda, a fruitful smile growing on their face.

"I was *very* right," Lucinda corrected. "We all needed to get outside and enjoy life instead of stress out about it. Sun, friends, and alcohol. It's the perfect refresher."

Lucinda had forced us out of the apartment to have brunch at a rooftop restaurant that she used to work at, and because she's still friends with the manager, the entire experience was comped.

We sat on top of the roof bathed in sunlight at a circular garden table. A golden pineapple mimosa in front of Macks, a hot pink strawberry mimosa in Lucinda's hand, and a bright peach Bellini in mine. With our food plates cleared away, we sat in each other's company and the comfort of bottomless drinks.

With my job stress, Lucinda's activism, and Macks' family drama, a day where we could get out of our heads was much needed.

Lucinda wore giant sunglasses and a black bob wig on her head. A long floral skirt draped down her legs, and a plain white blouse rested on her torso. She looked upward, embracing the light that radiated from the sky. "This isn't totally a selfless act by the way," she said before taking a sip from her glass. "I need to loosen you up for tonight. I can't have you killing the vibe."

"Were you worried that we would?" Macks asked. A hint of offense was woven into their tone. The necklace they received from their mother sat prominently on their chest, above an army green jumpsuit. Earrings made from the heads of miniature baby dolls dangled as they spoke.

"I couldn't afford to take the chance," she giggled. "But no, I wouldn't expect you two to be anything other than lovely."

"I don't think it's possible to be in a bad mood when you're performing," I told her. Lucinda had a reputation as a drag performer, working random bars all throughout the city. She had the amazing ability to hype up any crowd. Tonight was the debut of a monthly event that she'd be headlining. She was overflowing with excitement to be a regular performer and have a solid stake in nightlife entertainment. She had been planning and practicing her performance militantly for weeks, whenever she wasn't planning the protest.

Macks and I tried our best to be at every performance, but this one was big. Macks made sure to call off work at the theater so they could be there even before it started to get some footage of Lucinda backstage, in her element.

Macks was filming a documentary about the Cake'd scandal. Just their way of contributing to the cause. They were pretty sure the scandal wouldn't get the coverage it needed. Macks is a believer in art speaking volumes, and thinks this film, centering the Cake'd employees, could spread the message further than the news outlets that might forget about it once the buzz died down.

"Except when she turns our entire apartment into a performance venue," Macks teased, "and we're the captive audience."

"I've never heard you complain before," Lucinda shot back.

"Of course not," Macks responded. "How could you possibly hear over the music?"

"And the singing," I added.

"So much singing!" Macks squealed. We all erupted into laughter.

I almost didn't even notice the vibration coming from my phone. I lifted it, expecting to see photos of my little brother's wrestling competition, which was the only thing my mother was able to talk about last time we spoke. But the notification was not from my mom. It was a phone call from a number that I immediately recognized as the same number that called to set up my Divinity Magazine interview.

I swallowed a knot that immediately formed in my throat. The laughter at our table stopped, Lucinda and Macks looking at me with curious eyes.

"It's them," I said. The two of them nodded in response, knowing exactly what I was referring to. They sat in silence while the tables around us continued to chat and revel in their fun. I answered, preparing myself to hear the rejection. It was kind of them to call, rather than just ghost me like most employers who decided to pass on hiring me.

"Hello," I said, trying to sound chipper and dispel my disappointment.

"Hello! Is this Bryn?" It was the current assistant on the other end of the phone. "This is Mila from Elizabeth Stone's Office. I'm calling about the assistant position." Her voice was bright and airy like a cartoon princess.

"Yes," I managed to cough out. "Thank you for calling."

"Oh, of course," Mila said, and I could tell she was smiling. "Miss Stone was very impressed with you."

"Really?" I asked, unable to contain my shock. That was promising to hear. If I was going to be rejected, at least I was able to leave an impression. That could help me later in my career.

"Yeah, there were a lot of really good candidates but ultimately, she felt like she couldn't turn you away. And her instincts are, like, never wrong, by the way."

"Wait, what?" My ears stopped working for a second, my brain rebooting.

"She wants to offer you the position, Miss Gonzalez-Ortiz. If you're still interested."

"Absolutely," I said, almost choking on the knot that I thought I had swallowed, only able to get out that one word.

"Wonderful!" she cheered through the phone. "Can you come in tomorrow at eight? We can process paperwork and have you shadow me to get a sense of what your day to day will be like."

"Yes, I'll be there!" A smile stretched across my face, heart racing and warmth building in my chest.

"Cool! See you then!" Mila said. "Bring two forms of identification for the paperwork."

We said our goodbyes and hung up and Macks immediately jumped in.

"You got it?"

"Somehow, I guess I did." I was holding my phone as if it were a foreign object, like being offered a career starting job was something dangerous and unheard of. It felt like that, even though it's exactly what I wanted.

"I knew you could land it," Lucinda said with a tight smile.

"I didn't," I confessed.

"Well, you shouldn't doubt yourself," Lucinda said, seriously. "You're going to go on to do amazing things, and this is your start. I know it is." There was something in her eyes, something that felt grave and genuine.

"For real!" Macks called out, pulling my attention from Lucinda's earthy brown eyes. "Think about how far you've come. Where this all started. This is a major steppingstone."

When I was a child, my mother read me fairytales. One specific fairytale over and over again. It was my favorite and the only story I had any interest in hearing. I would beg her to tell it every single night. Objectively, it was nothing special. Just the least weird story from a book of Celtic fairy tales she bought at a yard sale for 75 cents.

The story of a lowly villager who lived in a world plagued by darkness. For hundreds of years, the people of the village found themselves at the mercy of this great evil waiting for a light to save them. One day a special villager was born but no one knew just how special she was. She was born with light inside her. But no one knew how to recognize the light, therefore there was no one to teach her to nurture it. And worse, while the people couldn't recognize the light, they were able to see there was something different about this villager and they shunned her for it. She grew up unaware of the power she had, ostracized from her community. One day, shortly after the villager reached adulthood, the darkness had accumulated to dangerous levels. As the darkness descended, the villager discovered a strength within herself and used it to pull out the light. She dispelled the darkness forever and saved the village. In the wake of her heroics the grateful people declared the villager a princess. Princess Bryn, bringer of light.

I could see the illustration, clear as day. A young woman, adorned with silver and gold armor standing on top of a hill holding the sun in her bare hands with an ocean of smiling villagers at her feet. I used to look at that picture and wonder what it must be like to hold light in my hands.

I wasn't sure why I liked the story so much. Not until some years later, after I had outgrown bedtime stories. Even though she stopped telling me the story, it remained in the back of my mind.

In junior high, we had Spirit Week where we would dress up according to a different theme each day. One of these days was called "Dress Like a Friend Day" where we were encouraged to come to school wearing matching outfits as our friends. Of course, Macks and I decided to be extra about it. Instead of dressing the same as each other, we would dress *like* each other.

We went to school early that day and met before the first bell rang. We sneaked into the single stall bathroom that was hidden away in the far corner of campus. We turned our backs to each other, removed our clothes and blindly traded the garments. This was a different time, before Macks was Macks, and when they dressed much more feminine. We thought there would be a humor in us existing in opposite versions of extremes.

"Okay," Macks said after we had finished adjusting into the new outfits. "Moment of truth."

We both turned to face each other in unison. I was expecting Macks to look like a foreign entity. My plaid shirt draped over them like a cloak, exposing my black undershirt that swallowed their torso like a void. My cargo pants clung desperately to their waist with assistance from my belt made from the material and buckle of a car's seat belt. The oddity I expected to see wasn't there. It was just Macks in ill-fitting clothes. Upon seeing me, however, their eyes widened, and they slapped their hands to their mouth to stifle a laugh. Excited to share in the joke, I turned to the bathroom mirror. Behind the scratches and marker graffiti, I didn't see a boy in girl's clothes. I saw me.

Embraced by a white lace shirt with ruffles that cascaded from the neck. A blue floral skirt that breathed life into me. A large pink scrunchie cuffed my wrist with a delicate tightness. I could have sworn I was glowing brighter than the fluorescent lights, my brown skin like shimmering gold, so bright it was blinding. Overwhelming.

This was why I had been so drawn to the Bringer of Light fairytale. Up until this moment, I had been a villager. Walking around in life, blind to a vital part of myself that had been hidden away, sad and closed off from others. In this moment, seeing the girl in the mirror, I had become a princess.

The girl looking at me smiled. I caught myself. I tried to turn the smile into a laugh, as if the sight were humorous rather than affirming. At the time, I barely knew how to explain this phenomenon to myself, and definitely not to another person. Under the watchful eyes of my closest friend, I had to pretend. There was no way for me to know that Macks would wholeheartedly understand and, in just a few short years, abandon the concept of gender completely. In that moment, I had to pretend to be a villager for a little while longer.

"This is going to be so great!" Macks cheered. "Everyone is going to think this is so funny."

A hundred-pound seed of worry planted itself in my stomach. The thought of this being nothing but a joke stabbing at me, lacerating my very soul. But I knew that one day a truer me would claw her way out of the wound and call herself Bryn Gonzalez-Ortiz.

Moving forward, when I later acknowledged my true self, my clothing was the armor I could utilize to affirm her. I could be the version of myself my soul wanted to be through my clothes. My relationship with fashion grew from there, and later mixed with my passion for journalism. And now, I was going to be working in the city's largest hub where those two worlds connect. Seeing how things work behind the scenes, studying people who have my dream job. Gaining knowledge and experience to get me there myself one day.

"Cheers!" Macks said, raising their mimosa. I raised my glass to meet theirs. Lucinda did the same.

"To your future," Lucinda said as the glasses clinked together. And as we all took a celebratory sip, Lucinda took in her entire drink in one smooth gulp.

Chapter 4

The Milky Way Nightclub rested in the lower level of an apartment building. Supposedly, way back in the day this underground bar was a safe haven for queer and trans people of color who couldn't gather out in the open. It had since grown from speakeasy, to dive bar, to cocktail lounge, to historic gay club.

The interior was a dark midnight purple, with silver glitter exploding on the ceiling, mirroring the beauty of a galaxy full of stars that stretched farther than the imagination could even fathom. Satin ribbons stretched from wall to wall, hanging overhead, creating an aurora made from every color of the rainbow.

The name, The Milky Way Club, was used in the guise of an astronomer's club, where intellectuals would come to chat in the past. While the front room did house stuffy academics socializing on any given day, at night the club's true patrons would knock at the back door and be allowed into a hidden speakeasy downstairs. Today, that front room was a passageway to the not-at-all secret nightclub downstairs.

The place was packed, sweaty bodies draped in

exuberant clothes writhed to the bumping music. The entire space was a dance floor, save for the actual bar, the DJ booth, and the stage for the performers. To walk anywhere, you'd have to navigate a sea of drunk queers dancing to the music that rained down from the speakers.

I sat at the bar, while Macks and Lucinda were somewhere backstage. Lucinda getting ready and Macks undoubtedly filming the whole ritual. It was my job to wait patiently until the show started and Macks could join me in the crowd, to continue filming. I wore a black crop top under a lettuce trim sheer top embroidered with gleaming stars. My black jeans were dusted with specks of silver glitter. The fit felt very appropriate for the location. Dressing to a theme was always a fun way to go out into the world.

"Excuse me!" I tried to call over the music to one of the three bartenders behind the long, crowded bar. She was a tiny girl in a red leather jacket, completely overwhelmed by the countless other voices vying for her attention as she poured a blended margarita into a glass. My attempt had gone unnoticed.

"What are you trying to order?" a smooth voice said next to me. The voice was steady and clear, somehow easily understood despite the fact that the person speaking was not even trying to yell over the explosive music.

I turned to my left to see a man. He looked tall, even though he was leaning on the bar, surely cutting off some height in that position. His dark hair was slicked back on the top of his head and shaved short on the sides. He wore a maroon-colored paisley suit, with a skinny crimson red tie. His muscular arms and chest nearly ripped through the fabric of his clothes. Perfectly manicured, coffin-shaped, sky-blue nails clung to his shoulder. The porcelain hand belonged to a tall and immaculate beauty.

Dirty blonde hair, slightly teased to convey stylized mess, framed a triangular face of blue eyes and shiny pink lips. They wore a white bomber jacket over a black top. The shirt was tucked into a skintight checkered pattern skirt, with a slit running up the left thigh, revealing a tattoo of a snake coiled around a bouquet of flowers. A black belt wrapped around their waist; three silver chains of varying lengths attached to the belt creating loops that accentuated their hips. They wore black knee-high socks over fishnet stockings. Black bracelets and garter belts with silver spikes clasped around their wrists and upper legs. It was giving grunge meets schoolgirl aesthetics.

I recognized them as Divine. They were well known in the city's queer bar scene. I had never formally met Divine, but I had seen them around and I had heard stories about them. A self-identified They/Them twink that frequented the clubs and always had men clamoring to bring them home. The man they were with tonight, I had never seen before.

"A Ginger Bitch," I answered him. The bar's take on a Moscow mule, mixing the ginger beer and vodka with watermelon flavored energy drink. One of their specialty drinks that felt dangerous and delicious at the same time.

The man raised a hand slightly, extending his pointer

and middle fingers. The tiny bartender quickly approached him and said, "What can I get ya?"

"One Ginger Bitch for my new friend," he said with confidence, nodding towards me. "I'll have a scotch on the rocks, and a cosmo for my date." He gave Divine's ass a squeeze and I couldn't tell if he thought he was being discreet or if he just didn't care that I could see the display of affection.

They gave him a pleasing smirk before looking at me. "You're Lucinda's friend, right?"

"We live together," I answered.

"Bryn, right? She speaks very highly of you," they said with a bright smile.

"You two know each other?" Lucinda had never mentioned Divine before, but she was a popular girl so it wouldn't have been surprising if they were friends.

"Our paths have crossed," Divine laughed, running their fingers down the man's arm. "My sisters and her perform at a bunch of the same shows. I'm Divine!"

"I've seen you around," I said kindly as the bartender put a tall glass filled to the brim with a red drink in front of me. "And who should I thank for this?" I asked, looking at the man.

"I'm Damon." He didn't strain to speak over the club's music, but he could still be heard smoothly and clearly. The bartender delivered a frothy pink cocktail and a stout cup of brown liquid to him before turning to the next people vying for her attention.

"What are we cheersing to?" Divine asked, lifting their cocktail glass.

"To finding each other," Damon said, lifting his glass and looking at me intently. I raised my glass to meet his, out of ritual, not to humor whatever his eyes were insinuating. His arm around Divine's waist, he pulled them close as they raised their glass. The three clunked together, spilling drops of each drink. We all pulled the rims to our lips and took the first sip. A strong fruity flavor swirled in my mouth, followed by a punch of spice and citrus.

"Welcome to Drag Night at The Milky Way Nightclub!" a man's voice called over the loudspeakers. The entire club cheered with excitement. In the corner of my eye, I saw Macks appear from the backstage entrance, their camera in hand and pointed at the stage. "Please welcome tonight's headliner, Nymph O'Mania!"

The crowd roared again. Divine clapped while turning to me with a joyous grin. I screamed loud, trying to send my voice above all the others, hoping Lucinda would be able to hear it like a beacon of support.

The lights dimmed even more than they had been, and the music changed to an upbeat tune with a hint of melancholy just under the surface. After a beat, a figure emerged, silhouetted on the stage. Moving forward, Lucinda came into focus. She wore a long flowing white dress, decorated with an explosion of flowers. She was adorned with so many flowers that the whiteness of her gown could hardly be seen. Every color imaginable was bursting off of her, various shapes of blooming flowers situated in organized chaos, from her neck to her chest, and all the way down to her feet. Her long sleeves were flowerless and hung like drapery. Rosy red hair hung over her right shoulder. Her face was decorated with bold swipes of color. Deep black lines outlined her blue eyelids, her face painted an earthy green, and her lips were a glossy dark red.

She began to sing an original song she had written years ago. Her voice a siren call, reaching out across the club. Her lyrics told the tale of a soul longing for a life out of reach, a home of sisterhood amongst nature, and how even though she missed the familiarity of that past life, she was doing something important. She never fully explained to me what this story symbolized but I always assumed it had something to do with the family she left behind for her life in the city.

As her voice swelled with the music, building to the climax of the song, she turned her back to the audience as she bellowed the final notes. There were no flowers on her back. Instead, her vibrant red hair fell down her back like a river. It was so bright it was nearly glowing. It glistened as if wet, like her back was drenched in fresh blood. The exaggerated hair hung off her like a cape of pain and heartbreak.

The audience bellowed at the reveal, eating up the artistry as the song came to a close. Lucinda struck a pose as the music shifted. No longer an original song, an 80's pop hit took over the speakers. Lucinda immediately ran across the stage, moving and grooving to the song as if it took control of her body. I was impressed that none of her flowers had fallen off. The audience continued to cheer, clap, and snap as she strutted along. Her face was shining with a show woman's smile.

"She knows how to use the stage," Damon said, sounding impressed. I nodded in agreement, taking my eyes off Lucinda for a moment to look at him. Divine was gone, and he sat beside me alone.

"Where'd your date go?" I asked, looking at the empty cocktail glass sitting at the bar. "They'll miss the show."

"We saw the opening acts," he responded with a smirk. "I sent them outside to wait for us."

"Us?" I laughed at his assumption. "I'm not going anywhere."

"I'm afraid you are," he said, unimpressed. "You won't be seeing the rest of the show." He stood up from his barstool and approached me quickly. His large hand wrapped around my upper arm with a tight squeeze. The swift movement caught me off guard, but I just sighed with annoyance. The threat of men at bars didn't entirely frighten me because I knew that they should be more afraid of me.

"I suggest that you give up on this and just walk away," I told him, looking directly into his dark eyes. He stood over me, a clear attempt at intimidation. I wasn't going to give him that power. "You don't know who you're messing with."

"No," he laughed. "But I know *what* I'm messing with." A devilish smile stretched across his face. I didn't know exactly what he meant by that, but the sentence sent shivers of discomfort running across my spine. I yanked my arm away from him, but his grasp stayed steady against my skin. I barely budged. His strength matched mine. And that was a terrifying thought.

I was someone who could rip doors off their hinges if I wasn't careful. I could shatter bones with the squeeze of my fingers. I've kicked holes into brick walls during childhood temper tantrums. I had never met anyone who could overpower me. My mind was racing. My chest tightened. What did this mean? Was he like me? Could he be linked to me genetically? Why was he coming at me with aggression? How did he know about me? The thoughts bounced around my head in a rapid barrage.

"Don't make a scene," he said in my ear. "Just walk out of here with me. Make it easier on everyone." He started to move, and I dragged along beside him. Still taken aback by what was happening, I didn't know how to react. In the past, if a man were to get handsy, it would be over seconds after it began. I always made sure of that. But here, now. This was a whole different situation that I wasn't prepared for. Something that I never imagined would happen.

He moved us through the crowd. I watched Lucinda dancing on stage and saw Macks filming with diligence. I wanted to call out to them, but I feared what might happen if I pulled them into a struggle with someone with my strength. My heart raced as we got closer to a door. It was not the main entrance. The backway that was once used for the secret parties, but now was likely a service entrance.

He pushed through the doors, placing us in a dark hallway. A pair of restrooms sat in the middle and a flight of stairs at the end. Without words he dragged me through the hall and up the stairs. A set of double doors rested at the top. He pushed me through and suddenly I was outside. The frigid night air clipped against me quickly. We were in an alley. Dumpsters and parked cars lined the walls. The music from inside was just a low hum now.

Divine stood in the moonlight, smiling when they saw us emerge from the doors. "Hey!" They sang. The joy in their voice and on their face faded when they examined us more closely. Their eyes darted between Damon's grip around my arm and the look of distress on my face. "What are you doing?" They sounded appalled. "If she's not into it, we aren't forcing her. I'm *not* down for that."

"Shut up!" Damon snarled at them. He flung me forward, releasing my arm and sending me to the pavement. "This isn't some sexual adventure gone wrong!" His voice was heavy and dark, like a low rumbling from the earth. He sounded almost inhuman. "It never was."

Divine ran to me, grabbing me by the arms and helping me to my feet. "What do you mean?" they asked him.

"It was a ploy, you idiot." Damon glared at us with eyes that grew darker by the second. "I needed to get this one alone," he spat at me, "and I needed a pawn." He looked at Divine, raising his right eyebrow. He stepped forward with aggression and my body reacted.

"Get back!" I yelled, unsure if it was directed at Divine or Damon. I stood between them and threw my fist outward. It collided against Damon's chest, an act that should have broken him. But instead, it just sent him propelling backwards. He lost his footing, falling flat on his back.

"Oh my God!" Divine screamed. They clutched onto my shoulders, their body trembling.

"Run," I tried to tell them. I had no idea what this man was planning but I didn't want them to be involved. I didn't want to be involved either, but I was the only one that stood a chance. "Go!"

Damon groaned as his body lifted off the ground. Lifted as if he was weightless and the laws of gravity had no ruling over him. His body straightened and his feet hovered over the ground for a second before he planted them down firmly. "You gals always want to put up a fight," he said. "And every time, I expect better from you."

"What the hell?" Divine squealed, squeezing me tighter.

"I don't know what you want or who you think I am," I told him. "And I definitely don't know what you are." He slowly approached us. I tried to step back but Divine's terrified body blocked my movement. I turned, planning to scoop them up into my arms and run for as long and as far as it took to get away.

Before I could even grab them, Damon was beside us. With one swift pull of his arms, he separated us. He looked at me and laughed. The bellowing sound that emitted from him left a vile taste in the back of my mouth. He took Divine's face in one hand, pressing into their cheeks with his fingers. He turned their face to look at his. They trembled as his eyes disappeared behind a swirl of red and black. Divine's body tensed and convulsed as their own eyes began to change. The whites and blues were overcome by solid black. Deep red veins stretched from the corner of their new black eyes across the sides of their face.

He released them and they stood completely still. The energy around them changed. As if they were no longer a person, no longer themself. A chilling husk stood where Divine once did. They turned towards me. A black fluid poured from their eyes. They opened their mouth to let out a wordless moan, and more sludge dripped from their lips.

Damon chuckled before speaking an order to them. "Get her."

Like a frenzied zombie, Divine arched their back and released a screeching wail, before running at me full speed. The black goo spilled from their eyes and mouth. I jumped out of their path, as they propelled forward, they tripped over my ankle. They tumbled into a puddle, sending droplets across the ground. Their skirt and jacket absorbed some of the water, taking on a brown tint.

"What did you do to them?" I asked as they mindlessly got back onto their feet, groaning incoherently.

"What I do best," Damon said, leaning against a white delivery van. "Corrupted them. I reached inside that fragile human brain and grabbed hold of darkness itself and pulled it to the surface."

"What are you?" I asked him, fear building in my bones, sending icy chills to every nerve in my body.

Divine lunged at me again. This time, climbing on my back, wrapping their legs around my waist. They raised their hands to the sky before bringing them down onto me. Their nails dug into my arms, ripping the flesh, and bringing dark red blood to the surface.

"Bryn!" I heard Macks' voice call as the club's back doors swung open. Lucinda, still in her performance attire, stood beside them.

"Get out of here!" I called to them as I grabbed Divine by the wrists and pulled, prying them off me. I tossed them to the side as lightly as I could muster. Their body rolled towards Damon, who stood there, observing but not reacting.

"What is going on?" Lucinda asked as Divine jumped to their feet. They crouched down and let out a scream, directed at the two of them. A river of black slime fell from Divine's face, splattering onto the ground at their feet.

"What the fuck?" Macks said in shock before immediately pulling out their camera and pressing the record button. They pointed it directly at Divine, who looked from them and then to me. Macks turned the camera to Damon, who responded by turning his head to obstruct the view of his face.

"Finish this," he called out.

Divine darted towards Macks and Lucinda, swinging their blood-stained nails like knives.

The two of them stood there, Macks recording the crazed attacker and Lucinda clutching her stomach as she looked on in astonishment.

I refused to let them get hurt. I reached out my arm just as Divine was passing me. Without enough time to react, they ran straight into my arm. I heard the air press from their lungs as their chest rammed against me. As soon as they made contact, I pushed back, only slightly. Their whole body moved away from my friends with extreme force. They made a series of gurgling noises, as if choking on their own madness, and attempted to run at my friends again.

I pulled my strength back, like I had been training myself to do for years. I focused on using just enough of it, but not too much. I tightened every muscle in my body as my mind concentrated on restraint. I imagined my strength pooling in my stomach, removing itself from the rest of my body, and only letting a tiny bit remain in my hand. I flattened my fist and sent it straight into the side of Divine's face, palm crashing into temple. Their body spun a full 360 degrees. After finding their footing, they wobbled slightly. Their face of empty rage melted away to confusion. The blackness of their eyes faded, bringing back the blue spheres. The red veins disappeared from their porcelain skin. The black gunk that spilled from their eyes and mouth shifted to a sanguine red. Even the slime that had already fallen to the ground turned to blood.

Divine immediately fell to the ground, unconscious.

"Oh my... Are they okay?" Lucinda asked, nearly screaming. She ran to check on them, wiping the blood from their face. Macks crouched down, capturing it all on their camera.

"I'm not sure," I answered, looking at Damon.

Macks shifted their camera's view to look at Damon once again.

"You passed the test," he growled as he straightened his tie. "But we will see if you're the one I've been looking for."

I opened my mouth to question him further, but before words could even form, he swiped his arm upward into the air. As if summoned by the action, a pillar of maroon-colored smoke materialized around him. It faded in an instant, and he was gone along with it.

I was speechless. I didn't know what to think or what to say. My life was full of the abnormal, but this night, this single moment was more unbelievable than my strength ever was. What happened here? And what did it all mean for me? Who was this man, who could do things far beyond feats of strength, and why did he want me?

"I can't believe I got all of that," Macks said in amazement, looking down at their video camera.

"I think they'll be okay," Lucinda said calmly, cradling Divine's head. A swollen purple spot was forming on their forehead. "They're breathing fine but a smack in the head from you warrants us calling an ambulance, just to be safe. Not to mention we have no idea what the side effects of whatever just happened might be."

"What did happen?" Macks asked, looking at me with wide eyes. "Do you know that guy?"

"No," I answered, catching a breath I hadn't realized I wasn't taking. "I've never seen him before, but he was targeting me, I think. How'd you know to come after me?"

"I saw you leave with him," Macks answered. "Almost missed it but I caught it out of the corner of my eye. And I know you wouldn't leave with someone without telling us details. And I knew you wouldn't leave in the middle of Lucinda's performance. So, something was up."

"Hello," Lucinda said into her cell phone. "I'm at The Milky Way club and there is someone in the back alley. They are unconscious but breathing. Send medical help immediately, they look like they might have been attacked or something." She hung up the phone and tucked it into her dress. "Let's get out of here."

"We can't leave," I said. "We should wait for the ambulance, and the police, to tell them what happened."

"I can show them the video!" Macks added.

"No, you can't," Lucinda said as she laid Divine's head down and stood up to face us. "We can't be here for the same reason you can't ever show anyone that video." There was a seriousness in her voice that made my heartbeat slow. "To protect Bryn and her secret. We can't be anywhere near this. On the off chance that they believe what we tell them, who knows what will happen to her."

Lucinda was right. In all the excitement I hadn't even thought about the aftermath. My parents had always stressed the importance of keeping my strength a secret. Now there was a disappearing man who can create sludge-spilling zombies. It was all connected somehow, which meant it was all a secret that needed to be kept. I couldn't let my parents' fears of me being hunted like a menace or locked up in some science lab come true, even if it meant we couldn't stay to make sure Divine was okay.

"She's right," I said. "We have to figure this out on our own."

"We go back inside," Lucinda instructed. "We make sure we are seen and then we make a quiet exit. By the time the police arrive and try to question people, we'll be gone."

"Right," Macks said, rushing to the doors leading back to the nightclub. I followed and Lucinda came directly after me. Once we were through the doors and descending into the club, she grabbed my wrist, stopping me for a moment while Macks continued.

"Are you okay?" she asked. The question was heavy, as if weighed down by something unsaid. I didn't know what to make of it, still barely processing what was happening.

"I'm fine," I lied.

Chapter 5

I could hardly focus on what was supposed to be a thrilling day. The events of the other night kept replaying in my head like an awful movie. "Her coffee order," Mila said as she led me to Divinity Magazine's conference rooms. "She only drinks iced, unless she's out of the office, then she drinks hot. Not sure why. Don't bother asking her."

We had gone over my onboarding before she gave me a brief tour of the facility. Now she was taking me to a meeting where I would shadow her, as she attended to her duties, and see how things work at the magazine. While we walked, she gave me tidbits of things I would need to know going forward.

I felt like a shell of myself as I tried to focus more on her and less on the insanity in my head. After getting home, Macks, Lucinda, and I unpacked that night as much as we could. We determined that I needed to show up to my first day, because the job was too important to screw up right away. But after the day was over the three of us would go try to see Divine. Our goal was to see if they could help us figure out who Damon was but also see if they remembered anything from that night. Specifically, about me. We needed to know if my secret had been exposed or if the whole event was just a hazy nightmare to them.

"Always almond milk," Mila continued. "And if it's a hot drink it needs to be sweetened with honey, iced drink needs to be sweetened with that, like, fake sugar stuff."

"Got it," I said as we crossed the hectic bullpen. The conference room was blocked off by glass walls, allowing for full transparency between those in the meeting and those who were working outside.

Mila opened the transparent doors, and all eyes shifted towards us. The long conference table was full of nameless faces I was sure to know soon. Only one seat was occupied by a familiar face. The girl I met in the elevator on the day of my interview. She gave me an acknowledging smile and as I returned the gesture, I realized that I didn't catch her name. She wore a black dress decorated with white polka dots, and black coils of hair cascaded from her head in every direction.

Elizabeth Stone stood at the head of the conference table, dripping with an energy that commanded attention and respect. A black and white color-block dress hugged her curves. Her muscular arms shamelessly exposed by the sleeveless ensemble. She wore two silver rings, one on the pointer finger of each hand. Both rings had bronze etchings, creating a geometric design.

She looked at us as we entered, giving a nod before speaking to the room. "This is my new assistant Bryn. She's shadowing Mila today. You'll be seeing lots of her in the future. So, if you can, take some time to get acquainted."

Murmured greetings echoed from the table before eyes shifted back to Miss Stone or the papers on the table. Mila opened the black padfolio she carried with her to a blank page and readied her pen.

"Alright, people," Miss Stone said. "We have just about everything squared away for the upcoming issue. We just need a featured story and cover."

Mila started to transcribe the information as a hand shot up from the table. A brown-haired woman in glasses sat tall as she waited for confirmation, or permission to speak.

"Go for it, Santana," Miss Stone told her.

She lowered her hand and said, "There was this up-and-coming designer, Gwendolyn Lynch, she went to her hometown in Maine a few months ago to get married. Apparently, her fiancé was killed, and she was kidnapped on the wedding day. We could do a piece on her and the tragedy."

"Investigative journalism? A crime piece?" a man at the table scoffed. "That's not what we do."

"No, just reporting on the events. I'm not trying to solve any mystery. It's an interest piece," Santana shot back. "People would be interested in hearing about it, and we've written about her in that Designers to Watch segment last year. So, there's a connection there too."

Mila continued to take note of the discussion. She looked at me, watching her, and whispered, "you'll want to keep track of everything in these meetings. Miss Stone will use your notes to move forward and keep track of next steps and ideas."

"Too gloom and doom for the cover," Miss Stone said to Santana with a sense of force. "But I do think it's a story worth doing. I think you should pursue it." She looked at the man who tried to argue the story idea. "Can you find room to include it in this issue?" It was a question, but she said it as if it was an order.

"Absolutely," the man choked, before flipping through the scattered pages in front of him.

"That's Quinton. He oversees layout and design," Mila explained as the meeting continued to unfold.

"For the feature," someone else said. A guy, with tattoos spilling across his arms from the edges of his short sleeve button-up, looked down at a handwritten list. "This model everyone's talking about..." He trailed his fingers down his list. "Hercules Nemean!" He called when he found it.

"We need an angle, Oli," Miss Stone said, looking at him intently.

"Legacy," Oli said simply, his voice deep and sturdy like the roots of a tree. "He's a third-generation celebrity. We can interview him and do a whole profile on his life, career, and family."

"Not to mention," the girl from the elevator added. "He is blowing up right now. Not just with his career. His is constantly trending on socials. People love him."

"And the people *will* buy the issue if he's on the cover!" yelled the man at the end of the table. He was tall and lanky.

He wore large sunglasses, despite being indoors, that were reflective like mirrors. A brown coat with tan fur at the neck and wrists made him look out of place in the conference room full of business casual attire. He flipped his long golden-brown hair, like a high school girl in a 90's movie. "And I'd love to work with him."

"That's Gianfranco Zanetti," Mila told me. "He's Divinity Magazine's head stylist." He needed no introduction. He was an icon. A fashion genius. A name associated with some of the most striking looks to ever grace runways and red carpets. His DNA was etched into all of Divinity's photoshoots.

"Do you think we can get enough out of this to get a feature length piece?" Miss Stone asked Oli. He nodded in response, and she followed with, "We'll get you in touch and see if he's interested. Be prepared with some backup plans if it doesn't work out. Have them on my desk tomorrow morning."

"I'm on it," Oli said with confidence.

Everything seemed to move so quickly, like the efficiency in the air was forcing the world inside this room to progress with sweeping motion. And somehow, Mila was keeping up with it all. Her hand moving in time with the meeting, her pen acting as an extension of herself. I wondered how long it would take me to become ingrained in this duty. I wondered how long it took her to solidify herself as a scribe.

"If everything with the print issue is squared away," a quiet voice said. She was the last to speak at the table. While most people in the conference room appeared to be in their thirties or maybe forties, she appeared to be in her twenties like Mila, elevator girl, and myself. "We need a subject for the Faces Of A Movement segment."

Two years ago, Divinity magazine started a social justice initiative. FOAM was an online exposé at the forefront of Divinity's website that examined activism and the people involved. A deep dive into a specific crisis or injustice, where a journalist would give maximum exposure to the events and implications. To make the issues hit harder for readers, they focused on specific people within the eye of the storm. By showing the problems of the world through the lens of someone's life, not just the thing that is happening, but a person and their experience before, during, and after, they tap into empathy that propels understanding and change.

"Minerva runs all our social media and manages our website," Mila said, her eyes focused on the girl. "Or at least, she's in charge of the team that does."

"It's London's turn to take the helm." Miss Stone looked at the elevator girl. "Do you have any leads?"

"I did," London began. Her face looked unsure, but her voice was overflowing with unwavering confidence. "I was looking into a unionizing piece. Employees of a local chain are trying to form but their employer is fighting them. I'm having a hard time finding someone to agree to be the face of it all."

"Might be better to put it on the shelf for now and revisit it in another month," Oli chimed in. "If they're afraid for their livelihoods, it might take time before they're comfortable."

"I like the corporate corruption angle though," Miss Stone said. "More incidents like this need to be addressed."

"Like the Cake'd scandal," I added, my mind making the connection and immediately expelling it through the mouth. Everyone looked at me, as if surprised to hear me speak.

"It's not really our job to contribute to these meetings," Mila whispered politely. "Just take notes and grab lunch."

"No, no," Miss Stone said immediately. "It's alright. Go on, Bryn."

Suddenly my body felt heavy as I tried to get words to come out of my mouth. "Well, it's just this super popular bakery, and they pride themselves on being a queer-owned business and they think that is some sort of shield that protects them from the fact that there are multiple instances of racism and sexual assault from the owners."

"I have been hearing a lot about this," Miss Stone said, nodding intently.

"My housemate is one of the ex-employees leading the protests against them," I told her, looking at the whole table. "And it's not just her, there is a small group, they might be willing to do FOAM."

"The Cake'd thing is a hot issue right now," said London. "And it's local, in the heart of the city. I can follow it. I can do coverage of the protest alongside the profile on the workers. I can try to get enough info on the owners to do an article there too."

Miss Stone stood, unresponsive, for a moment. Her right hand caressing her neck, holding her elbow in her left hand. The artificial light of the room clung to the rings on her fingers. "I like it," she finally said. Excitement filled my body, the satisfaction of helping on my first day. "You'll be there, Bryn?"

"Yes Ma'am," I said, fighting not to let my excitement show.

"If you're willing to make some introductions for London, we can count it as billable hours for you."

"Sure," I said, swept up in the thought of assisting in the endeavor.

"Perfect," Miss Stone responded. "I'll leave it to you two." She swiftly moved to their next order of business.

After the meeting was over, Mila hung back to go over her notes with Miss Stone, after informing me that this is what I would need to do after each meeting and Miss Stone would likely have a list of follow-up tasks for me. When I tried to follow Mila, to listen in on this aspect of the job, London approached me.

"Welcome to the team, thrilled you made it," she said with a smile, extending her hand and I gave her mine on instinct. She led the handshake with three crisp up and down movements before letting go. "I was her assistant once, before Mila."

"Really?" I asked, surprised but happy to hear it. Seeing where she was now, having started from where I currently stood, was a promising thing.

"Yeah, I did it while I pursued my degrees in journalism," she said, and I wasn't sure if she was bragging or not. "After I graduated, I applied to the next available position. And since I knew extensively how this place worked, I think it helped."

I wondered if she looked at me and saw someone that could, one day, be where she was. In her eyes, were we the same, just at different stages in time? Would Miss Stone be able to see that potential in me as well? God, I really hoped so. My heart and soul were practically salivating, yearning for this. A future that was standing right in front of me.

"Anyways," London said like a breezy song. "Here's my phone number. Let's keep in touch about this protest." She handed me a card, an official piece of Divinity Magazine stationary, with her name, phone number, and email printed in white ink on black paper. "Or if you have any free time today, stop by my desk."

"Absolutely," I said, rubbing the thick and sturdy paper between my fingers. It felt so serious. Holding it in my hands felt like I was in a dream. I got the job, I was in that meeting, my voice was heard by a room full of people who are doing what I dream of doing, I came up with an original idea that was immediately accepted, and I've been handed a direct line of communication to a person who got her start where I currently was. It was all crashing down on me in a beautiful avalanche.

"Bryn," I heard Mila's voice behind me. "If you're ready, I can run through a few more things with you."

London smiled and turned towards the sea of desks and computers, and I turned to continue with the first day in this new chapter of my life.

Chapter 6

"Girl, tell us everything!" Lucinda called out, arms in the air as I approached her and Macks. She wore a gray faux fur coat over black jeans and a floral blouse. She was wigless, showing off her perfectly shaved scalp. She towered over Macks, like a massive tree, in her platform shoes. Macks wore an oversize shirt and baggy shorts, both in a matching shade of hot pink. Two large silver stars hung from their ears.

"It was…" I stumbled, not finding the right words that encapsulated just how amazing and full of potential I felt. "It was really good."

"Okay, I see you!" Lucinda exclaimed. "That smile! You're beaming!"

"You'll have to give us the full rundown later," Macks said with excitement.

"Something kind of big did happen," I said, cheeks hurting from the grin I couldn't contain. "I suggested the Cake'd protest for FOAM!"

"Oh my God!" Macks called out with a cheer. "And they took the suggestion?"

"Yeah! Isn't that incredible?" I looked at Lucinda,

expecting joy. What looked back at me was cold brown eyes and a stone-faced expression. I didn't understand.

"Why would you do that?" she asked, a sharp sting in her voice.

"To help," I answered. "I thought that would have been obvious. You know how popular Divinity is. This segment on their website will give y'all so much visibility. For the cause. To hold Cake'd accountable."

"Thank you," Lucinda said, not sounding thankful at all. "But no. I can't be the center of a Divinity article."

"Why not?" I asked her, baffled by what I was hearing.

"Because!" She stammered over her words, looking me up and down before her eyes fell onto Macks, who was watching us like a wide-eyed child. "Macks is filming their documentary!"

"So?" I asked, louder than I intended.

"Their film is like the same thing as FOAM, showing this political moment, focusing on the people leading the charge, or whatever," she explained erratically. "Macks is our friend, this could make their film, like, obsolete."

"I doubt it," Macks said with a squeak. "I think it's better to have as many projects focused on this as possible. Maximum exposure will hold them accountable. Bryn has a point. Divinity Magazine is so much bigger than me. They can carry your work much further than I can. If they overshadow my film, so be it. I care more about seeing this creep burn, than I do about how many people watch my film."

"See," I said, gesturing my arms at Macks. "You don't have to worry about them."

"So, I'm just going to be Divinity's Black trans poster child?" There was a sharp disdain in her voice, cutting at me like a blade.

"You know I would never offer you up as a token," I said, hurt that she'd even think that. "I'm only trying to help. I thought you'd be into this."

"You should have asked…" She looked at me, unblinking and jaw tight, holding something back.

"Excuse me?" a nurse in crisp blue scrubs grabbed our attention. I had been so absorbed in our discussion, I almost forgot we were in the waiting room of a small hospital. Fluorescent lighting, dingy chairs, and a television screen playing old game shows on mute decorated the area. An elderly woman sat in the corner, stirring coffee in a foam cup with a wooden stick. "You can see them now."

The nurse directed us down a long hallway, past rooms of patients, letting us know how to reach the door we needed. Divine sat up in bed, wearing a hospital gown. Their hair was unkempt, and their makeup was undone. A pale and hollow shell of themself. They used a remote to flip through the static channels of the TV on the wall. They looked at us, their face drained of color and emotion, and dropped the remote on the bedside table.

"Hey," Lucinda said, taking the lead. "How are you feeling?"

"I'm alive," Divine said, looking at us as if they were unsure how to proceed. "When I heard you wanted to visit me, I was surprised." Lucinda had reached out to Divine's sister and asked to be put on the visitor list so we could check in on them. The fact that Divine was surprised by this was probably a good sign. They might not remember that I was connected to their accident. Or they were surprised because they did remember and didn't know what to make of the whole situation.

"This happened at one of my shows," Lucinda said swiftly. She approached them and sat at the chair posted at their bedside. "I felt bad and wanted to make sure you were okay. And maybe try to figure out what happened."

"The doctors say my adrenaline was spiking through the roof and my amygdala was practically on fire. They are running tests trying to figure out what might have caused it or if there are any side effects."

"Do they have any leads?" I asked, trying to see on their face if they had any sort of inkling.

"They swear it's drugs. But I don't do that shit," Divine scoffed. "So, if it was drugs, that jerk must have drugged me."

"The guy you were with at the bar?" I asked them.

"Yeah, Damon," they answered, narrowing their eyes at me. "We were talking to you at the bar. That's the last thing I remember before things went hazy." Relief flooded my chest. "Did you see anything?"

"No!" I lied. "You two disappeared during the show, I just thought maybe you left."

"Damn," Divine cursed. "I thought you might have some answers for me."

"How do you know this guy?" Macks asked, leaning against the threshold of the door.

"We had just met that night. He was really hot and charming and real thirsty for it. I assumed he'd be a guaranteed good time, but…"

"Things took a turn," I said. "You don't remember anything after the drinks at the bar?"

"No, things just kinda go dark after that. Although…"

"What is it?" Lucinda asked, leaning in.

"It's not so much a memory, but a feeling. Like I remember being angry and afraid. Like, consumed by it." They looked down at their hands, shivering slightly. "Like, whatever happened to me or whatever I was drugged with made me blackout but left that behind. I don't know if that makes sense."

"It sounds scary," Macks said.

"Yeah, and then I woke up here with a killer headache and this!" Divine pointed at the large bruise I left. A black and blue welt on the side of their head. "If he did drug me, he either got rough or I hurt myself in the drugged-out haze."

I felt terrible that they had gone through this. I felt terrible that it was because of me. I felt terrible that I had to hurt them. But I also felt really glad that they had no memory of the events. My secret was safe, which was one less thing to worry about. But there was still so much to worry about. So many unanswered questions. And it was looking like Divine was not going to be a lead towards answers.

"Is there anything about this guy that would help track him down?" I asked, hoping. "A phone number or a last name, maybe."

"No," Divine said. "None that I can remember. Why are *you* trying to track him down?"

The three of us exchanged looks before Lucinda jumped in with a save. "We want to help find him just in case he is truly responsible. Justice for you, and maybe save people he might target next."

"Let's be honest, the evidence seems to point that he is responsible," Macks pressed.

"Don't turn this into a crusade," Divine sighed. "That's sweet that you want to help but you don't have to get involved with this. Besides, aren't you already dealing with your own thing?" They looked at Lucinda, eyebrows raised.

"The Cake'd thing," Lucinda nodded.

"Yeah, everyone is talking about it," Divine said. "It seems huge. You're already out there fighting the good fight. Don't worry about me."

"I guess," Lucinda said, accepting the pushback.

"See!" Macks chirped. "You've got people rallying to get this done. Think about how much more you can do with FOAM."

"Macks! Not now." Lucinda said.

"FOAM! Like, Divinity Magazine's FOAM? They want you?" Divine asked with excitement.

"I just started working there and suggested the protest as the upcoming feature. But Lucinda is trying to turn it down," I said. If this was a dead end in the pursuit of our mystery man, I could at least use the visit as further fuel to support Lucinda's protest.

"First of all, you lucky bitch," Divine said to me. "I love Divinity Magazine. They did an issue with only nonbinary models back in the day, which was huge for me. I named myself after the magazine after I came out." Light was coming back into their face. They turned back to Lucinda. "You have to do it! If you really want this protest to mean something, to accomplish something, Divinity is offering you exactly that."

"I already tried to tell her that the exposure would bolster the cause," I said, feeding off the excitement in the room.

"Why on earth would you reject this?" Divine asked.

Macks, Divine, and myself all stared at Lucinda, who sat there looking directly into my eyes, stone faced. "This will open up a can of worms," she said. "An inevitable one that's already begun. So, maybe you're right. I should just go for it. I would never forgive myself for hindering the protest because of my own fear." She sounded defeated and somber.

"You're going to do it?" Macks asked. I didn't think it would be that easy to change her mind.

Lucinda looked at Divine. "We clearly have the attention of our community," she said. "But we can go further, go harder. We can reach the public. I'd be an idiot to turn that down."

"This will be good for you," I said, hugging her. "I promise."

"It will be good for the cause," Lucinda said, pulling back and grasping Divine's hand. "Thanks for the encouragement. And for letting us check in on you."

Without another word, Lucinda exited the room.

"I hope you feel better soon," I said, as Macks quickly followed Lucinda.

"Thanks," Divine smiled. "She seems pretty anxious about this FOAM thing. But I can tell y'all are good support. She'll be just fine."

I nodded before exiting the room and catching up with Lucinda and Macks down the hall.

"It's good that they don't remember anything," Lucinda said as we entered the waiting room again. "But this guy, if he was targeting you, he'll probably show up again. And you need to be ready for that."

"I don't know how I would prepare for it," I said. Lucinda continued to exit the hospital, leading us into the lobby. "But if he does show up, he won't have the element of surprise again. That's for sure."

As we exited the building, Lucinda turned to Macks and me. "A storm is coming. And you're at the center of it. I just wish I could protect you."

"This storm might be a blessing," I told her. "This might tell me where I come from. Or where my strength comes from at the very least."

Lucinda nodded. "Until the storm hits, I guess we just carry on with our lives."

"Working this new job," Macks said. "Leading this protest, doing FOAM, and making this film. Lots to keep us going until we figure out what's next with the mysterious stranger."

"I guess we should reach out to Divinity," Lucinda said. "Let them know that I'm all in for what's to come."

Chapter 7

Sunlight rained down on the crowd, making everyone shine like silver. The heat burrowed into every person and onto each surface like a parasitic disease. A long black river of asphalt flowed through the veins of metal giants, carrying hundreds of faces emitting thousands of voices.

Bystanders muddled along the sidewalk capturing the moment with their cellphones. Police officers stood in small groups, dispersed through various points in the mob of people, stiff and unamused but ready to deliver brute force if the building passions reached combustible levels. At the center of this spectacle, the facade of red brick and pristine windows. A large hot pink sign adorned with the word "Cake'd" in white calligraphy sat on the storefront like a crown.

Pouring from the bakery like the petals of a blooming flower, a mob dripping with rage. Wielding posters reading "NO MORE SILENCE," "Consent, Not Cake'd," "End Sexual Assault," "Boycott Cake'd," and more. They were ready for war. Each demonstrating body wore a pink shirt mimicking the Cake'd logo with a blood red circle and diagonal slash laid over it. The uniform of the movement.

Lucinda stood, elevated above the crowd, gallantly holding the words "Hands off my Cake" high in the sky. Her pink shirt cut into a crop top. Lavender curls cascaded from her head, framing her terracotta brown face. This was the hair she wore when she needed to be seen. Lucinda was an unapologetic force of nature. Her voice fell over the crowd, feeding the chants like logs to a campfire.

Macks stood beside me, their video camera pointed upwards at Lucinda. They maneuvered themselves to get a view of the waves of people behind her. When filming, the camera was merely an extension of Macks. Not a device or a tool. They melded with the machine and together they would birth footage that would evolve into a documentary.

There were other cameras present. Bigger, more professional than Macks' equipment. They captured footage and testimony from anyone they could. One such camera focused on a woman who stood in front of Lucinda. She wore a dark gray pantsuit with a sleek black turtleneck underneath. Her blonde hair was tied in a braid over one shoulder. This was Judith Campbell, a face that made a daily appearance on every television screen in the city.

She spoke into her microphone with a crystalline voice. "I'm here at the Anti-Cake'd protest, with demonstration leader Lucinda Marsean."

Lucinda jumped down from her raised placement, even on the same ground, she stood a few inches taller than the reporter.

"I hate when they do that," I scoffed. Macks turned their camera to face me. Although I was unprepared to give anything to the camera, I allowed my thoughts into the world. "They make this sound like the problem is with this one business in this single moment. It is so much bigger than just this." I felt like my explanation was unsatisfying. As if I didn't deliver justice where justice was due.

Macks gave me a smile as if to say that I delivered a moment of truth, and that truth was exactly what they wanted. They turned their camera back to Lucinda, who was taking Campbell's first question.

"Richard Owens, Owner-operator of one of New York's most prominent bakeries has been under fire due to accusations of sexual harassment from alarming numbers of current and previous employees," the reporter began. "What do you have to say in response to Mr. Owens' most recent statement that all of this is merely haphazard cancel culture?"

Lucinda scoffed. "I'm not a fan of zero tolerance for inexcusable acts being labeled as cancel culture. Here's the tea: you don't want your business shut down? Don't inappropriately touch people, your employees. Boom. Case closed." She looked into the camera with a fire in her eyes, like she was laying down a curse on anyone who would watch the footage. "The bar is on the ground and yet here we are, tripping over a damn toothpick."

The crowd, who had settled for the news crew, erupted in cheers.

"Men really love throwing around the term 'cancel culture' when they really mean 'dealing with the consequences of their shitty actions.' How disgusting," Ceci said, seamlessly slipping through the crowd and joining Macks and me as we watched Lucinda go to work.

Statuesque and dressed in black, Ceci stood out in the field of furious pink. She watched over the roaring people with a blankness on her face. She was lost in it. The sight put her deep in her mind and disappointment seeped from her, in the form of contained tears, glossing her sage-colored eyes.

"Thanks for coming," I told her. "I'm sure it means a lot to Lucinda."

She looked down at me, her large black sun hat framing her face. "I wouldn't miss this for the world."

"What you said just now," Macks jumped in. "It would make a good sound bite. Would you mind giving your thoughts to the camera? I'm making a film."

Ceci chuckled softly. "Sure, I wouldn't mind leaving my own mark here."

"Cool, let's head over here," Macks pointed out past the crowd. "We could get a great shot of the protest behind you."

The two of them walked away, leaving me to watch Lucinda speak with the news crew as London appeared holding a notepad, pen, and her phone which she had been using to vigorously record statements.

"I think I talked to all of the coworkers Lucinda pointed out to me," she announced.

"Are any of them willing to do FOAM with her?" I asked.

"I got one for sure, Karla Pierce. Everyone else is either thinking about it or declined."

"Damn," I said. "I thought you'd have more people interested."

"It can be tough, agreeing to be the literal face of a movement. It's a very public thing. We are used to this with FOAM," she explained.

"Lucinda was against it at first too," I told her.

"Well, I'm glad she changed her mind," London said. "I think she's a great subject for this. People will respond to her. I'm excited to do the interview."

"When is that happening?" Macks asked, joining us.

"I think I can get both Lucinda and Karla today. Sounds like they can both swing by the office after the protest," she answered. "You're making a film about all of this, yeah?"

"I am," Macks said, holding up their camera.

"Maybe we can join forces," London suggested. "I could interview you about your efforts and how you support what's going on here with your art. Maybe the film can even go up on our site. I could probably get you paid too."

"That would be incredible!" Macks said.

"I have to talk to the boss first, but I'll let you know what she says." London handed Macks her notepad with the tilt of her head and a smile. "Give me your number and I'll be in touch."

"Where did Ceci go?" I asked as Macks jotted down their digits.

"She went off into the crowd somewhere, talking to

people," they answered. It was cool to hear she was engaging with the protest. The sense of community and unified purpose was palpable.

"This is going great so far!" Lucinda said, approaching us after the reporter finished her questions. "So many people showed up."

"You did that!" Macks cheered.

"And it's only the beginning," London insisted. "Will you two be joining us at Divinity later?"

"I can't," Macks said with a shrug. "The theater is hosting this Indie Film Fest tomorrow and in exchange for not working today, I agreed to come in tonight to help close and set up for the event."

"Sounds dreadful." Lucinda rolled her eyes before turning to London and me. "Will I come face to face with Miss Divinity Magazine herself?"

"Probably not," London answered. "We'll be there a little late. The office will likely be empty."

"So why go there for the interview?" she promptly responded. "Sounds positively drab!" She spoke boldly, with an exaggerated hand clutching imaginary pearls, like she was on a stage projecting to an audience.

"It's just a nice neutral location," London said, unfazed by the dramatics. "And we like to record these interviews and we have a whole set up at the office."

"Well, fine," Lucinda agreed, a sense of satisfaction on her tongue. "Can't argue with that."

Just then, a voice called out to Lucinda, and she disappeared into the crowd, immediately swept away by her duty, by her cause. London followed, pen and paper in hand, ready to envelop the continuing moment. Macks was still by my side, but completely absorbed into their camera and the images it captured. As I watched the mob of people ebb and flow, their chants washing over the streets, I caught a glimpse of Karla Pierce.

I didn't know Karla well, but I had seen her a handful of times while she and Lucinda worked together. I had heard that she took the brunt of the assaults, and later intimidations, lobbied against the Cake'd employees.

In this moment, it seemed like the crowd parted slightly, framing her in view. She stood amongst them, her hot pink shirt like a suit of armor on the battlefield. Fire red hair rolled in curls down her neck. Freckles like warpaint decorated her cheeks. She brandished her sign, meticulously painted with a pristine glossy finish on a study poster board.

In the same hot pink as the warrior uniform, it read, "Sexual harassment: The secret ingredient in your cake."

Chapter 8

The office was quiet. I had never seen it like this in the short time I had been working. Quiet. Empty. Eerie.

London had taken Lucinda and Karla to conduct the interviews, something she asked not to have an audience for. While I waited for Lucinda to finish, so we could go home together, I decided to be productive. I was wandering the bullpen, examining every desk, and testing my memory of the people who sat at each one. Conjuring up faces in my mind and associating them with the nameplates at each desk. Miss Stone was already sending me around to deliver or retrieve things from random people, the sooner I knew who everyone was, the sooner I would reach peak delivery girl efficiency.

As I was about to begin my second round of desk studies, I heard footsteps approaching. I looked to the hall where Karla stood. She looked out of place, arms crossed over her chest, squeezing herself into a tight ball as if to make herself as small as possible in this space. Her face was contorted, brow furrowed and the corners of her mouth twisting downward. The whiteness of her skin had a greenish tint.

"Is everything okay," I asked her gently.

She looked up at me, as if shocked that I was speaking to her. "Yeah," she sighed. "This is just…a lot. London said I could take a breather."

"I can't even imagine what you must be feeling," I told her. "But I know for a fact that you're doing the right thing. This needs to be exposed and he needs to be held accountable." I knew I was saying things she was already aware of, but I still hoped it might reassure her. I wasn't even sure if my words registered in her mind. She just stood there, staring at the ground. I noticed that her left hand was caressing a dark green jewel that sat on her right wrist in a black metal band with a design of crescent shapes laid across the surface like bricks.

"That's a beautiful bracelet," I said, thinking that changing the subject might be a more effective way to make her feel better.

She smiled at me. Quick like a flash and then the smile was gone. "Thanks," she hissed. "Someone at the protest gave it to me, saying it was a testament of my strength and resilience. I liked the thought, so I took it, even though I don't really *feel* strong or resilient."

"Everything you're doing is exactly that," I argued. "It takes unbelievable strength to stand up against the ugly shit in this world, and it takes incredible resilience when the fight seems impossible to win but you choose to fight it anyway. I believe that, with my entire soul." I was practically pleading with her to take my words to heart, but once again she seemed like my voice didn't even reach her.

"Where's the bathroom?" she asked me, tightening her lips like she had eaten something sour.

"Right past the elevators," I told her, pointing towards the opposite hallway.

"Thank you," she said quietly before scurrying away and disappearing from sight, past the large potted plants that stood at the office's threshold. I turned to continue my mental exercise but heard movement behind me. I looked back, expecting to see Karla again. Miss Stone stood there instead.

"Oh!" I said, straightening my posture at the realization that it was her. "I didn't know you would be here."

"I wasn't going to be," she said. There was a fogginess to her voice. Almost like she was trying to choose her words carefully. "But London emailed me to let me know you'd be in the office after hours and I wanted to come by." She wore a white jumpsuit with burgundy-colored vertical stripes and a V-cut at the chest.

"That's so nice of you to check in," I said. I felt like most bosses wouldn't drag themselves back to the office on their own time just to check in on their employees when they can easily do it the next morning during work hours. "London is working on the interviews now. The protest went really well. I think the only downside was that London was hoping to try to get a statement from the owner, Richard Owens, but he didn't even show up." The words came out in a nervous sputter.

"I'm not surprised," Miss Stone said, shaking her head. "Men have trouble coming face to face with their demons.

Especially when others are trying to bring them to light. But I must admit, that isn't why I'm here."

"Oh," I said. "Is there something you need? Anything I can help with?"

"I know what you are."

Fear collected in my throat. Pleasant things didn't usually follow that sentence.

"I felt it, the moment we met." She approached me, weaving through the maze of desks without taking her eyes off me. "I thought when you came here, when you applied for the position, you knew what I was. But some time has passed, and you have said nothing to make me believe that this is the case."

"I don't understand," I told her.

"Exactly my point!" She yelled with vigor. "And that seemed strange to me. And then you started talking about the protest and your friend, and I investigated the scandal more because it was going to be on our site. And then I saw her and then it all clicked."

"Saw who?" everything she was saying was making less and less sense. She was throwing around pieces and I didn't know how to connect them.

"Bryn?" a familiar voice called out to me, instantly instilling some calm. Lucinda stood in the hall, looking at the two of us with wide eyes. "I was coming to check on Karla."

"It really is you," Miss Stone said, looking at Lucinda in utter disbelief. "Which means…" She looked back at me.

"They told me you wouldn't be here," Lucinda said,

looking like she had just been caught doing something completely depraved. A deer in the headlights.

"You two know each other?" I asked, putting two of the pieces together, still unable to complete the puzzle.

Miss Stone approached Lucinda now, putting herself halfway between us. "You're avoiding me?" she asked. "You have had her, been with her this whole time, and you've been avoiding me?"

"I..." Lucinda sounded like she might cry. "I wasn't ready. I knew the second you knew who she was, things would change. I was just holding onto her, to us, for a little while longer."

"It was inevitable!" Miss Stone argued.

"I know," Lucinda shot back.

"From the second she walked into this building; it was inevitable!"

"I know!"

"Can someone please explain to me what is happening?" I called out to them. They both looked at me, a swirl of emotions on their faces.

"Your job was to watch her, not befriend her," Miss Stone said to Lucinda but looked at me. "You were supposed to bring her to me when the time came. And you prolonged it because you put your feelings above duty."

My head was spinning. I didn't know what was happening, but it sounded bad. Like, Lucinda had targeted me for something. Something connected to Miss Stone. Maybe something tied to me getting this position. Maybe this was the whole reason Lucinda was even in my life. Like she was never a real friend. I could feel in my gut that this had something to do with my strength. I couldn't explain how I came to the conclusion, but it was there, plain as day. Also there, along with my suspicion was the fear that whatever secret they had was something sinister.

"Don't lecture me," Lucinda said, anger forming on her face. She stepped forward, a large visible breath building in her chest. Before she could form that breath into words, a loud crash grabbed the attention of all three of us. We looked towards the hall that led out of the office.

The restroom door. It sounded as if it had been thrown open, as if in anger or a hurry. I expected Karla to come running into the room, but she didn't. The hall was quiet and still for a moment. Then the sound of something dragging across the floor came trickling against my ears.

Scraping. Continuous scraping. Growing louder. A shadow emerged in the corridor. A large shapeless blob. The sound stopped and the shadow took shape. A body lifting upward, as if standing up. But something about the silhouette felt off. There were no defined legs. The lower part of the shadow's body was just one solid form, wider than the torso and waist.

"Hello?" Miss Stone called. "The office is closed."

There was no answer.

Just a sharp and prolonged sibilant whisper.

"What the hell?" Miss Stone said as the shadow lurched forward, making the body casting it visible.

A massive…*thing* came into view, so quickly I didn't even have time to question what I was seeing. A woman, or a woman-like creature. Her skin was a pale green, and her naked body was covered in patches of a brown scaly rash. Her lower half, completely covered in the brown scales, was a large tail of a serpent that extended from the office and disappeared into the hallway. Her arms extended much farther than that of a human, going from shoulder to elbow to forearm, and then to a second elbow and forearm before ending at a hand of dull yellow metallic talons.

Her face was erupting in more scaly patches, like muddy fireworks in a green sky. Where a nose should have been, there were only two triangular holes that slowly pulsed as she took in breaths. Two large sharp fangs protruded from the upper jaw of her closed mouth. Her eyes were shut tightly, pulling at the skin around her eyelids. Attached to her bald head was a mound of writhing red snakes.

The snakes, too many to count, wiggled and squirmed in every direction, looking at their surroundings. The monstrous woman let out a low growl. And I was speechless.

"Both of you, get behind me!" Miss Stone said, turning her back to the creature. As she faced me, Lucinda ran towards us. Some of the snakes on top of the woman's head put their focus on Lucinda's movements and the creature backed away slightly in response.

Lucinda grabbed at my arms, attempting to pull me even further away from the creature but she could not move me. I just stood there, staring at the monster before me. It was three, maybe four, rows of desks away. Kind of far, but definitely too close for comfort. It was twice the size of a person, not counting the section of its tail that stretched across the ground. The smell of ashen smoke wafted off of it.

It was terrifying.

But Lucinda and Miss Stone didn't seem particularly taken aback by this thing. They seemed surprised. But not afraid or confused or particularly mind blown like I was.

"What is going on?" I asked, eyes focused on the creature.

"Bryn," Miss Stone said, placing a hand on my cheek and turning my head to look at her. "You shouldn't look at it."

"We need to get you out of here," Lucinda insisted.

"What's happening?" I asked them both.

"No time to explain," Miss Stone said before glaring at Lucinda. "Thanks to you." I felt Lucinda's body shudder beside me.

Miss Stone raised her hands to her chest, creating a X shape with her arms. The identical silver rings that rested on each hand began to glow slightly, intensifying with every second before culminating in a bright flash. When the light dissipated, the rings were gone.

Elizabeth Stone stood before me holding two curved blades. Each hand grasped a S shaped bronze hilt which was connected to sharp silver crescents. She spun around quickly, throwing each from her hand as her body continued the movement and placed her back in her original position, facing Lucinda and me. Her eyes opened when her circular turn ended, meaning her eyes must have been closed when she threw the blades.

Each blade flew towards the creature, slicing clean through sections of the pack of snakes. The creature roared and ducked down, bringing her hands to cover her face as five snake heads fell to the ground followed by a spray of red blood.

"Stop looking at it!" Miss Stone commanded, bringing my attention to her and away from the monster.

She extended her hands upward as the blades came flying back like boomerangs, catching them with so much ease that she barely glanced at her hands.

My heart was racing. I didn't know what was going on, but I knew we were all in danger and I knew that I could help. The sooner the danger was gone, the sooner I could get answers.

There was sudden movement behind Miss Stone, the creature rising and pouncing forward. Miss Stone put her two blades together at their hilts, creating one circular blade, with the hilt crossing through its center. She tossed the weapon backwards, this time not even turning her body. The snakes on the creature's head hissed and the monster, eyes still closed, raised its hands to shield its head. The circular blade clanged against the monster's brass claws and it ricocheted to the ground.

I reached for the nearest object I could find. A desk. I bent down to grip the bottom of the piece of furniture and flung it forward with one simple tug. Computer, office supplies, and knickknacks fell to the ground as the desk crashed into the creature, sending it backwards. As it fell, its tail whipped forward, landing at our feet. Miss Stone grabbed the tail with both hands and heaved the creature up and tossed it clear across the room and into the far wall with a mighty grunt.

"You're strong?" the question formed on my lips before I could even think it.

"You and I," she said with a heavy breath. "We are the same."

My heart leaped into my throat.

We are the same.

What I was, she was.

The strength that plagued me was the same strength she seemed to wield with precision. After years of feeling alone, even amongst my support system, I finally found someone else who was like me. And it was someone I aspired to be. Someone so incredibly brilliant and talented and accomplished. Who, at least on the surface, lived a normal life amongst normal people.

Before I could even dare to unpack that further, a voice called out. A voice belonging to someone I had completely forgotten about in all of the chaos.

"Is everything alright?" London called out with concern. Her voice, and the following crashing footsteps came from the hall that led to the interview room. The hall that the monster now laid directly in front of.

Instantly, as London turned the corner, she screamed at the sight. The snakes on top of the monster's head all looked at her with a sharp turn, inviting London to scream even more. The monster's body lifted, and its arms reached out, grasping her in its claws, pinning her arms to her side and lifting her into the air.

"The snakes on its head," I gasped.

"They see for her," Miss Stone finished.

London's screams of fear quickly turned to a bellow of anger and determination. She raised her feet and brought them crashing down into the monster's face and against the head of snakes.

"We have to help her!" I yelled.

The creature shook her violently, immediately stopping her fighting and screaming. It pulled her forward, bringing them face to face. The monster's eyes slowly peeled open.

Suddenly, I felt Lucinda's hands against my face. Her familiar warmth against my eyes, shrouding my view in a dim blackness. I heard London scream again, this time a scream that sent ice water through my veins. And as quickly as the scream came, it stopped. Immediately, as if cut off mid breath. And then a loud thud as something heavy and solid hit the ground. I heard the creature slithering against the ground, not towards us, but further away.

I pulled Lucinda's hand away, to see London on the ground. Her mouth wide open, eyes bulging, her body stiff. Every inch of her was caked in a stone-gray substance. Her skin, her eyes, even the inside of her mouth looked like they were made of stone. Like she had been turned into solid rock.

The pieces clicked in my head in a shocking revelation. "Medusa?" I wasn't even sure who I was asking the question to. But I had to say it. This was a pretty popular figure in mythology. I had learned about her in various literature classes in the past. But this was never something that was supposed to be real.

"Not quite," Miss Stone said, looking down at stony London. "She died quite a long time ago."

"This is a Gorgon though," Lucinda said, a comforting hand on my back. "Which is what Medusa was." Their response took me off guard. So assured and readily available. Not only were they confirming what this thing was, but they spoke about it like it was common knowledge to them. Which made everything seem even more surreal.

"London," I said, afraid to ask what this means for her.

"There is time to save her," Miss Stone said. "A Gorgon's petrification is only permanent after the following sunrise. If the beast is slain before tomorrow morning, the process should reverse."

"What?" I asked, taken aback by what felt like a nonsensical rule. "Why is that the way it works?"

"I don't know!" Miss Stone spat, as if I was crazy for asking. "That's just how it is."

I looked at the monster, who seemed to have retreated to the other side of the room. It sat there; eyes closed again. It opened its jaw, revealing more sharp teeth beneath its fangs. Breathy words fell from her mouth.

"Richard Owens," she hissed. "Where is Richard Owens!"

"Owens?" Lucinda asked, dismayed. "What does this thing want with my sleazy ex-boss?"

"He must pay," the monster said breathily, a long forked tongue flapping with every word. "He is who I seek to curse. Give him to me and no one else shall meet the fate." The creature extended her lanky arm to point at London and I saw something that went unnoticed before. A black metal band with a snakeskin design and a dark green jewel sat on her wrist.

"That's Karla!" I screamed out. Miss Stone and Lucinda looked at me, confused.

"No longer!" She hissed. "I am something new. Something more. And he will taste vengeance."

"You can't kill her," Lucinda pleaded to Miss Stone. "She's…she's a victim. Whatever is happening to her, she's reacting to trauma. It's not her fault."

"The life of an innocent person is at stake," Miss Stone said, biting at the air. "My employee. We can't leave her like this."

"Is there another way?" I asked. "Like, how did she turn into this? There has to be some way to reverse it." Gorgon-Karla seemed to sit there impatiently, clicking her brass claws together rhythmically.

"Medusa was a witch," Miss Stone said, lowering her voice. "She was…abused by a god. She and her sisters used black magic to give themselves the power to get vengeance."

"She was violated and felt powerless, so she turned to transformation magic. Feels topical," Lucinda said. "Which is very powerful stuff. If Karla did it herself, she would have had to have performed the proper ritual. But she's been at a protest and in an interview all day. And this kind of thing doesn't come from nowhere."

"So, someone else had to have done this to her," Miss Stone said, feeding off of Lucinda's analysis. "Someone gave her the strength to get revenge on your old boss."

"Strength!" That word kept reverberating in my life. "She told me that someone gave her that bracelet to represent resilience and strength."

Miss Stone and Lucinda shared a glance with raised eyebrows. "That could be it," Lucinda said, as if she was just going with the flow.

"Enough chatter," Gorgon-Karla demanded with a raspy yell. The snakes atop her head glared at us. "If you won't give him to me, you are an obstacle that must be eliminated. I will find him myself!" She began to slither forward with swift speed.

"We need to get that bracelet," Miss Stone ordered.

"I can hold her back for a minute," Lucinda said, stepping forward. "It's been a long time since I've done this." She took a deep breath and put her arms out, palms facing the ceiling. As the monster got closer, Lucinda lifted her arms, and I heard a shattering sound. The potted plants at the hall had been broken, soil spilling out onto the clean floor. The roots of the plants were erupting from the dirt and shards of ceramic. They stretched forward and continued stretching. Like tentacles, they grabbed Gorgon-Karla and pulled her back, suspending her in place and pulling her arms upward. As the monster squirmed, a few of the roots wrapped around the top of her head, creating a barrier in front of her eyes.

"What the actual fuck?" I looked from the spectacle before us and then to Lucinda. And then back and forth, trying to make sense of it all.

"Bryn," she said, sounding strained, arms still extended. "There is so much you don't know. But I promise you, you will understand it all very soon."

Miss Stone ran at Gorgon-Karla but every snake on her head let out a furious hiss, directed right at her. Gorgon-Karla whipped her tail around, knocking over a few desks before crashing into Miss Stone. Without missing a beat, she wrapped her arms around the tail and held on tight like a determined hug. Gorgon-Karla tried to pull away, but Miss Stone tugged on the tail even harder.

"We need you," Lucinda said, with an urgency. I didn't know what she needed from me exactly, but I felt there wasn't time to ask questions.

I felt my feet moving before I had decided what action to take. I ran forward, bent my knees, and shot myself upward into the sky. My feet landed on top of the giant tail, right above where Miss Stone stood. I pushed off and found myself back on the ground, right in front of the monster, squirming to get free. I reached for the bracelet. Dozens of snakes snapped their jaws at my fingers but couldn't quite make contact as I grasped the jewelry and pulled it from the wrist with one pull. I backed away, holding the green gem in my palm.

Gorgon-Karla roared. Her body jerked and contorted.

Her tail lifted upward, taking Miss Stone with it and then slammed her against the ground. I looked over my shoulder just in time to see the impact. I watched as the tail came towards me. No time to move, I did the first thing that came to my mind.

I squeezed.

The gem crumbled in my hand. Tiny specks of green fell from between my fingers and rained down onto the floor. Gorgon-Karla froze instantly. She convulsed and groaned as she ripped free of the roots holding her. I heard Lucinda wince behind me. The beast curled up on the floor, shrinking in size as a green fog poured off of her. The colorful mist covered her body from view and then faded away, leaving Karla behind.

Normal, non-monstrous Karla laid on the ground unconscious.

"How did you know breaking it would break the spell?" Lucinda asked, approaching me.

"I took a chance," I said, turning to find London also knocked out on the floor. She was no longer petrified in stone. Her skin was back to umber-brown, her hair was once again black curls, and her body moved softly with every breath. "Will she be okay? Will they both be?"

"Yes, they should be," Miss Stone said, pulling herself to her feet.

"Good," I sighed with relief. "So, is it finally time for you two to tell me what's happening here?"

Chapter 9

"I don't even know where to start," Lucinda said. She was looking at me like her heart was breaking.

"The beginning," Miss Stone said plainly. "We are Amazons."

"Amazons?" I asked, my mind instantly went to imagery of tribal women wearing leather and riding horses with medieval weaponry in their hands.

"We are a race of warriors, unknown to the natural world," she continued. "We are born from Ares; the god of battle and war, and we follow the teachings of Artemis; the goddess of the hunt, and Athena; goddess of military strategy and victory."

"This sounds insane," I said. The words came from my mouth, but part of me knew there was no point in trying to argue with what she was saying. I looked at the girl on the floor who had just been turned to stone, at the girl who had just turned into a creature from myth, and at my best friend who apparently had magical powers, and my new boss who had the same super strength I have had since childhood. "I'm listening."

"A very long time ago, Ares sought to create the

greatest supernatural army the world will ever see, in order to protect the world from powerful evils, and also fight on behalf of the gods if a war was ever waged against them." Miss Stone leaned against an overturned desk. "So, he vowed that his daughters would be born with unmatched strength that they would then dedicate to this army. For centuries, we've done exactly that. We live in a society hidden away and our army has a network that stretches through various corners within the world. And we act as a line of defense between the supernatural and the humans that don't know it exists." She spoke with pride. Her back was straight, her shoulders taut, and a smile stretched across her face.

"So, I am the daughter of a god, and I'm supposed to be in some warrior woman army?" I asked her. The words felt bonkers.

"No no no," she laughed. "You're not his daughter. Neither am I. His daughters are born Amazons. And so are their daughters and their daughters and their daughters after them. This is how we grow as a society. After centuries we have multiplied by the thousands."

"So, my birth mother…" I couldn't finish the sentence.

"Yes," Lucinda said.

"You're one too?"

"No, sweetie." She bit at her lower lip, as if she was trying to hold something inside her mouth that was fighting to get out. "I'm something else."

"But you knew about me?" I asked her. My lungs felt heavy. She didn't answer. "You both did?"

"I did," Lucinda said. "I was supposed to bring you to Miss Stone when your strength emerged. So, you could train."

"I didn't know you when my strength came," I told her. I don't know why I was telling her, as if she didn't know this already. But the look on her face told me that she knew that I was wrong.

"I've been…I've been watching after you since you were a baby."

"Watching me?" Chills spread across my skin.

"Not watching you," she said, sounding apologetic. "Watching over you. Just to make sure you're safe and to take you in at the right time. But I found a soft spot for you and the life you built. So instead of bringing you into the danger of a looming war, I let you be. And then, when you got older, I forced a meeting and became your friend and that spot in my heart grew so much bigger. I couldn't put you in danger."

"Stupid and reckless," Miss Stone scoffed.

"Wait," I said. "If you've been watching me since I was a baby…"

Lucinda was only a few years older than me. The math was another impossible thing.

"I'm a lot older than I look," she shrugged. "You know, Black don't crack." She caressed her cheeks with her fingers and smirked.

I wanted to laugh but I didn't let myself. It was just like her to try to throw humor into a situation so serious.

"And she was supposed to bring me to you?" I asked Miss Stone.

"Yes," she answered. "I'm a trained warrior, one of the best. I was chosen to make you one of the best. And it seems when Lucinda didn't do her job, fate decided to bring us together instead."

"Fate?" I'm not sure why the idea of fate seemed so unreasonable next to everything else I was being told.

"There are forces in this world far beyond our understanding," Miss Stone said with a graveled tone.

"So, fate made me follow this career path, and put this assistant job on my radar?" Miss Stone didn't respond. She just looked at me. "And how did a mythical warrior woman end up at the top of a fashion magazine, anyway?"

"When we are sent into the world, to live amongst humans, sometimes we are assigned roles to fill within their society. Sometimes we are allowed to follow our own interests. I was one of the latter, and this is my interest." She threw out her arms, gesturing to the half-destroyed office. "It's possible that fate put me on this path, knowing that we'd intersect here one day. There is no way to know."

I felt sick. Woozy and wobbly. "So, this is where my strength comes from."

"Yes," Miss Stone said. "When an Amazon begins to come of age, her strength comes shortly after. I imagine for you, it coincided with when you recognized your own womanhood." She was right. I never connected the two events until she pointed it out. My power came around the same time I realized that I was a girl.

"And this whole time, you knew?" I asked Lucinda.

"It's complicated," she said. "There's so much more to this."

"The whole time I was dealing with this thing that made me feel like a freak of nature, you could have told me where it came from? All this time I spent not knowing and just living in mystery and darkness." I was fuming. Hurt and betrayed. I felt like my whole life was a lie and the liar had been standing right in front of me the whole time. And I was just the fool who never saw it. "And it takes attacks from a mythological monster and a superpowered bar creep for you to tell me the truth?"

"What creep?" Miss Stone asked, perking up slightly.

"Some dude turned someone into a zombie-thing and tried to…kill me, I think," I explained. "It didn't make sense at the time, but it has to be connected."

Miss Stone's face went grim and blank, as she looked off into nothing. "There have been stories in recent years. Some mystery man with a lot of power targeting Amazons. They've rarely died but they have been forced to kill humans that this man seems to brainwash into fighting for him."

"You think he turned Karla into a Gorgon?" Lucinda asked.

"Gorgons are not a common beast. This can't be random or coincidence. It feels targeted," she said, still deep in thought. "If someone was at the protest, giving her that hexed charm, it's possible that they used the protest and your connection to it as an opportunity to launch an attack."

"I'm not directly connected to the protest though," I

said, once again not making the same connections that she clearly was.

"Not you," she said. "Lucinda."

"Me?" Lucinda sounded baffled by the suggestion. "You think I was the target?"

"It's possible that Karla was made into this monster because someone figured out you'd be together. Maybe whoever caused this expected her to take out those around her during her rampage against your boss," Miss Stone said. "Did you witness this man and his attack?"

"Yeah," Lucinda said. "I was there. With our friend Macks."

"He corrupted someone at the bar and made them attack me," I added. "I managed to snap them out of it. They're recovering in the hospital."

"If this is the same man who has attacked our sisters, he doesn't let witnesses last long after the incident."

"Oh no," Lucinda said. "Does they are in danger?"

"Quite possibly," Miss Stone said.

"They're all alone, defenseless," I said. Tension grew in my body.

"Go to them," Miss Stone ordered. "We can finish unpacking all of this when your loved ones are safe."

"But what about all of this?" I asked, looking at the unconscious girls laying in the aftermath of the battle that was fought.

"I'll make some calls," she answered plainly. "We have connections. People…fellow Amazons to clean up messes and make up cover stories. I can also have some of us keep an eye on your friend at the hospital."

I didn't bother to probe her further. I trusted that she had the situation handled and that we'd hash everything out, because I was owed that. But the fear of Macks being in danger outweighed what I was owed. So, I left, determined to make it to them.

Lucinda followed quickly behind. Nothing between us but our mutual concern and my resentment towards her.

Chapter 10

"So, you knew my birth parents?" I asked Lucinda as we ran down the sidewalk, the dimming sky above us. The theater Macks worked at was a little far from the Divinity office but trying to wrangle public transit would have taken too much time. I had no problem running a few blocks. I have always had pretty good endurance, which must be due to my Amazon blood.

"No," Lucinda huffed as she tried to keep up with me. "I only met your mother the day you were born. I never knew her very well. And your father…well. Amazons don't have much use for fathers after conception."

"You are going to tell me this whole story when we know Macks is safe!" I demanded. I hadn't spoken to her for the entirety of the run. But my mind begged for that question to be asked, so I spat it out as we approached the theater.

"Of course," she wheezed. The Larson Theater was a large but quaint brick building adorned with curves and arches that made its facade stand out in comparison to the boxy apartment and office buildings it was sandwiched between. Under the curvatures of its roof were stained glass windows that usually decorated the lobby with euphoric lighting during the daytime. The name Larson was spelled out in giant red letters right above the list of films in their current slate. Most of them were independent titles I had never heard of before.

I reached for the double doors and immediately felt resistance as I grasped the handles. Locked.

"Should we knock or something?" I asked.

"Babes, you can get yourself through any door with minimal effort," Lucinda pointed out, hands on her hips.

"Right," I said. It was surprising to hear that as her first suggestion. When it came to my powers, she had always been the most cautious person in my life, other than my mother. When Macks would encourage me to embrace the strength, Lucinda was in the other ear preaching restraint. I always thought she was trying to protect me, in her own way, but now I questioned if she was just overcompensating with my secret because of the guilt she felt over her own.

I pulled the door, slowly, hoping that I wouldn't just rip the handle straight off. I heard the snap and clank of metal as the locking mechanism gave in to the pressure. I looked around, afraid someone might have seen. A force of habit. As if there was something strange about a girl opening a door. But the street was quiet. I ushered Lucinda in and followed behind, allowing the door to close behind us.

The large circular lobby was dimly lit and devoid of people. Tables sitting next to large movie posters and cardboard standees were scattered around the space. A large red and white banner hung over the unmanned concessions stand that read "Murphy House Independent Film Festival."

"What are you two doing here?" I heard Macks' voice before I saw them. They entered the lobby with a broom in hand, quickly scurrying to a nearby storage closet, storing it away before crossing the room to meet us. "Did you break in here?" They looked at the door, slightly ajar. Their cupcake earrings, which they wore as a topical statement to the protest, swung back and forth as they shook their head in disappointment.

"We can explain," I told them. Although I wasn't quite sure exactly how to convey everything yet.

"This is my job," they whined anyway. "Like, I would have unlocked the door for you. How am I going to explain the broken door to my boss?"

"It was important, Sweets," Lucinda said gravely. "We thought you might be in danger. We didn't know if there was time to wait."

"Danger?" The stress that was plastered on Macks' face quickly turned to curious worry. "Why would I be in danger?"

"We think the man from the bar might be targeting us," I said. "There's a lot that went down earlier. We were attacked."

"By another one of those..." Macks stopped, stammering to find a word. "Those spiller things."

Spiller. Clearly named for the spilling black sludge that came from Divine's orifices. It was simple, yet clever, and a little gross. Pretty on brand for Macks.

"Something a lot crazier actually," I said.

A sound called out from the hallway that led to the various screening rooms. An exasperated groan. Macks turned quickly to face whoever was entering the lobby.

Three people. A man and two women. All wearing a black polo over jeans, just like Macks except for their amulet hanging at the center of their chest. The man was older and balding. One of the women appeared to be in her mid-forties, with weathered skin and long brown hair with a stylish gray streak. The other woman, judging by her small frame, had to have been a teen. Maybe a college freshman. She wore her long black hair in pigtails on either side of her face. A style I almost never see in people old enough to do their own hair.

"Hey guys!" Macks called out. The nervous tremor in their voice was immediately recognizable. "These are my friends, just stopping by to check out the festival prepping. I figured it was okay, as long as they weren't in the way."

There was no answer.

"Macksy," Lucinda breathed. "How many of you are here tonight?"

"Just the four of us. Why?" they responded.

"Just wanted to know how many spillers we had on our hands."

The three theater workers stepped closer into view within the lobby.

Black eyes. Red veins on their faces. Black blood pooled at the corners of their mouths.

"Fuck," I said to myself. Or maybe the universe. Or perhaps the gods, because apparently, they're real now.

As if thinking in unison, all three of them rushed towards us. The small woman tackled Macks to the ground, the man swung his arms at me in rapid succession, and the older woman grabbed Lucinda by the wrists and flung her into a nearby table.

Doing my best to dodge the blows that were coming at me, I looked around, expecting to see Damon lurking, and watching the fight. But unless invisibility was one of his powers, he wasn't there.

"What do we do?" Macks asked, struggling underneath their attacker as black slime fell from her mouth onto their face.

"Same thing as last time, I guess." I shoved the man, and he fell backwards, catching himself in a crabwalk position and launching himself back to his feet. "When I knocked Divine out, it seemed to reverse whatever this is."

"So, we just have to knock them out," Lucinda said, backing away from her attacker. "Easier said than done."

"Couldn't you do your…whatever that was from earlier?" I asked, as the man ran at me again.

"My powers are plant based, and there is not a single plant in this lobby. It's like a wasteland," Lucinda complained.

"Powers?" Macks asked, bewildered, as they kicked the woman off them.

"You missed a lot," I said, swinging at the man. He ducked down, dodging my fist, and grabbed me at the waist.

With the power of momentum and surprise, he lifted me into the air and slammed me down onto my back. Pain shot through my body like an earthquake, forcing any air I had out in an avalanche of coughs.

The second I was on the ground, the other two left my friends and pounced onto me. The women held me down by the arms while the man pounded into my abdomen with his fists. Each blow was another tremor in my body.

Unlike a comic book hero, my super strength did not come with invulnerability. As a kid, I always thought that was stupid. At this moment, I completely agreed with my younger self.

I lifted my arms with as much force as I could muster through the pain. The women flew into the man, crashing into him like the bread of a spiller sandwich. "Get Macks out of here!" I told Lucinda.

She ran to Macks and helped them off the floor. The two of them ran for the door, a path that cut between me and the spillers. Breaking from their disorientation, the spillers grabbed at their bodies. The older woman had Lucinda by the throat. The man pulled Macks' arms behind their back. The young woman reached for Macks' neck, but they struggled with their whole body, causing her to miss slightly. Her hands clasped onto Macks' shirt and amulet.

I didn't know which of them to go to first. Macks who was outmatched or Lucinda who was caught in a death grip. I hoped that Macks could struggle long enough that I could afford to get to them second.

I ran forward and brought my forehead down into the

side of the woman's face. I had never headbutted someone before, but the act came as if it was instinct. I didn't even feel the collision of our skulls. Must have been the adrenaline.

The woman fell to the floor in an instant. Her limp body made a thud as she landed. Eyes closed, the red veins on her face began to fade and the black liquid that dripped from her began to turn red.

I held onto Lucinda to sturdy her wobbly stance as she composed herself and took in some breaths. "Thank you," she said, massaging her neck.

I didn't bother to answer. I turned to put my focus on Macks, who was thrashing and kicking in the arms of the spillers. I tried to assess which one to attack first; the one holding them back or the one attempting to claw at their neck. Before I could make a move, Macks began to scream.

"Enough!" They yelled, elongating the word into a powerful cry. As their voice trickled down, another sound built up. An audible vibration surrounded us, and it got louder and louder every second. I looked around, trying to locate the source but it was fruitless. It was coming from every direction.

With one loud burst, shapeless blobs of darkness came flooding into the room through the air vents in the ceiling and the door that I had busted opened before. The blobs all formed together, like floating spills of liquid, above our heads. The shapeless mass spun around like a cyclone, and that's when I recognized the sound.

Buzzing.

Swarms of unidentifiable black and brown bugs were flying through the air in a unified hive mind. The swarm dived down towards Macks and the spillers, creating a wall of insects surrounding Macks. The spillers swatted the air as a barrage of bugs pelted them.

The young girl spiller backed towards me, twisting, and turning. Taking the chance, I swung out my arm, backhanding her across the face. As she hit the ground, the black sludge still on Macks' face had shifted to red.

The flying bugs moved like a wave of water crashing into the last spiller. With incredible force, he was lifted into the air and dropped into the concession stand. The back of the head hit the counter, and he slid to the floor.

All of the bugs flew in a million different directions, all exiting the lobby through vents, doors, and corridors until not a single one was left. By the time they were gone, the man's spiller effects had faded.

There was no danger, but I was left questioning my reality once again.

Macks stood in front of Lucinda and me, wide-eyed and looking at their hands as if they were covered in filth.

"Did you do that?" I asked Lucinda, trying to fight off my assumption.

"No," she said, sounding like she was in just as much shock as I was.

Macks brought their hands to the amulet around their neck, grasping it tightly. The beetle inside of it was practically calling attention to itself.

"So, you too?" I asked Macks, betrayal flooding my

insides.

"I have no idea what just happened," Macks insisted. I wanted to argue, but the look of fear and desperation on their face gave me pause. They were physically staving off hyperventilation. Their eyes were collecting water. Their mouth trembled with every word. "I really don't."

I looked at Lucinda accusingly. "I promise you," she said. "Macks has nothing to do with what you've learned today. Trust me, I would know."

"Trust you?" I asked, almost laughing.

"I've lied to you. I'm not proud of it. But that's all over now," she said sternly.

"What is happening?!" Macks screamed. A few tears escaped them.

"We'll explain but we should get out of here," I said.

"What about them?" Macks asked, looking at their coworkers.

"Leave them. They'll be mostly fine when they wake up. They'll get themselves to a hospital and they'll be told the same thing Divine was," Lucinda said, grabbing Macks' hand. "You finished up and left them here, and they were fine when you left. That's the story you'll tell when anyone asks."

Macks didn't answer verbally, they nodded their head and allowed Lucinda to walk them toward the exit.

As confused as ever, I followed.

Chapter 11

"So…you're an Amazon?" Macks asked for the fourth time. Lucinda and I gave them a hushed recap as we made our way home. We had finally made it into the apartment as they were wrapping their mind around the whole thing. "And so is your new boss?"

"Apparently," I said. "And Lucinda, who isn't human, knew this and has been watching me since I was born and forced herself into our lives so she could watch me from a closer view." I was pulsing with anger.

"So, what are you?" Macks asked Lucinda, falling into our sofa.

"I'm a tree nymph," Lucinda said, leaning against the door. "Us nymphs, we are like handmaidens to gods. We serve them, they give us tasks, and we follow them."

I wanted to laugh at the joke, but I knew it was reality. This was my new reality.

"And a god told you to watch over me?" I asked her.

"Yes," Lucinda said. "You are an Amazon that grew up amongst humans and you were always meant to be brought into the fold when the time was right."

"And you let me just sit and rot outside of the fold," I

said. "You were supposed to give me the answers I've always been missing but just didn't. You're supposed to be my friend and you…" I couldn't finish the words.

"Okay, but what about me and the bugs?" Macks asked.

"I have no idea, Hun," Lucinda sighed. "I've never seen that before. But I'd bet money it has to do with your new jewelry. So maybe it's time to reach out to your mom."

"What are the odds that my mom knew something about this when she sent the amulet?" Macks asked. "What are the odds that my mom dragged me into some supernatural mess around the same time you two are dealing with Amazon shit?"

"The odds are irrelevant when fate is involved," Lucinda said, almost sounding nurturing.

"You know what," I groaned. "I can't do this. Not tonight. It's been a long day and I'm not sure how much more I can take."

"Sweetie," Lucinda argued, trying to pull me back in.

"Don't call me that," I told her. "You can't act like things are normal right now."

"Nothing has changed for me," Lucinda said.

"Well, it has for me," I shot back, letting the sentence hang in the air. I turned to Macks, who sat on the couch looking back and forth between Lucinda and me. "I'm sorry, Macks. I promise we will figure this out, I just need some time to breathe."

I quickly left them. I entered my room and shut the door between us. I shut out the ever-changing world outside with the lies and the revelations. And I just stood there. It was like I didn't know what to do with myself. Now that I knew what I was, I was stuck in a kind of pause. My heart needed comfort, and my body took me to comforts long forgotten.

I went to my closet and shoved my hanging wardrobe to the side and pulled out a box that I had packed up when we moved in, but never opened. I pulled off the lid and removed stuffed animals and dolls I hadn't thought about in years. I hugged the plush elephant I used to sleep with every night. Holding its soft squishy body to my chest didn't seem to push off any of the bad feelings I was trying to fight. Defeated, I started to put it back into the box but something else caught my eye. At the bottom of the cardboard box was a tiny lavender notebook with my name written out in bubble letters. Holding it in my hands, I flipped it open and began to read the pages inside. Like a rush, it all came back to me. I decided I would try to make sense of things in the same way I tried to make sense of life when I was a child.

I went to my desk, grabbed a pen, and began to write.

Entry 47

Hey Journal,

It's been a while.

I'm sure you're probably wondering where the hell I've been and what I've been up to. Well, you'll be happy to know that I survived my freshman year of high school. (I was just reading entry 46 and YIKES! I really made teenage drama sound apocalyptic). I didn't just survive freshman year; I made it through the whole damn thing.

I'm actually living with Macks now! They moved in

with us after they hit a rough patch at home. And then Mom and Dad moved to Vermont a few years after that. So Macks and I found a place in the city with Lucinda, who you don't know yet. Together, we are the sun, moon, and stars. An ever-expanding cosmos, larger than life, but still home no matter what. At least that's what I thought. I recently realized I had been overlooking the deep all-consuming darkness that rests beneath the stars.

But let's not go there yet.

I got an AA in journalism. Yes, I stuck with journalism. After that, I kind of threw myself into the workforce. I realized that learning how to do things sucks, but actually doing the thing and getting the experience is where I wanted to be. So, I spent some years jumping from job to job. Nothing entirely satisfying. Nothing that truly merged journalism and fashion, which was the goal.

And then a few weeks ago, I applied for a job I would never get, and then I GOT IT!!! I am now Elizabeth Stone's personal assistant. The head, face, and soul of Divinity Magazine saw me and decided I was worthy to follow her around all day. This is a job that could propel me in the industry if I made a good impression.

All of that should be great, but you know it's not. Why would I be writing in you if I wasn't in a crisis? I recently found some clarity. Learned some things about myself. And now I question everything. My sense of self, my job, my relationship with one of the people I thought I could trust most in this world.

So naturally, I looked through a box of my childhood

things. Wondering if this reality changes my past. And that's when I found you. Writing these entries helped me through teenage angst, transitioning, and heartbreak. So, I hope you can help me work through this too.

I finally found out where my strength comes from, and the thing I feared most as a kid has been confirmed.

I'm not human.

I wrote for what felt like hours until all my thoughts and anxieties were on the page and I was able to stomach the idea of sleep.

I woke to an email from Miss Stone. It was addressing the entire company, stating there was a break-in and vandalism at the office. She told everyone to work from home while the office is cleaned and repaired. I immediately got a second email, from Miss Stone's personal account. One sentence in all caps.

SAY NOTHING.

"Hello?" London said through the phone.

"Hey!" I tried to sound cheery and nonchalant. "I wanted to see how you were doing. Are you okay?"

"I'm fine," she said, a bit of inflection at the end of the sentence. "Are you asking because of the break-in?"

"Uh…" I didn't know what to say yet. "Yeah."

"It's a good thing we all left before it happened. We must have just missed it." I could hear a sigh of relief. "It was such a long day. The night is kind of fuzzy, I barely remember coming home. I woke up with the stiffest back, probably from just standing at the protest all day. But I would take brain fog and back pain over coming face-to-face with whoever broke into the office, ya know?"

"Oh absolutely."

"How are you?" she asked.

"I'm fine," I answered.

"Hmmm." She took a long pause. "I feel like when people usually say that they aren't actually fine."

"No, no! I am," I lied.

"If you say so." She let out a soft chuckle. "Oh! I'm glad you called actually. I wanted to let you know that I'm going to meet with Miss Stone and talk about featuring your friend Macks' documentary in F.O.A.M. And if it goes well, maybe Divinity can hire them on as a videographer or video editor or something. We have been looking for ways to make F.O.A.M., and the web section of the magazine in general, more engaging. We've bounced the idea of video around before so it's not too much of a stretch."

"That's incredible!" I said, feeling a spark of joy breaking through the murk. "Thank you so much."

"It's not a sure thing yet. But we'll see," she said quickly. "Don't say anything to them just yet."

"Yeah, no problem," I told her.

"I should get back to work," she said. "But we should do lunch or coffee. All four of us. You and your friends seem cool." She hung up before I could respond. Leaving me alone and without a distraction.

I was sitting at the center of my bed, dressed in the matching patchwork denim jacket and shorts I made back when my sewing machine was still in commission. I had gotten dressed as if I was going to go out into the world, but I was too afraid to even leave my bedroom. Afraid to confront Lucinda. Afraid to wonder how Macks fits into all of this. Just afraid.

But I was a monster-fighting warrior woman now, apparently. So why was this more terrifying than that? I swallowed my hesitation and jumped from my bed. One foot in front of the other, I approached my bedroom door and opened it to the world on the other side. Macks and Lucinda sitting on our couch, looked up at me before standing to their feet.

"I'm still mad at you," I told Lucinda. I knew the question about where we stood was sitting at the forefront of her mind. A plush purple robe clung tightly to her body. No makeup, no wig. Just Lucinda, bare and vulnerable. "But I think I am long overdue for a full explanation."

"I will happily-"

"Not from you," I interrupted her. "You've been lying to me this whole time. Miss Stone came to me with the truth almost immediately after meeting me."

"That's fair," she said plainly.

"What about me?" Macks asked softly. They wore flannel pjs, their family amulet prominently displayed under their neck. I was surprised they were still wearing it.

"Perhaps, I can try to help you figure it out while Bryn talks with Miss Stone," Lucinda offered.

"Still don't want to call your mom?" I asked them.

"Not if I don't have to," they said with a shrug.

"I've been around a long time. We can do some digging

and I might be able to point you in the right direction at least," Lucinda said. "Then, if you aren't satisfied with what we uncover, I'll be by your side if you decide to give her a call."

Macks silently accepted her offer with a smile on their face. I was jealous that whatever Macks was dealing with wasn't directly related to a lie that Lucinda told. Macks could still look to her for comfort when all I saw when I looked at her was bitter betrayal.

"I'm with you too," I told Macks. "You're not alone."

"Neither are you," Lucinda said, stepping towards me.

"I'm going to go." I stepped back as she got close. I left the apartment, standing at the front door after I closed it. I took in three deep breaths, feeling like I should go back inside and ask them both to come with me. My gut instinct said to have them both by my side when I was told the great mystery of my life. But I resisted it. I set off alone.

Miss Stone said in her email that she would be in the office to oversee the cleanup and repairs. So, I took a chance and hoped that wasn't a lie as well.

After successfully convincing the building's security and receptionist that Miss Stone was expecting me, despite the floor Divinity was on being closed for the day, I rode the elevator up to the office. When the elevator doors opened, I walked into the office and was shocked to see it looking exactly as it did before last night's attack.

There were no overturned desks, the broken pots and spilled dirt and elongated roots had been cleaned up and replaced with identical potted plants, and the cracks and dent in the wall from where Miss Stone chucked the monster into it had vanished. The room was in complete and perfect repair.

"Hello, Bryn," Miss Stone said. She stood at the entrance to her personal office wearing a floral blouse tucked into black dress pants. "Come on in." She sat behind her desk, and I took a seat in front.

"How did you get everything fixed so fast?" I asked her.

"Cleaners," she said simply. "Some of us seek out male witches to have children with. This results in Amazons with the ability to do witchcraft. They take on the role of Cleaners. They enter human society and take jobs as first responders, politicians, construction workers, sometimes even actual cleaning jobs, or whatever else might be helpful to us. Whenever something like last night happens, they come in and clean up the evidence. They make up cover stories, repair damage, erase memories, what have you."

Amazons with witchy magic! Witches were real too. It was all starting to not even surprise me anymore. Instead of being shocked, I found my mind making connections. I noted how these special Amazons would explain how London had no memory of what happened. I imagined Karla would probably have the same hazy memory. Is this what it felt like for this kind of thing to be normal?

"So, you have people just infiltrating all parts of society?"

"*We*," she said, "have people all over so we can best do our job of protecting the human world from supernatural threats. We are quite organized. In the next five to ten years, we project that one of the Amazons we have within the United States government will become the first woman to hold the position of President."

Hearing that these people were controlling and manipulating institutions as large as the government felt more shocking than the idea of monsters and witches.

"This is all a lot to take in," I told her.

"I'm here to make sure you understand all of it," she said. "Ask me all of your questions." She leaned back into her chair as if to hunker down for what was to come.

"Start from the beginning, I guess," I said. "How does this all work?"

"Well, I've already explained our origin and our purpose," she began, looking at the painting of paradise on her wall. "Our home is an island, gifted to us by Ares and magically hidden away from the world. We live there in secret. Some of us are sent away to live amongst humans. And we either implant ourselves in society or reproduce and return home to raise our daughters."

"What about the sons?" I asked her.

"In the old days, we would return them to their fathers or leave them in the woods," she said, sounding ashamed. "But those were archaic times. These days, we leave them with their fathers or place them up for adoption. We've actually come a long way in terms of reproducing. There are quite a few Amazon-owned sperm banks whose supplies we can utilize as we see fit."

"Adoption?" I asked her. "Is that why I was put up for

adoption instead of raised on this magical island? Because they thought I'd grow up a boy?"

"Oh, my sweet girl," she said. The stoic expression on her face melted into a look of sympathy. "No. You would never have been shunned away for that. Our oracles can foresee a child's gender long before they are born. Even a transgender child. We take home any child who is destined to be an Amazon."

It was reassuring to hear that they were progressive and accepting at least. "So, what happened to me?"

"The oracles foresaw a threat," Miss Stone said, shutting her eyes tightly. "A threat that I believe could be this man you encountered. A man with great power who sought to wipe out the Amazons."

"What does that have to do with my adoption?" I asked.

"Bryn," she said gravely. "Your mother wasn't just an Amazon. She was…she *is* our Queen. Just like her mother before her, and so on and so forth going all the way back to the very first Amazon."

"Queen?" I asked, springing to my feet and backing away from her desk. I wasn't sure what I was running away from exactly. "So, what? I'm a princess or something?"

"Exactly," Miss Stone confirmed. "The oracles declared you were next in line for the throne. And they knew that a newborn Queen would be a prime target for this looming threat. If this man were able to wipe out all of the first Amazon's descendants, there would be no one to birth future Queens."

"When the man at the bar attacked, he did mention I might be the one he was looking for," I told her.

"That likely confirms what I've feared," she said grimly. "This man and the prophesized threat are one in the same."

"God damn," I sighed. "So, I was sent away so some evil psycho wouldn't murder me as a baby."

"It was the only way to protect the royal line and ensure the safety and survival of the Amazon race," Miss Stone insisted, standing up as well. "She had to separate everyone of royal blood. She stayed on the island. She sent your older sister away to an undisclosed location and forbade her to return. And sent you away to live a life safe and unknowing."

"I have a sister?" The question zapped the energy from my body, and I felt my knees buckle a bit.

"A half-sister. I never knew her."

"And she's not the next Queen?"

"The throne is not automatically passed to firstborn daughters," she explained. "The oracles and their future sight tell us when a new Queen is born."

She opened her mouth as if to speak but no words materialized.

"What?" I asked her, point blank. I wasn't sure if I was ready for this other shoe to drop.

"In order to protect the future of the royal line, the three of you were separated, so in case one of you were found the others would survive," she said slowly.

"You said all this," I told her.

"It was decided that the nymph would watch over you and bring you to me for training when your strength developed," Miss Stone continued. "So that you may defeat this dark threat and save the Amazons. And in saving the Amazons, you ensure the safety of the human world."

I laughed.

I let out an audible cackle.

I wasn't proud of it, but I couldn't contain it either.

"It's all been foreseen by the oracles, who speak on behalf of the gods," Miss Stone huffed. "And as it is spoken, so it shall be."

Hearing her talk in absolutes, as if my free will had no place in the discussion, was irksome.

"So, I'm supposed to train to be a warrior woman so I can defeat some mystery man who can turn people into zombies to ensure the survival of all other warrior women and take my place as princess under a Queen that threw me out like trash the second I was born?" I raised my eyebrows, waiting to see if she would address the absurdity of it all.

"She never wanted to give you up," Miss Stone said with a low and smooth voice. "It was something she had to do, not something she chose to do. When you were born, she said herself that she would be looking forward to the day you reunite."

"It doesn't matter," I said, shaking my head. This was something I dreamt of. Hearing that my bio family wanted me. Like, somehow that kind of validation would lessen the pain of being different. Perhaps part of me thought that being different might be worth it in the long run if I wasn't also rejected at birth. But this didn't feel as satisfying as I imagined it would.

I liked to say that I never needed or wanted them. I tell myself that because it makes me feel better. I convince myself that I would be betraying the parents that raised me if I were to go looking for the parents that created me.

But it's impossible not to wonder.

Growing up, people would tell me that Matthias and I looked nothing alike, leaving me to wonder if I had a brother out there that actually looked like me.

When my father's mother would visit, she would never quite look me in the eyes, because I was a granddaughter she didn't recognize. I didn't know if she refused recognition because of my identity or because her blood wasn't in my veins. This was something my father didn't have the nerve to address with her, and she died without ever having to discuss her hesitation toward me.

At her funeral, I was pestered by thoughts about what my biological grandmother might be like. I created an image of her in my mind. In reality, I took the aspects of my mother and attributed them to some elderly goddess-like figure with a tray of oatmeal cookies. I was always curious about how accurate this image could have been.

Once, our entire family caught the flu except for me. My father, barely strong enough to speak, asked my mother if she noticed that I had never actually been sick before. They didn't know I could hear their conversation through our paper-thin walls.

He sounded concerned about something I thought any parent would consider a blessing. I heard my mother blow her nose and let out a groan. "Your daughter can flip a truck with one hand, and you're worried about her perfect health?" The two of them sat in silence before she continued. "Bryn is special. There is no point in searching for explanations that are beyond us."

That always stuck in the back of my mind. An explanation really did seem beyond our scope then, but surely the answers we wanted weren't beyond my biological parents. They had to know something. They had to be like me. I was convinced of that as a kid. I think we all were. We just had no way of finding the people who held the answers to our family mystery.

So, we…

So, I was left with questions while they embraced not knowing. And at some point, I joined in that complacency.

I had somehow ignored all of that pondering, all of that yearning, and convinced myself that if I had a happy life then I wasn't missing anything. I wired my brain to think that not knowing was better than wondering. And for the most part, it worked. But sometimes, every once in a while, the wondering would break through. And then I would quickly bury it.

"Would you like me to tell you about her?" Elizabeth Stone asked me. Her facial expression seemed to resist the weight of that question. "Your biological mother."

An offering I never thought possible rested at my fingertips, so red hot with enticement that I could feel myself blistering.

"No," I said, halfway surprised by my own answer. I knew that the more I learned about this woman, the more real this was all going to become. There would be this image of her in my mind, not a fantasy but a real idea of her. She would exist there with my true mom, the one who raised me. And I didn't know how to make that space in my brain a shared one. That scared me. So, I decided to lean into something much scarier. The perfect distraction. "But if you're supposed to train me to be an Amazon, let's start there. Maybe we can work our way up to the mother stuff."

A smile stretched across Miss Stone's face. A smile I didn't quite know what to do with. "Oh, I won't just train you to be an Amazon," she said. "I'll train you to be a warrior. I'll train you to be a future Queen."

Chapter 12

Miss Stone was adamant about starting immediately. She refused to let me leave the office. I sat around while she rescheduled meetings and made some hushed calls. When she was finished, she escorted me out of the building, and we got into a sleek black car that seemed to pull up as soon as we hit the sidewalk.

I didn't know exactly what to expect with warrior training. But I did not expect a library. The building was tall and circular, made of yellowish bricks and decorated with long columns. Above its towering doorway, "Jerimiah Greenbrook Private Library and Museum," was carved into stone.

As Miss Stone's personal driver opened the door for us to step out of the car, another identical vehicle drove up.

When that driver exited the car and opened his own back door, a head of long braids in a spiral of black and hot pink hair emerged. Under the colorful hair, Lucinda looked at me with a bright smile. But my facial expression must have been much less pleasant because her smile quickly went from a look of shocked recognition to an averted glance of shame.

Macks followed Lucinda out of the car, looking at the large library building with wild eyes and a dropped jaw. Their beetle necklace and the two tiny hands that showed off the middle finger hanging from their ears forced my eyes to travel in a triangle.

"What are you two doing here?" I asked.

"I arranged for the nymph to meet us," Miss Stone said, sounding charged. "I *didn't* arrange for a guest."

"I wasn't going to leave them alone," Lucinda said to me as if I was the one accusing her of stepping out of line.

"Why did you send for her?" I asked Miss Stone, trying my best not to give Lucinda anything other than the cold shoulder.

"The Oracles foretold that both of us would be by your side on this journey," Miss Stone answered. "And any words from an Oracle should be considered the future, written, or an order from the Gods, best not ignored."

Lucinda scoffed. "Oracles. I don't take orders from them."

"Not a fan?" Macks asked.

"You know how my people are servants to the gods?" Lucinda began, rolling her eyes. "Oracles are powerful psychics who guide the gods and sometimes speak on behalf of them as well. That closeness inflates their egos."

"And they said nothing about your presence being needed." Miss Stone said, looking down at Macks with intense eyes. "Who are you?"

"My name is Macks, Ma'am," they stammered.

"Macks has recently developed powers," I explained to

Miss Stone before turning my attention to my friends. "Were you able to find anything out about that?"

"Lucinda said there are different kinds of nymphs, so I thought maybe I was one of them," Macks answered.

"But, there are two major problems there," Lucinda said. "This started when you got the necklace, but nymphs are chosen by a god, and agree to be in their service. So, you would know if you were one. And I've never heard of bug nymphs. mountain nymphs who control stone, forest nymphs who turn into animals, water nymphs who command water, and tree nymphs like yours truly." Lucinda gave a dramatic bow.

"You control insects?" Miss Stone asked Macks with a raised eyebrow.

"Uh, yeah, I think so," Macks said, touching the amulet around their neck. "I only did it once and I can't seem to make it happen again."

"Well, perhaps it's good you came along," Miss Stone said. She didn't really seem surprised that this seemingly random person in my life also had some sort of connection to the supernatural. I thought back to how both she and Lucinda seemed to lean on the idea of fate. I wondered if this thought system just made them accept everything without question. "The Greenbrook is the largest supernatural archive on this side of the country. If you need to make a discovery, this is a good place to start."

"Supernatural archive?" I asked, looking up at the building in front of us. "Just out in the open like this?"

"It is a secret," Miss Stone laughed. "While it seems

conspicuously placed within the city, access is restricted, and you can only find it if you know exactly what you are looking for." With that, Miss Stone marched forward, tackling each stone step leading to its door with vigor. The three of us followed, but it didn't feel like our footfall on the steps had the same musical tone.

She opened the door into a massive circular room with brown and beige walls covered in bookshelves and banners that sported the image of a skeletal owl hanging from the ceiling. Wooden tables and chairs flooded the space in neat rows. At the end of the room, a long desk stood before three corridors. A woman sat at the desk, typing at a computer. She looked up as the door opened and stood to her feet.

"Can I help you?" the woman asked. She was blonde with an oval face and stiff composure.

"My name is Elizabeth Stone. I have an appointment with your leader." Miss Stone always seemed to speak with such assuredness, as if she had control over the world around her. "I just left something here quite some time ago, and it's time I collect it."

"I have no meetings scheduled," the desk woman said, without even referencing her computer. "She's actually quite busy. It's a hectic time."

"I spoke with her today," Miss Stone said without missing a beat. "She is expecting me."

"I didn't put it in my schedule," another woman said as she exited one of the corridors and approached our group. She was tall and thin with a triangular face and hooked nose. "This isn't the kind of thing you add to the calendar. I'll take it from here."

"Yes, Miss Patel." The blonde woman sat back down and began typing away at her computer.

"Miss Stone," the new woman said, sounding professional and rigid. "I must admit I was surprised but glad, to hear from you. As you heard, we are in the middle of a stressful period."

"This is Bryn, the girl I told you about. And these are her companions," Miss Stone gestured to us. I wasn't sure if that was the right word for whatever Lucinda and I were at the moment.

"And this is Kathrine Patel." She gestured to the woman who stood in front of us.

"Are you an Amazon too?" I asked the woman.

"Oh no," she said plainly. "Not at all. I'm human. I am the head of a society of scholars who work to understand the supernatural world and keep it a secret. We are called The Strix." She turned and began to walk down a nearby hall. "Follow me," she said.

"So, the secret race of warriors is working alongside this secret society of human librarians?" Macks asked as we walked. The hallway held various doors that lead to rooms of books and glass cases with strange-looking objects.

"I had an object of importance that I needed to be hidden," Miss Stone said. "I'm familiar with what they do, but the Amazons and the Strix have no relationship whatsoever. So, I decided this would be the perfect hiding place."

"A genius move," Kathrine Patel said. "No one would guess that the Amazons would trust a human organization with their divine weapon."

"Divine weapon?" I asked Miss Stone. "Like, your rings?" During our battle against the Gorgon, Miss Stone's rings had turned into deadly weapons.

"Those are magic, but not divine." Miss Stone answered. "Many Amazons have weapons that are enchanted to transform into something hidden."

"A divine weapon is an object forged by a god, using their very essence," Patel lectured. "Through this process, it is imbued with immense magical power, such as the ability to kill a god."

"Ares crafted a sword, infusing its metal with his own blood," Miss Stone added. "He gifted it to the first Amazon, your ancestor, Bryn. And ever since then, that sword has been passed down from Queen to Queen. It is how we officially recognize the title, for only those in the first Queen's bloodline can use the sword's true potential."

"If it belongs to the Queen, how did you get it?" I asked her.

"Your mother wanted you to have it, for the battle to come, so she eventually left it with me so that you may have it in hand while I train you."

Patel stopped walking, and we all paused with her. "The battle to come?"

"Someone out there is seeking genocide against us," Miss Stone told her. "His first target is the Queen's bloodline."

"Well, I hope you win this battle," Patel said to me. "This would be a terrible time to lose an army such as the Amazons."

"What's that supposed to even mean?" Lucinda asked, sounding offended by the vagueness.

"We are preparing for a threat like no other," Patel continued. "It would certainly be helpful if the Amazons were in our corner."

"What kind of threat?" Miss Stone asked with narrowed eyes.

"The kind that threatens the world, both human and supernatural," Patel answered. "I can brief you later, perhaps."

"Please do," Miss Stone said. "I'll bring it to the attention of our Queen as soon as our people's safety is secured and she's able to properly lead us, once again."

"Wait," I said. "So, I'm doing this battle against a homicidal douche just so your current Queen can get her sword back and lead her army? Why doesn't she just do this fight herself?"

"A few years after you were born, she hid herself from the world, so that she may live on after the threat has passed. Taking part in it herself is too big of a risk."

I hated hearing that. The risk was fine for me but not for her. It sounded like I was expendable.

"And the oracles have seen you at the forefront of this conflict," Miss Stone added. "I trust their visions. If they say you are meant for this, I have no reason to doubt them."

"We heard whispers that the Amazons have restricted

travel from their island," Patel said. "Preventing anyone on the island from leaving and anyone away from the island from returning."

"Yes," Miss Stone said. Her voice was almost a whisper. "It was done for the greater good. But once this is all over, it will have been worth it just to see home and those I love once again." She looked off into the distance, dreamily gazing at a nearby wall. I knew she wasn't looking at the library's interior design. She was seeing home, and the faces that lived there. For as long as I've been alive, she and so many others have been separated from their society. Their family. Their home. This journey I was about to take on was not just about preventing genocide, it was ensuring an end to heartbreak and separation. They were counting on me.

"So," I said with a deep breath. "This sword?"

"Oh yes," Miss Patel said, straightening her glasses to sit properly on the bridge of her nose. "Right this way." She continued to lead us down the hall and stopped at an open door. Upon entering the room, we were surrounded by blades mounted on walls or sitting on tables under glass cases, most of them looking archaic.

At the far end of the room, against a bare wall, was a vertical standing glass case. A long onyx black blade sat on display. Its edges were sharp, even to the eyes, with impeccable straight lines meeting at the end to make a tip that came together at a pristine point. The sword's deep red hilt held two horn-like protrusions on both sides. At its center sat a symbol of an old-fashioned warrior's helmet with a prominent A printed on the forehead.

"This," Miss Stone said with a sweeping gesture, "is the Queen's Sword. Your birthright."

"I must say, I'm sad to see it leave our possession," Miss Patel said before I could even think of a response to the whole birthright thing. "Thank you so much for allowing, and trusting, us to hold onto it. Giving us a chance to study a divine weapon, even if we couldn't activate its true potential, is very much appreciated."

"Full potential?" I asked. "You keep saying that."

"This divine weapon has the ability, when held by an Amazon Queen, to transform into any weapon known to man." Miss Stone didn't take her eyes off of the sword. "As long as she can will it."

"Woah!" Macks called out. "That sounds badass!"

"It certainly is," Miss Stone laughed. For a moment she almost seemed like a person, rather than a boss or a warrior.

"I wish I had super strength and a transforming weapon," Macks groaned. "All I have is a necklace that conjures bugs."

"Bug magic?" Miss Patel sounded intrigued.

"Sorry, I wasn't trying to distract us from the magical god weapon," Macks said with a hurried tone.

"No, it's okay," Lucinda insisted, flipping her braids over her shoulder. "We are trying to figure this all out."

"We don't know what their power means," I told Miss Patel. "It kind of just sprang up and we were hoping you might be able to shed some light on it."

"Well…" She seemed to ponder things in her mind for a long moment. "It's possible that your necklace is a cursed or enchanted object. Or it's possible that your necklace has unearthed some sort of latent magical ability."

"We gathered that much," Macks said, sounding kind of sad.

"One of our leading experts on enchanted objects is actually on site," Miss Patel said. "Perhaps, if he examines your necklace, he can tell you what it is."

"That would be incredible!" Excitement found its way into Macks' voice.

"Come with me," Patel said, before turning to Miss Stone. "I'll leave you to the sword."

"Thank you," Miss Stone said, giving a half bow before Miss Patel began to lead Macks out of the room.

"I'm going to go with them," Lucinda announced to me. "But, Honey." She grabbed my hands, squeezing my fingertips. "I want you to know, once you take that sword in your hands…the life you knew will be over. You won't be this girl chasing her dreams and having fun with her friends. You will be a Princess, a future Queen, destined to fight battles she never chose. And that is exactly why I chose not to bring you into this life."

I pulled my hands from her grip. "I don't think I have much of a choice," I told her. The sentiment was nice. She sounded like a friend, like the friend I thought I knew before all of this. She was someone who wanted what was best for me. But her idea of what's best left me in the dark in a period where I wanted nothing but the truth. "Oracles and fate, and everything else."

"There is always a choice," she whispered. "Just, try to remember that."

She turned and followed Macks and Miss Patel out of the room. Leaving Miss Stone and me alone with the Queen's Sword.

"What your nymph fails to realize is that our choices have consequences," Miss Stone said bluntly. "You may choose to turn your back, much like she chose not to bring everything to light the moment your strength emerged. And these choices have reverberations that affect more than just the person making them."

Miss Stone approached the glass case. She undid the latches on its side and swung the transparent door open. Her fingers wrapped around the sword's hilt like a mother holds her child, soft enough not to hurt it but firm enough to keep it safe and secure.

She pulled it from its case and gazed upon it, raising it into the artificial light of the library. She turned to me, presenting the sword with one hand flat under the hilt and the other flat under the blade. I reached out, not sure what to do with it once I had it, but I was taking things one step at a time.

My fingers wrapped around the handle, and I lifted it from Miss Stone's hands. It was heavier than I expected. Not physically heavy. Metaphysically heavy. Something red hot and burning rushed through my veins. Like I was carrying the fate of an entire people, a purpose, pure power. All of it was in my hand.

It was invigorating but also terrifying.

My knees buckled under the pressure and my lungs tightened. Miss Stone caught me at my elbows before I even realized I briefly lost my ability to stand upright.

"To wield the power of war is not a burden to be taken lightly," she said, holding me tight as my legs regained their strength. "It takes a heart of true courage to bear it."

Miss Stone always seemed so serious. As if she didn't want you to know what she was thinking or feeling so she made sure not to wear her emotions on her face. As if her humanity was something that needed protecting under a suit of armor. But in this moment, the armor was stripped from her. The look on her face. The smile, wide and bright. Her eyes, soft and glossy. It was joy. It was hope. So bright it was almost blinding. But there was something else too. A smidge of something underneath. Something dark under the brightness.

Chapter 13

"So, when do you teach me the magic stuff?" I asked Miss Stone as we traversed the halls of the massive library.

"The Queen's Sword is a tool of great power and leadership," she said without looking back at me. She was a few paces in front of me. I was struggling to keep up, afraid to walk too quickly with a very large sharp object in my hands. I could hear my mother's voice lecturing a much younger me about running with scissors. "It's better if you learn to use it as a sword before transforming it."

"If this thing can really be whatever weapon I want," I began to argue. "I should be learning a lot more than swordsmanship."

"You start with the basics!" she said sternly. "I had to become accustomed to my blades before they were enchanted into jewelry." She waved her hands above her head, drawing attention to her rings, still not looking back at me. "This sword has the power to kill a god. It's not something to play with. We have to go about this the right way."

"Kill a god?" I stopped walking. Killing seemed so surreal. It was an aspect of this I hadn't really considered.

And then you throw killing a *God* into it. That sounded so…huge. "I have to kill a god?"

Miss Stone stopped now. She turned halfway, catching me with only one eye. "Along with protecting humanity, Ares also created the Amazons and that sword on the chance that a godly war might come. But hopefully, it doesn't." She took a deep breath. "All divine Weapons have the ability to kill a god. It's not a guarantee, or even likely, that you'll have to use it as such. This threat we are facing probably isn't a god. They are fairly absent these days."

"Have you ever gone up against one?" I asked her.

"No," she said, turning and continuing to walk. "I've never even held a divine weapon before your mother handed me that sword."

"So, you've never used a weapon like this, but you're going to train me to use it?" I asked.

"I have, like most Amazons, extensive training in combat, weaponry, and warfare. I also understand the Queen's Sword, as it is my duty as a woman who would be expected to follow it into battle. While I have never used a divine weapon, I am the best person suited to teaching you to do so. I will train you to be a warrior."

As she finished her explanation, we entered the large lobby again. The front desk woman stood at her station, back towards us as she spoke to someone on the other side of her desk.

"I'm sorry sir," she said, sounding annoyed and persistent. "This is a private facility with exclusive access. I cannot let you in without proof that you belong to this organization or have received permission to enter."

"I have no interest in what you do here," a man's voice said. The familiarity of it sent a hot white chill down my back. "You have someone visiting today. I just want to see her, that's all."

The blonde woman prepared to argue, standing up even straighter. As she moved, the view of the man was no longer obstructed. Damon stood on the other side of the desk. Dressed in a black coat over a black suit, his dark hair falling loosely at the sides of his head, curling slightly. He made immediate eye contact with me and a smirk sprouted on his face.

"Ah, there she is," he sang. He raised his hand in the air and what looked like, maroon-colored lightning shot from his palm and rammed into the receptionist's chest, sending her flying backward. As she hit the ground, the stench of charred fabric and flesh wafted into the air. The center of her torso and part of her right shoulder had been singed to an ashen black, and she laid still on the ground with wide-opened eyes that focused on nothing. "Hello, Bryn."

I wanted to scream. It was the first reaction my brain commanded of my body. But there was some sort of disconnect that neither anticipated. Instead, I just stood there, staring at the lifeless body on the ground.

"Damon, I presume," Miss Stone said, neither shocked by what we just witnessed nor concerned about the man's overall presence.

"Elizabeth Stone," he laughed. "A titan of the industry and Amazon warrior. It's a pleasure to meet you."

"You know of me, but I'm not too familiar with you," she said, still sounding cool under the pressure.

"Damon is just my most recent alias," he said. "I'm sure you've heard my true name and the various names the humans have stuck me with over the years."

"And what is your true name?" she asked him, slowly crossing in front of the desk. They stood face to face, and I stayed glued to the same spot.

"Deimos," he answered with a wicked smirk.

Miss Stone stepped back. A slight gasp fell from her lips. "Deimos, demigod of terror," she said to me before turning back to him. I was thankful for the clarification, but I had no idea what to do with the information. "As the son of Ares, there should be no qualms between us. We are daughters of Ares."

"I'm aware." His smirk turned to a grimace. "Daughters, granddaughters, female descendants. I'm very familiar with who and what you are, Amazon. And I assure you, I have many *qualms* with your kind."

"Any chance you'd like to talk it out?" Miss Stone asked as her rings started to glow and transform into her circular blades. She raised the weapons to her torso in a battle stance. "Perhaps we can avoid a fight."

"Isn't that what you're made for?" he asked, leaning forward and positioning his face inches from hers, clearly unafraid of her blades. "Created to fight my father's battles. Meant to combat supernatural evils in his name. Destined to march in his army. Daddy's perfect little soldiers." He tilted his head towards me, not taking his eyes away from Miss Stone. "And she has been named the next Queen. It's my mission to watch you crumble, and the only way to do that is to squash your Queen's line. So, we have nothing to talk about."

"So be it." Miss Stone shrugged lightly before raising her leg up and delivering a roundhouse kick into his chest. He toppled backward, falling beside the reception desk.

"What do I do?" I asked her, my fingers gripping the hilt of the sword so tight I thought my fingers might break.

"I want you to stay back!" she barked. "Demigods are not to be underestimated. We have no way to know what he is capable of." She threw her blades at him as he rose from the ground. Before the blades could plunge into him, he disappeared in a brownish-red smoke. The blades embedded themselves into the far wall as the smoke moved across the room, and he materialized at the front door of the building.

"You've seen what I can do. And we both know it's more than enough to handle you and your ilk," he said. Crimson lightning danced between his fingertips. "I can harness fear itself, turn it into pure and devastating energy."

He raised his hands, and the red sparks came flooding directly at me. I raised the sword, out of panic or instinct, I was unsure. The blade acted like a lightning rod, absorbing the energy before it could touch my body. The midnight black metal took on a glowing red hue as it vibrated for a moment.

Deimos looked at me with shock and awe. "Is that my father's sword?" He sounded offended. "How dare you? You aren't fit to even hold such a weapon, much less fight with it."

"Your father bestowed it to the first Amazon," Miss Stone said. "He wanted it passed down to her descendants. It is his wish that it is wielded by our Queens. Who are you to defy him?"

"I'm someone that can see the bigger picture," he scoffed. "And I'm going to prove to him that he chose wrong."

"The gods are gone," Miss Stone said. Her curved blades freed themselves from the wall and flew back into her hands. She put them together at the hilts, forming a full circle. "How do you attempt to prove anything to someone who isn't here."

"The gods aren't gone for good." He shook his head. "They are just off in their own world. Literally. But my holy crusade will force him to take notice."

"Like a child throwing a temper tantrum to get daddy's attention?" My words came before I could consider the implications of taunting a demigod. He looked at me with a glare.

I wanted to show him I wasn't afraid. Even though I was. My entire body was screaming at me. My knees were trembling. My breathing was weak. My heart was pounding. But I refused to let him see it.

I attempted my best battle stance. I squatted slightly, solidifying my position. I raised the sword with bent elbows, and I looked him square in the eyes. I felt the blade's vibration and the warmth of its glow beside me. Something about it inspired me to make a move. I felt something guide me, like someone else with me taking my arms and directing my movement.

I sliced at the air and a wave of dark crimson energy released from the sword and barreled towards him. Red sparks flew in every direction and the energy collided with Deimos' body in a bright flash. He grunted in pain as he fought to remain on his feet. His jacket and suit were shredded to ribbons, hanging off his body like the branches of a willow tree revealing alabaster skin tightly pressed against the toned muscle underneath.

"How did you do that?" Miss Stone asked, placing herself by my side. "I've never heard of the sword displaying this ability before."

"I'm not sure," I said. "It just absorbed his energy and I let it go, I guess."

"This power comes from Ares," Deimos said, looking at his hands. "It seems that this sword made from his blood acts as some sort of a beacon."

"It can devour and repurpose the corrupted energy. This will be a powerful tool in the prophesized conflict," Miss Stone said with a chipper inflection.

"That's annoying," Deimos spat. "Unexpected, but I'll persevere." He stretched his arms as if making a dramatic gesture to the room around us. Multiple pillars of his muddy red smoke appeared and disappeared, leaving behind a dozen bodies to join us in the library lobby.

Standing in front of us was a mob of enraged faces with black ooze dripping from their mouths and solid black eyes, red veins stretching across every inch of their bodies, and ghost-white hair.

"I have been keeping an eye on you. When you came here, I didn't expect that sword to be the purpose. I always assumed it was on that disgusting island!" He was screaming, almost foaming at the mouth. As he continued to speak, the group of spillers all spoke in unison with him. "But now that I know it's obtainable, I'll make sure to pull it from your corpse. I know it can act as a key to the land of the Amazons. I'll use it to get to your home and drive it through the chest of your bitch Queen, and as she takes her last breaths, I'll make sure to tell her how her daughter suffered."

"Bryn!" I heard Macks and Lucinda call out from behind me, pulling my focus from the demigod for a brief second. The two of them were alongside Kathrine Patel under the threshold of one of the deep halls. Miss Patel quickly ran to check on her desk worker. She seemed to shrink into herself as she came to the realization of what had happened. She placed her hand on the woman's face and pulled her eyelids closed.

"Good!" Deimos cheered, alone this time. "You're just in time to die with your friend!" He raised a hand, pointing a finger in our direction before disappearing into the dark red smoke. The white-haired spillers all ran at us, swarming without mercy.

Chapter 14

Hands and arms twisted around me. Inky black sludge and strands of white hair obstructed my vision. I lost grip of the sword as I fell to the ground with a vibrating clang.

"What do we do?" I heard Macks call out in a panic.

"Same as last time," I grunted, shoving my assailants off of me. Two men fell in front of me, their limbs twisting and contorting as they snarled. "Knock em out to cure them."

"That won't work this time," Miss Stone said as she swung her curved blades, slicing the arm of a white-haired woman, and spilling black blood onto the ground at their feet. "When the veins stretch across their whole body and hair turns ghost white, it means they are fully corrupted, to the point of no return." She shoved her blade into the woman's chest before tossing her deceased body to the side.

"So, are you saying what I think you're saying?" Lucinda asked. She stood behind the desk, positioning her body as a shield in front of Macks and Miss Patel. Three white spillers stood on top of the desk, ready to lunge.

A whizzing sound carried one of Miss Stone's blades through the air, slicing the throats of the White Spillers one at a time before curving back and finding its way into her hand again. Rivers of black blood poured from the three as they fell over like dominoes, falling from the desk to the floor in a puddle of midnight.

"Oh god," Macks gasped, cowering behind Lucinda at the very sight of it. Lucinda seemed to stand taller in response, as if the grizzly sight was confirmation that things would be alright. Miss Patel looked down at her fallen employee, a stone face of acceptance resting with her.

My breath caught at the center of my chest. A gruesome wave of fear and bewilderment rushed over me. I had never seen someone die before. I had never had to kill before. And that's what needed to be done here. That's what was going to be expected of me as a warrior. As a future Queen.

The white spillers I had pushed away rushed me along with another, robbing me of the time to process what I had just seen. A pair of hands wrapped around my neck. Two more pairs grabbed each of my arms, putting them in different directions. I was thankful that, despite being supernaturally altered, they did not also have supernatural strength.

As the woman who had my neck tightened her grip, I could feel her nails piercing my skin. I pulled my arms upward, lifting the men who had me in their grasp. I flung them downward, momentum loosening their grip. I kicked at the woman, and she let out an inhuman grunt as she fell back. Throwing my arms forward, I dropped the two men into her.

They stood quickly, barely phased by my efforts. The

man at my right rushed forward and then stopped with a sharp inhale. His swirling dark eyes went still, and all of the rage melted from his face before he fell forward, flat onto the ground. Looking down, I saw one of Miss Stone's circular blades embedded right between his shoulder blades, black blood seeping from the wound it created.

The other man roared, grabbing the blade and yanking it from the corpse of the other spiller. He ran for Miss Stone, who had her own collection of dead spillers at her feet. The man lunged at her, swinging her own blade through the air. Miss Stone lifted her arms, shielding her face.

The blade sliced through the sleeves of her blouse like butter but stopped as if met with resistance. The blade clunked and scraped off of her as if she were wearing armor. Leaving unbroken brown skin underneath the tears of her sleeve.

"How?" I asked, flabbergasted.

"Now is not the time!" She yelled, grabbing the wrist of the hand that held her weapon and twisting. The man's hand turned so unnaturally that it made my own fingers twinge in pain. He dropped the blade on the floor and Miss Stone delivered a swift elbow to his head. A loud and alarming crack could be heard before he fell lifeless to the floor. "Stay alert!"

Taking my eyes off her, I saw the two spillers in front of me begin to approach. They moaned as if annoyed, releasing more black blood, dripping down their chins. I stumbled backward, terror building. Fear of them, and fear of what I needed to do.

As they prepared to pounce, I was met with another oddity. The Queen's Sword flew through the air from where I dropped it, landing in my outstretched hand.

I looked down, surprised. I hadn't even realized I put my hand out.

But like Miss Stone said, now was not the time. This wasn't the place to question how I managed it, this was the time to act. I raised the sword high and charged forward, my heart nearly pounding a hole through my chest.

The spillers swung their gnashing hands at me, but I dodged and weaved to the best of my ability. Some of their blows landed nothing but air while others scratched at my arms. I slashed the sword through the air, cutting at their blows, slicing black leaking cuts into their limbs.

I was hesitant even to attempt a finishing blow. The thought of killing made my throat burn. But as the spillers closed in, seemingly unafraid of the threat of death, I knew I had no choice. I gritted my teeth and swung the sword with all of my might.

The man fell to the ground with a groan, black blood spilling from his gut and onto the polished floor. The woman spiller, who also took part of the blow, refused to fall. Her left arm dangled to her side, half attached at the elbow, black goo pouring from the joint. She jumped forward and I yelped as I thrust the sword forward. Her body fell into the blade, and I felt the resistance of her insides. Like shoving a stick into the thick mud and hitting something hard underneath. My knees buckled slightly under the weight of what I had done. Her dark eyes drifted closed and her animalistic growl lessened to a whisper as her body went limp. Impaled like meat on the skewer.

I pulled the sword away, feeling more resistance on the way out than I did on the way in. She fell to the ground, laying still next to the man. The pool of inky blackness around them turned to a human red. I stood there for a moment, panting and sweating, clutching the sword tightly between my hands.

I had never killed anything before, and the experience left me feeling shaken. I collapsed to my knees, looking around at the carnage. Bloodied bodies scattered around us. They had been human. At one point, these things were people, and we killed them. I felt a pang of sadness in my gut. The feeling shot upwards, erupting from my mouth, manifesting as yellow bile, burning my throat as it made its way to the ground.

I felt hands on my shoulders, and I didn't need to look to know the person behind me was Lucinda. She pulled my body close to hers, in an embrace that felt all too comforting. An embrace I welcomed on instinct.

She held me in silence, and I melted into her as I looked at what I had done. As horrified as I was, I was also alive. My friends were alive. And I knew if I had been more prepared, the woman I watched die might not have had to suffer that fate. I had done good, even if it didn't feel like it. I channeled my strength and courage, and I did what was necessary.

Miss Stone approached us, panting slightly. "You did well," she said.

"The power of a demigod," Miss Patel said, still cowered behind the desk. "You truly are dealing with an insurmountable threat."

"More than we realized," Miss Stone said. "Thank you again, for holding the sword. Now that we have it, this will all be over soon."

"We should go," Lucinda said, lifting me to my feet. I was still barely processing.

"Yes," Miss Stone agreed before turning to Miss Patel again. "I'll call my people and arrange for a cleaning crew."

After a hushed conversation between the two of them, Miss Stone made a phone call, and we were on our way.

"Wait," I said while the four of us sat in one of the fancy cars deployed by Miss Stone's car service. Miss Stone sat beside us, still on the phone with who I assumed were more women in the Amazon network. The Queen's Sword sat between us. I turned to Macks. "Did you get the information you needed?"

"Um, sort of," they said with a timid air around them. "The guy she sent us to said the situation sounds like sorcery. Apparently, some sorcerers channel their magic through an object, unique to them."

"Sorcery is apparently a very niche magic though. He couldn't tell us any specifics," Lucinda added, looking out the window of the car. "But he told us how to find someone who could help us more."

"A sorceress who they outsource for magical services,"

Macks said, handing me an index card with handwritten scribbles. I looked down at the paper, surprised to see the address of our building and Ceci's name right above it.

Chapter 15

I was so tired of this shit. The constant twists and turns and revelations. I didn't know how much more I could take. I marched into our building, practically running. I approached the door of the first-floor apartment, unsure of what I would even say in the interaction to come.

It took every ounce of my self-control to not put a hole through the wood as I knocked. Macks and Lucinda stood behind me, tension radiating off of them. Miss Stone, holding onto the sword for safekeeping, left us to follow this thread on our own.

"What's the plan here?" Macks asked.

"Figure out what's going on," I said as the door opened slowly.

"Hello," Ceci said with a satisfied smile. She leaned against the threshold of the door, draped in a fuzzy black robe, olive tanned skin underneath, the only ounce of color on her was her sapphire red lipstick. "I received a call from an acquaintance a little while ago. Some old contact that has hired my services on occasion. He said he was sending someone my way. A young soul in need of information. Imagine my surprise when he told me the name of this wayward soul." She looked down at Macks with a growing grin.

"Was it a surprise?" I asked.

"What do you mean?" she asked, not taking her eyes off Macks.

"I'm new to all of this," I told her. "But it seems that everyone around me is supernatural. This can't be a coincidence."

"My dear," she said, turning her gaze to me. "You live in New York. Magic is literally around every corner."

"So, you're not connected to any of what's happening?" I looked to Lucinda for confirmation.

"I didn't know about her," Lucinda said. "Just like Macks."

"And I have to admit," Ceci began. "I'm not even quite sure what I'm being accused of here. Why don't the three of you come inside? We can sit and make sure we are all on the same page."

She opened her door and led us inside with a wave of her hand, so inviting and assured that we entered without a thought. Her apartment was a studio of three white walls and one wall of exposed red brick. Her large circular bed sat against the brick wall. The center of the room held a sofa and coffee table, while the far end of the room housed a small kitchen. Shelves filled with books and small wooden chests lined the walls.

She directed us to sit on the couch, which we did, and she sat at the edge of her plush bed after picking up a coffee mug from her bedside table.

"So," she began. "What has your panties in a twist?"

I didn't know where to begin.

"I recently found out that I have magic powers, I guess," Macks spoke first.

"Yes," Ceci said. "I got that phone call earlier. And it sounds like the whole crew has magic." Her eyes wandered to Lucinda and me.

"I'm a nymph," Lucinda said, ripping off the Band-Aid.

"Fascinating!" Ceci cheered. "Your kind is quite rare. Truthfully, I didn't even know if you were still around" I felt Lucinda shift beside me as if trying to distance herself from the statement.

"And I'm an Amazon, apparently," I said, reluctantly. "But the thing is, I just found out, from my boss who is also one apparently. And then Lucinda tells me what she is and that she's known about me since before we even met. And then shortly after all of this Macks gets these powers, and apparently it's unrelated. And then to find out that you, of all people, are a sorceress when we were referred to you by some secret society of supernatural librarians. I'm not sure how to make sense of all of this."

Ceci looked unfazed by the info dump. "When you moved in here, I thought I sensed something off of the two of you. But I'm not in the business of prying into other people's identities," she said calmly. "This all sounds…like a lot to deal with all at once. But I promise you, it's purely a coincidence that we live in the same building."

"Or fate," Lucinda said. "Fate maybe brought Macks

into your life, and fate maybe put us in the same building as someone who can help Macks figure their shit out." She was talking to me, practically ignoring Ceci's presence.

"And I would really like to figure this shit out," Macks sighed.

"What would you like to know?" Ceci asked, sipping from her cup. "I can't help you with all the other stuff, but I can help you with anything sorcery related."

I looked to Macks, giving them the space to find their answers.

"What even is sorcery?" Macks asked after a moment of reflection. "Literally all I know is from the movies."

"Well, a sorceress…" Ceci stopped herself with a sharp breath. "Sorcerer… Hm. I guess neither of those terms really reflects you."

"Sorcerex?" Macks suggested with a shrug of their shoulders.

"I like it," Ceci nodded proudly. "A sorcerex is a person with the ability to control arcane magic."

"Like, witchcraft?" Macks asked.

"Don't ever compare what we are to that filth." Ceci's words were etched in inky blackness and her entire body became stiff and rigid for just a moment, as if she lost herself. She regained her composure and put softness back into her voice. "All humans can tap into magical energy that permeates the world, they use it when they pray in their churches or when they check their phones seconds before they get a notification. Witches have magical energy in their veins. While they can tap into the magic and control it more than humans, they are still just human-plus. We have magic in our bones. We aren't simply using the magic as a tool, we are the magic. As a result, we are much stronger and can do so much more. We aren't confined to potions and spells."

"What does that mean?" Macks asked, leaning forward. "What can we do?"

"Each sorcerex has a specialty," Ceci said, basking in her own words. "An aspect they use to channel and manifest their power. For example, a fire sorcerer would be able to command flames, manifest them, and also utilize fire to do things far beyond its normal capabilities. Or an animal sorceress, like myself, can use creatures as conduits for her magic, command them, and borrow or distribute their physical and spiritual abilities."

"So, what does it mean if I do…bug stuff?" Macks asked. "An animal sorcerex too?"

"It's hard to say," Ceci answered. "You could be. You could instead be a sorcerex of pestilence. An insect sorcerex. Or even something as uber specific as a sorcerex of tiny things."

"Is there any way to know for sure?" Lucinda asked, reaching over me to grasp Macks' hand.

"You weren't born with your magic?" Ceci asked them. "Most of us are."

"No, it just showed up. Right after I got this." Macks grasped their grandfather's necklace.

"Some of us are not born," Ceci said plainly. "Sometimes our power is given to us, from beings far more powerful. Or some of us are born with dormant powers and they need to be awakened. When this happens, an object is usually connected to the emergence of our magic. This is where the magic wand mythos comes from. But it doesn't have to be a wand. It can be anything." She looked at Macks' necklace with intense focus. "Where did you get it?"

"From my mother. It's a family heirloom."

"Ah!" Ceci screamed with excitement. "Well, that settles it! It runs in the family, and this gaudy accessory activates it. All you have to do is ask your mother, she should be able to tell you exactly what kind of sorcerex you are."

"It's not that easy," I sighed.

"We don't talk," Mack's said, sounding defeated.

"You don't, or you can't?" Ceci asked with a raised eyebrow.

"What kind of question is that?" Lucinda shot back.

"All I'm saying is," Ceci answered, raising her hands in defeat. "If you want answers, that's the best person to get them from. I'll help you as much as I can but nothing could beat the source."

"You don't have to talk to her if you don't want to," I told Macks. "If it would be too hard, it might be better to just leave it. Especially since you have a choice here. You aren't being chased by some magical higher duty. You can just walk away from all of this if you want." I envied them for that.

"Right," Macks agreed. "But *you* can't walk away. You have this huge magical destiny. And I can't just let you deal with that alone. If I can help, I will."

Macks' determination and dedication took me off guard. I didn't even know what to say. Ceci stepped in before I could manage a response.

"What magical destiny are you so insistent on helping with?"

I didn't know if I should be telling Ceci this, but we had already told her so much. And she must be trustworthy if she's associated with the Strix. "I'm an Amazon princess, the next Queen," I said, cringing at the words. "And a demigod is trying to kill me and the entire Amazon race."

Ceci sat with that for a moment, in a silence that commanded us to embrace its uncomfortable aura. She stood up and approached us.

"A demigod is nothing to take lightly. I can't just send you off into battle against something like that," she said solemnly. "If you truly insist on doing this, go get answers from your mother, and then come back to me. Once we know the extent of your power, I will teach you to be the best damn sorcerex you can possibly be."

"I can't expect you to fight this fight," I said, standing up to meet her face-to-face.

"No no no," she insisted. "I am most definitely not joining you in battle. Self-preservation is always my number one concern. But I cannot, in good conscience, let an untrained mage blindly walk into something like this."

"I'll do it," Macks said, standing up as well.

"Let's think about this for a minute," Lucinda said, quickly joining us on our feet. "We don't know her."

"Do you know anyone else that can teach me sorcery?" Macks shot back.

"Well, no," Lucinda sighed.

"Bryn is going to be getting Amazon training, and you're a fully realized badass nymph," Macks said. "If I'm going to help, I need to do this. So, I'm going to call my mom."

Chapter 16

Macks sat at a large bay window, gleaming white sunlight beaming through. The gem-encased beetle beneath their neck seemed to glow in the light. They wore yellow corduroy pants with a tucked-in denim shirt. Two chocolate donut-shaped earrings hung from their ears. These were the first pair they had ever owned, given to them by their mother. There was an absence on their face as they gazed through the glass. Not pain, not nervousness. Just nothing.

"She's here," Macks said with a quiver in their voice. They stood up, facing the door of the cafe. Lucinda and I stood beside them.

A woman with toasted brown skin and a smooth black bob came through the threshold. She wore a teal floral dress and carried a large black purse. She looked around, scanning the room, before laying eyes on us. She gave a toothless smile, although her eyes lit up her face brighter than any smile could. I wondered if Macks also saw it. I didn't know what we were in for, but I felt like that was a good start at least.

"Macks," she said as she approached. She reached out her arms but pulled them back in hesitation before Macks put out theirs as well. They embraced. Macks' body was stiff like a board, their mother draped around them like she'd never let go.

"Hi Ma," Macks said, still being held. "Thanks for coming."

"Of course," she said, letting go. "I'm glad you called."

"Hello, Miss Liwanag," Lucinda said with a polite nod.

"Hello," she responded, stepping away from Macks.

"Hi, Sheila," I greeted her. Lucinda and I hadn't seen her since Macks' dad's funeral last year. Which was also the last time Macks saw her.

She gave me a hug. "Bryn! You are looking well. How is your family?"

"They are doing good, thanks."

"Let's sit," Macks said, leading their mother to the seats we had chosen. "We really need to talk."

"I know," she said, joining Macks at the bay window while Lucinda and I took the nearby chairs. "I know I haven't been the best mother. But I am trying. Ever since your father passed, I had been thinking, reflecting. And I want to do better. We are the only family we have left now."

Macks looked stunned. "Oh wow," was all they could manage to say at first. "Are you saying that you're okay with me being me?"

"I want to be," she said, grabbing her child's hands. "I'm trying to be. I joined one of those parent support groups last year. But I wanted to give you space to come to me. One of the other moms suggested it after I told her our situation."

"That sounds really lovely," I said, amazed at what I was hearing.

"Yeah, Ma. That's great, and I appreciate it," Macks stuttered. "But that's not actually why I called." They removed their hands from their mom's fingers and touched their necklace.

"Ah," their mom said. "I kept that from you for far too long, back when I didn't understand you. When I refused to. It wasn't right, and I wanted to give it to you as the first step in undoing my wrongs."

"Do you know…do you know what it is?" Macks asked, in a hushed tone. "What it does?"

Their mom looked at Lucinda and me with wide eyes, shifting between us and Macks.

"They know," Macks said, gazing at their mom with a look that could only be described as awe. "They were with me when it first happened. Judging from your reaction, you clearly know too. Why didn't you tell me?"

"I thought you'd get in touch with me before…before the spark ignited," Sheila said. "I didn't expect it to be so soon. I thought this meeting would give me the opportunity to explain."

"Well, you're in luck," Macks sighed. "Explanation is exactly what I need."

"Are you sure you don't want to do this privately?" she whispered.

"Bryn and Lucinda are my friends and they are here to support me," Macks said sternly, looking at their mother with a cocked head.

"Okay, okay," Sheila said in a disarming voice. "We come from a long line of Mambabarangs. My father, my grandmother, and her mother too. It passes down the family, through that necklace, to one person every generation." Macks looked at their mother with a puzzled look.

"What does that even mean?" they asked.

Their mom chuckled. "One of our ancestors was a sorcerer in the Philippines. He used magic to help his community. Healing the sick and injured, protecting them from dangers, even enacting revenge on their enemies."

"With bugs?" Macks asked with a curled lip.

"The story goes that his love was very sick, a poison that she got from the sting of an insect. He couldn't bear the thought of losing her, so he sought help from a powerful being to heal her. When he found such a creature, it recognized the love in his heart and bestowed him a gift. A single beetle that crawled into his mouth to live inside him."

"Gross," Macks scoffed.

"I know," Sheila laughed. "With this beetle inside him, he went back to his love and commanded the insect that stung her to suck the poison from her body, healing her completely. After his love was saved, the beetle left his body but the being that bestowed the gift was so impressed by the act of love that it encased the beetle in a necklace and let him keep the power."

"That's not how bug stings work though," Macks said.

"It's how magic works," Lucinda said with a dreamy look.

Sheila looked at the three of us with a suspicious glance. "You all are taking this very well," she said.

"I can be very open-minded," Lucinda said with a forced smile.

"It's a long story," I said. "But lately I've had to open my eyes to a lot of things."

"Like I said," Macks jumped in. "They were there when the magic first came." They didn't want to tell their mom everything that was going on. They told us before they called her, that they wanted us to keep our secrets secret, to focus on the mystery at hand.

She nodded, accepting our vague explanations. "This necklace unlocks the ability to use insects in ways that could never be done naturally," Sheila continued. "As a baby, my father would carry me through the air on a bed of butterflies. He did the same for you too actually, before he died." She looked down at her hands, a smile on her face.

"So, are you one too?" Macks asked, ignoring the joy in their mother's voice.

"No," she said with sadness. "I rejected the necklace when I came of age. Your grandfather swears it's because I was born here that I rejected tradition. He says I was too American to appreciate the gift." She laughed at the memory.

"Why did you reject it?" Macks asked.

"When I was a little girl, our neighbor's dog got loose. It was an untrained vicious thing. They had been looking for it for days and it must have wandered back and found its way into our backyard. We didn't realize it until it was already running at me. The thing nearly tore my face off." Her voice was shaking.

"That sounds terrifying," I said, trying to be supportive.

"Something even more terrifying came next," she said. "Before it could touch me, a swarm of…I don't even know what kind of insects swooped down from the heavens. They circled the beast like a black fog and devoured it in mere seconds. I watched a living creature turn into a pile of meat and blood and bones. And I saw my father with his hands raised and a look of anger and concentration on his face." She paused, looking at Macks. "I feared the power after that. And he was never happy about my fear. But he learned to live with my decision. Although, he insisted that I'd give my child the choice when the time came."

"And now here we are," Macks sighed.

"Macks," their mom said, taking their hands again. "This power is like a flame and the necklace is its spark. Your flame is igniting but you can take it off and let the flame die out before it can become stable and cultivated. But if you keep it, and let the flame grow, it will be with you forever, whether you wear the necklace or not."

So I was right. Macks could turn away from this if they wanted.

"I don't think I want to give this up," Macks said, nodding to themselves.

"If that is what you want, I'm sure it would make your grandfather very happy. But you should know," their mom said. "He always told me that because I never took the necklace, my spark never had a place to go. It would be in there with your own, igniting your flame into an inferno stronger than anyone's who came before."

"So, what does that mean?" Macks asked her.

"I can't say for sure," their mom said. "But I would like to be by your side as you come into this power. And I would love to be in your life again."

"Yeah," Macks said with a smile. "I think we can make that work. We can do a weekly lunch or something and go from there."

"Yes," Sheila squealed, hugging Macks tightly. She jumped up. "I will go get a coffee, and maybe we can catch up. With all three of you"

"Sure," Macks said, and Lucinda and I agreed, following their lead.

Their mom scurried away, and I excitedly turned to Macks. "This is great, isn't it?"

"Yeah, I guess," they said.

"You guess?" Lucinda asked inquisitively.

"This is just…she's making it all so easy," Macks said incredulously, looking off into the distance, at their mother peering at pastries at the coffee shop's counter. "I've thought about this moment for so long, and I always imagined a fight. Now that it's here and she's done the fighting on her own and comes out better at the end, it's like I don't even know how to feel."

Chapter 17

It was weird, going to work like everything was normal. I wasn't sure how Miss Stone did it. I didn't understand how Lucinda looked at me every day, knowing that all of this was coming, and pretended it wasn't. I couldn't see how Sheila could raise Macks and bear keeping their family secret. I didn't know how I was supposed to go on. But I was, somehow.

"Today, I'm going to have you support Oli," Miss Stone said as she looked over some papers. "With the model interview today. He should be arriving soon. I'll have you collect him downstairs and bring him up. And be ready if anyone needs assistance during the interview."

"Um…" I struggled to find a way to say what I needed to say.

"What?" Miss Stone said, looking up from her desk. We were alone in her office. "I thought that was pretty clear."

"No, it was! I got it," I said quickly. "It's not that. I just…a lot happened the other day and now we are just here. In the office."

"For now," she said, leaning back in her chair. "And later, I will begin your training."

"Where you'll train me to do what you…what we did, again."

"Where I will train you to fight, yes." There was a dismissive tone in her voice.

"To murder people," I said. I still felt sick about being pushed into something so dark. "People who are innocent victims, literally brainwashed to act against their will.

"Amazons do not murder." She spoke every word like it was its own sentence. "We are warriors that act in battle, as we must. We kill if the situation calls for it, and we are protecting the lives of ourselves or others. Murder is an unnecessary act that comes from anger or darkness, not duty for the greater good."

"Is that what they teach at Amazon school?" I asked her, not entirely satisfied with her justification.

"As a matter of fact, it is," she said with a tilted head. "And perhaps you should take into account that I have actually been here before. I am a fully realized Amazon who has gone through 'Amazon school.' I've led armies through war. I've fought in more battles than you can count. So, do your best to consider that I know what I'm talking about before you get snarky again. It will make your training much easier on the both of us."

"I'm sorry," I said, sinking into myself. "I just, I need time to think like that, I guess."

"Time might not be a luxury we have. We don't know when he will strike again," Miss Stone sighed. "But, keeping up with appearances and our lives is important, even when other things seem so much more pressing. There is a reason for everything we do. You'll see that eventually. Please get to work."

"Yes, Ma'am," I said, biting down everything I wanted to say.

"You'd think working with an army would prepare me for having a protege," she said to herself as I exited her office. There was a swirl of pride in my chest after hearing her call me that. But it was quickly snuffed by the fact that she likely only meant as an Amazon, not as a journalist. Was this my life now? Was everything I wanted going to be smothered by my Amazonian status?

I tried to force the thought out of my brain as I went down to the lobby of the building. I approached the front desk, and the security guard looked up at me with a smile.

"Hi, Matt," I greeted him. "I'm supposed to bring a guest up to Divinity."

"Sure," he said with a nod directed behind me. "He's already signed in and issued his guest sticker. Remember, he can't go anywhere in the building without a badged employee."

"Thanks," I said as I turned to the gray sofas perfectly arranged around a marble coffee table on the other side of the room. A broad-shouldered figure sat there, alone, as if the various bodies in the lobby arranged themselves to put a spotlight on him. Curly bronze hair covered a face that looked down on a cell phone while his fingers scrolled. He wore a monochrome fit of salmon sweatpants and sweat jacket and even sneakers to match.

"Excuse me," I said as I got closer. "Are you Hercules Nemean?" I cringed at the name. I was having enough of mythology, now I had to babysit a model who named himself after a god. And what did it say about him that he chose *this* figure for his celebrity name game?

He looked up and immediately stood to face me. He was taller than I expected, prompting me to look slightly upward to make eye contact.

He looked like a dream. I had seen his pictures before, I even saw him in that cologne commercial that set the internet on fire because he was depicted in a throuple along with a famous actress and football player. But in those he looked like only a fraction of what I saw before me.

His face was perfectly square as if sculpted for symmetry. Green eyes illuminated his face like moonlight. Soft button lips curled upwards in a smile.

"Hey." His smile was intoxicating. "Are you the interviewer?"

"Oh, no!" I laughed for about a second too long. "I'm Miss Stone's assistant. I'm going to be providing support during the interview."

"What kind of support would be needed during an interview?" It was unclear if he meant that to sound as insulting as it felt.

"Picking up the subject from the lobby so he can actually get to the interview," I said, gesturing to the elevator.

"Right," he said with a raspy giggle. "That sounds, like, pretty important."

"Oli will be interviewing you," I said as we walked to the elevator, and I scanned my access badge. "I don't know him too well, but I've read his work. He's great." The elevator doors slid open, and we stepped inside.

"You never told me your name," he said, leaning against the wall with his forearm. I pushed the button to the Divinity floor.

"I'm Bryn," I said politely.

"Nice to meet you, Bryn." He smiled again and I tried not to look directly at it. "I look forward to receiving your support during this interview." He winked, so fast I nearly missed it, and looked to his feet as he pushed away from the elevator wall. "I tend to avoid interviews. So boring just talking about myself and answering the same questions over and over again. But it's been a hot minute, I'm actually kind of excited."

"You don't like talking about yourself?" I asked, surprised. "I thought that was every famous person's favorite topic of conversation."

"I try to keep things focused on my career, but reporters love gossip so they always find a way to ask about personal stuff. My life is…it's not fun to unpack. Especially repeatedly." I resisted the immediate urge to ask what he meant by that. "So I actually promised myself last year I wouldn't do them anymore."

"What made you go back on your promise?" I asked him.

"I know your boss," he said with disappointment. "And I couldn't stomach saying no to someone I know, ya know?"

"I get that," I told him. Miss Stone was truly a force to be reckoned with. Her connections allowed for an interview with someone who swore off interviews.

The elevator doors opened and spat us out into the Divinity office. I led him to the interview room. It was a large photo studio, a big open space with sectioned-off areas of stark white walls and floors. Tall studio lights were scattered around the room. A table of assorted snacks lined one wall. Two clothing racks sat beside a group of chairs, facing one of the white sections that housed a single stool.

Minerva, wearing a bright pink fur coat and sleek black jeans, stood by a collection of camera equipment, talking to a photographer whose name I didn't know.

Oli, wearing chocolate brown pants and a simple black tee, listened intently as Gianfranco Zanetti waved his arms dramatically as he looked through the clothing racks.

London waved at me as we entered, ushering me over to the refreshment table. I smiled at her, acknowledging the request but continuing to lead the model where he needed to go.

"And he has arrived!" Gianfranco called out. "We met briefly during fashion week last year. I'm *so* looking forward to dressing you this evening."

"Yeah," Hercules said. "Should be fun."

"This is Oli," I said, stepping to the side. Hercules and Oli exchanged a handshake.

"Thank you for coming," he said with an air of gratitude. "Let us show you what we have planned."

"I'll be here if you need me," I said as they discussed clothes and interview logistics. I turned and joined London at the food table.

"Hey!" She handed me a plate with tiny cubed mangos, blueberries, and a mini croissant. "Welcome to your first interview-slash-photoshoot."

"Thanks," I said, taking the plate. "It'll be cool to see how this all goes down."

"I've been on multiple sides of this," she said, tossing a candied almond in her mouth. "A Journalist, like Oli, and an assistant, like you. It's not going to be the most glamorous thing for you right now but it will get there."

I spent the next two hours fetching outfit pieces for Gianfranco, cataloging what was worn in each photo, and bringing Hercules a water bottle whenever he got thirsty.

After the repeated outfit changes, poses, and flashing lights, the shoot was nearing an end. Gianfranco had put Hercules in an assortment of looks, including a ball gown, with a bodice that cradled his pectoral muscles too perfectly and a suit jacket hanging from his shoulders. Hercules seemed particularly fond of a yellow chunky knit polo and shorts combo. There was a fit that consisted of nothing but an expensive brown leather jacket and designer underwear that I particularly enjoyed.

Now, Hercules was in the final fit. A silky red shirt, unbuttoned low to his chest, and black jeans with embroidered roses. Something more casual for the interview. He sat on the stool provided for him, facing the camera with a brooding look while the photographer snapped pictures.

Gianfranco had left with all of the finished clothing to get a head start on putting things away. Oli sat in a chair beside the photographer while Minerva set up her phone on a tall tripod to silently watch and record the interview. She wouldn't post the whole interview, but footage of any particularly good sound bites could be posted online to encourage people to read it. After the photographer finished, I began to attach a small mic to Hercules' shirt to better enhance the audio of Minerva's video. Oli prepared his own audio recorder.

"Thanks for all the help," Hercules whispered in my ear as I clipped on his mic and checked to make sure it was on and ready to record.

"It's my job," I said.

"Thanks for doing your job," he sang, followed by a small laugh. I smiled and returned to London who had been watching the whole shoot with me.

"Is Hercules Nemean flirting with you?" London asked in a hushed tone.

"No," I scoffed. "He's just being overly charming. He's probably like this with everyone." He seemed like the type to schmooze for the sake of schmoozing. The kind of guy who knows he's attractive so he tries to make people swoon for fun.

"He keeps looking at you," London said, raising her eyebrows. I glanced over at him to see his green eyes firmly locked onto me. He smiled and raised his hand slightly, while Oli began the interview.

"He probably just wants another snack," I said, thinking back to the three times he asked me to bring him something from the refreshment table during the fifteen-minute break from shooting.

"So, you've taken the world by storm in just a short amount of time," Oli said. "You've only been modeling for four years, but you're already dominating the industry."

"I guess you can say that," Hercules chuckled. "I guess people like what I have to offer."

"What do you think that is?" Oli asked.

"Oh no, self-evaluation straight out the gate. I feel like you should at least buy me a drink first," he joked, bringing a laugh out of Oli. "I don't know, really. I guess some people would say I'm just a pretty face. But I don't really think that's it. That's not what modeling is. It's a confidence. It's standing in front of a crowd or a camera and saying 'This is who I am. Take it. Revel in it.' And there is something about that that I really like. I just, kind of, feel at home in that kind of confidence."

"Is that the key to this business? Confidence?" Oli asked.

"Partly," Hercules said. "You're delivering a fantasy. You want people to see you wearing clothes or using a product and you want them to yearn to be you in those clothes and using that product. And if you bring that confidence to the table, people will want that every time. People are constantly seeking the courage their lives are missing. I might not be able to give them that but I like to think I give them enough courage to buy that shirt they like, or the watch that will make them feel good, or to finally book that vacation they've been dreaming about. All because they saw me living in their fantasy." Hercules didn't look at Oli, as if gazing into a dream.

"Fantasy," Oli said, pulling Hercules' eyes back to him. "That's the family business, isn't it?"

"It is!" Hercules said with glee. "I always say I caught the fame bug from my family."

"You're a third-generation household name," Oli said.

"I don't know if I would call myself that," Hercules argued.

"Well, your grandfather certainly was," Oli countered. "The great Henry Nemean. World famous and undefeated boxer. Families would gather around their TVs to cheer him on as he fought in front of sold-out crowds."

"Yeah, that's him," Hercules said. "He was fantastic. It's a shame he passed away before I could meet him."

"And his stage name was Hercules," Oli said, leaning in. I was surprised to hear his name was real, coming from his family, and not just something he used for the camera. "What was it like, being named after him? Did you feel the need to keep his name in lights?"

"No," Hercules said after a minute of thought. "Although he is largely forgotten now, which I think is a shame, I never considered him the reason I chose this career. My dad had a collection of old memorabilia, though, from his fights and stuff. I look back on it all sometimes. He was definitely a cool guy."

"And your dad," Oli probed. "Adam Nemean, a world-famous movie star of the '90s and teen heartthrob of the '80s."

"People say I look just like him." Hercules straightened up in his seat, puffing up his chest, and boasted a proud look.

"You do," Oli said. "People also say you got to where you are through nepotism. Do you think there is any truth to these claims?"

"Maybe," Hercules said with a serious tone. "But it's not like I intentionally used my family to become famous. I couldn't really use my dad's connections, even if I wanted to. He died young and he was very private. People didn't even know I existed until, like, 20 years after he was gone."

"Which is around the same time you got your first big modeling gig," Oli pointed out.

"Right," Hercules said, stone-faced. "I guess, in that regard, my family name could have contributed to my success. But I'd rather think of it as upholding a legacy rather than benefiting from nepotism."

"Why is that?"

"The Nemean Foundation," Hercules said. "My dad started his nonprofit in the middle of his career to offer support and grief counseling to those who have suddenly lost a loved one, as well as to educate professionals who work closely with those who are grieving." He sounded like he was reading from a script. "Throughout my very short career, I've spread his message and donated to his organization. The same organization that helped his own family after his death. I'm not just keeping our family name alive, I'm keeping our family name alive through his work. I hope to run the organization one day."

"Why not now?"

"I'm nowhere near ready to be in charge of something so massive," he said. "I've got a lot more living and learning to do. For now, I volunteer. Fundraisers, support group meetings, advocacy."

"I had no idea he was doing all of that," I whispered to London. "Yeah, I guess he doesn't advertise it much. If anything, it always seemed to me like he was trying to distance himself from his family."

"What do you mean?"

"The same way his dad hid the fact that he even had a kid," London said with a shrug. "Homeboy doesn't publicly talk about his dad much. I'm surprised he's doing it now."

"So, if that's the plan for later, are there any plans for the near future? Career, life, or otherwise?" Oli asked.

"I don't know," Hercules laughed. "I'm kind of just vibing. My career is still taking off. I'm open to new things as they come." He glanced over again, this time our eyes locked onto each other's. And just for a second, I was lost in that moment, like looking into the eyes of someone who truly sees you. Something I've only ever seen in a few pairs of eyes before. Something I couldn't possibly see in the eyes of someone I just met.

No. I was seeing things. Letting a crush warp my perception. I refused to be that girl.

I ignored the glances and the gorgeous green eyes for the rest of the interview. Even when I wasn't looking at him, I could feel him looking at me.

"That was great," Minerva said as she packed up her recording set up. "Really great stuff. The team will go over the magazine layout, and I'll craft together a campaign for the socials. People are going to love this."

"I'm happy to hear it," Hercules said.

"We'll send the interview and magazine over to your people once it's ready," Oli said, giving him one final handshake. "And we will leave you in Bryn's capable hands." He and Minerva left the room, chatting about their next moves.

"I should go with them," London said, skipping over to Hercules. "But I just wanted to meet you. I'm London, and that was really great. I'm excited you're our next cover."

"Nice to meet you," he said, with a charming smile. "Can I ask, what happens now?"

"You're free to go. Bryn can take you back downstairs or she can give you a tour of the office before you go." London shot me a mischievous look.

"I was actually hoping to see Miss Stone," he said, looking at me. "She reached out and said she'd drop in during the interview.

"Oh, she didn't mention that to me," I said. I knew every meticulously planned detail of her day and she hadn't planned on being here for the shoot. But she did leave a slot in her schedule open for directly after. "Maybe she forgot to tell me. I can take you to her office. She should be done with her phone calls by now."

"No!" London said. She turned to Hercules. "You two stay here. I'll go let her know and have her swing by."

"It doesn't make sense to make her come to us," I pointed out.

"Trust me. She has been cooped up in her office all day. It'll do her some good to stretch her legs and see a different room." London turned and scurried away before I could argue further. Leaving me and Hercules alone in the photo studio.

"I should get changed back into my own clothes," he said after a moment of silence where I still attempted to avoid eye contact. He walked to the changing partition set up for him. "So, tell me about yourself, Bryn." I looked over to face him, but he was no longer in view. Articles of clothing began to be flung onto the partition, sloppily hanging like discarded rags.

"Not much to tell," I said. "I'm Miss Stone's new assistant."

"And who were you before?" I heard rustling behind the partition. "And who will you be after?"

"Before, I was just me. I dreamt of an opportunity like this. And after, I hope to be the one asking questions instead of fetching water bottles."

"And Elizabeth says you only just found out you were an Amazon." Panic shot through my spine like a rocket. "What was that like? I can't imagine."

"What?" I could only manage one word.

"Oh come on," he said, stepping into view. He was wearing his colorful sweatpants, but his sweatshirt rested in his hands. My eyes traveled across every inch of him. His bare and protruding chest, rising and falling with every breath, the veiny mountains on his arms, the lines that sketched bulging muscles along his stomach, pointing down into his low riding waistband. For a second, I could no longer even manage one word. "We are alone now. We don't have to pretend."

I put it all together in an instant. But I had to hear it from him before I could believe it. "So, you're the real Hercules?"

"Heracles," he said with a confident smile. "But the Romanized version is more popular these days, so I adapt with the times."

"Jesus Christ," I exclaimed, turning away. Partly because of rage, partly because I didn't want to be distracted by the sight of him. "It just never ends. Things just keep on coming."

"Wait, did she not tell you who I was?" I could see him step closer in my peripheral vision.

"No!" I told him.

"And you didn't figure it out from the name?" He laughed.

"I didn't think the real Hercules would be a model! I don't know what gods do."

"You're adorable," he continued to laugh.

"Why are you even using your real name?" I asked him,

feeling brave enough to look at him again. "Shouldn't you be trying to be discreet? Miss Stone tells me how important that is."

"I've used fake names in the past. But a name is such an important part of your identity, you start to miss it after a while," he explained. "People these days give their kids all kinds of wacky names, no one is going to bat an eye at a guy named after a myth. So after some time as Henry, and Adam, and countless other names, I decided to use my real one."

"Wait…" I said. "Your father and grandfather?"

"Don't exist," he said quickly. "They were me. It's a common tactic amongst immortals. Live a life, fake your death, and come back a few decades later as your own kid or grandkid. It's either that or constantly moving around with a new name and backstory, and that gets old."

"And you choose to be a celebrity all the time?" I asked. "Isn't that risky?"

"Not always. But I like the fame. It's riskier now, with the way everything is documented and living on the internet these days," he said with a shrug. "But people aren't ever going to figure it out. The truth is impossible, and most people don't go looking for the impossible explanation."

"People just assume you have really strong genes," I said.

"Exactly," he nodded.

"You must have lived so many different lives," I said, unable to fathom all he must have seen and done.

"You should let me take you on a date sometime," he said with a smirk. "I can tell you all about it."

"Aren't we, like, related?" I asked. I didn't know much mythology, but I knew who his father was supposed to be.

"What? No!"

"Ares is my ancestor, and Zeus is your father," I said. "That makes my ancestor your brother?"

He laughed. "God genetics don't really work like that."

"How do they work?" I asked, already dreading the explanation.

"Gods are metaphysical beings without bodies or DNA," he explained. "When two gods create another god, they are pulling their power together to dream a new being into existence. Brand new, also with no body or DNA."

"So, we aren't actually related to the gods?"

"Well..." he dragged the word on. "Demigods are a different story. Gods can come into the physical plane by possessing a body that exists there. When they do that, they physically become that being, fusing together in all aspects. When a god is possessing a human, they can get together with another human and make babies the old-fashioned way."

"So gods share no relation amongst each other but demigods share relation to gods?" I asked.

"Exactly!" he cheered. "So Zeus and Hera created Ares, who then fathered your ancestor. So you share blood with him. Zeus fathered me with my human mother. So I share blood with him. But Zeus didn't father Ares, so Ares and I share no blood. Which means you and I are free to—" He leaned in close. The heat of his lips grazed mine before I even realized what was happening. Breath caught in my chest like a vice, I placed my hand on his chest, stopping him just before contact was made. His skin tingled beneath my palms.

"Thanks for the lesson on godly genetics," I scoffed. "But you're still getting way ahead of yourself." I stepped back, putting an appropriate distance between us.

"Oh come on," he sighed dramatically. "I don't usually have to work this hard."

"This hard?" I asked, shocked. "This is literally our second conversation."

"Exactly," he smirked.

"You're a little cocky, aren't you," I said, shaking my head.

"Do you like cocky?" he asked with a smile that made my knees weak.

"Not particularly," I said. "Hopefully you have more redeeming qualities."

"Only one way to know for sure," he said, looking down to the ground and for a brief moment his armor-like gaze was off of me. "Let me take you out."

"I have to train to fight a demigod," I argued. "I can't date right now."

"Says who?" he laughed. "I'm one of your trainers, and I say it's okay."

"You're my what?" I asked him in disbelief.

"When Divinity reached out for this interview and I

agreed, Elizabeth asked if I could stick around and help," he explained. "She really didn't tell you about me?"

"No," I said. My mind tried to make up some sort of reason for the secrecy, but I couldn't think of anything.

"Well, now you know," he said. "And you should also know that training and war is a lot of stress and pressure. It's important for you to take the edge off. A social life, which includes dating, could help with that. In fact, I heavily encourage it." He smiled as if he expected a laugh but I didn't want to give him the satisfaction.

"I guess I can't argue with that," I said after a minute of thought. I didn't really want to argue. One date couldn't hurt anything. It could even turn into more.

His smile grew twice as large as he pumped his fist slightly.

"I see you two have already become acquainted with each other," Miss Stone said. I turned to see her tall figure leaning against the threshold of the studio door. She looked at us both up and down with one raised eyebrow.

"Elizabeth!" Hercules called out, quickly putting on the rest of his clothes. "You finally showed up."

"I had some work to do," she said, leaving her perch and approaching us. "Thank you for coming and agreeing to help. We have a lot of ground to cover and we don't know how much time we have to do it."

"I'm looking forward to lending a hand," Hercules said, stealing another glance at me. "So, tell me what you're dealing with."

Chapter 18

"Before we begin," Miss Stone said as she led Hercules and me up a stairwell in the Divinity office building. "London proposed that we hire your friend to do video work for the magazine. She made a very convincing argument."

"Wait, really?" I said. "Did you agree with her?"

"I had Macks come in today and fill out the paperwork." Miss Stone looked over her shoulder, peering down at me. "They officially start next week."

"I don't know what to say." It was exciting to hear Macks would be working at Divinity and even more exciting that Macks would be working with the art form they love.

"I trust London's judgment," Miss Stone said. "Plus, it might help to keep your friend close if they insist on being part of the coming conflict."

"So, you're just going to let some random pal join a fight against a demigod?" Hercules asked, dripping in disbelief.

"Macks just found out they have magic," I explained. "They could be useful."

"After seeing what this Demigod is capable of," Miss Stone said as she pushed open a door at the top of the stairwell. Dim daylight poured over us as she led us to the roof. A big open space overlooking a domino of buildings across Manhattan. "We might need all the help we can get."

"You still haven't told me what demigod you're fighting," Hercules said, crossing his arms. Miss Stone turned to face us.

"Deimos," she said with a curled lip.

"What?" Hercules cried out. "No way!" He shook his head as if trying to wake from a nightmare.

"You know him?" I asked.

"We crossed paths a few times," he said. "His father created the Amazons and Ares had always favored them over his other children. And yeah, Deimos resented them for that. But I don't believe it would drive him to genocide."

"Well, believe it," Miss Stone insisted. "It's happening."

"He attacked us," I told him. "And he told us exactly how he felt." Hercules stared at me, his green eyes glazed over as if watching something play out in his mind.

"If you know him, you might be of more help than I originally thought," Miss Stone said. "You might be able to add some insight into fighting him."

"I've never fought him," Hercules said with one quick breath. "It was never like that."

"Do you know anything?" Miss Stone asked, tilting her head.

"Just that he can corrupt people. He can amplify their fear and rage until it consumes them completely," he explained. "It turns them into something…different."

"We've seen it," I said. "It turns them into these zombie things."

"And he can also take fear and anger and convert it to pure energy," Hercules added.

"The rage lightning," Miss Stone said. "We've seen that too."

"So you can't tell us anything new," I deduced.

"I guess not," he said, biting his fingernail.

"That's okay," Miss Stone said, raising her hands in defeat. "You're here to help me turn Bryn into a fighter."

"Where do we start?" he asked, looking me up and down with a glance that felt entirely too judgmental.

"Defense," Miss Stone said. "And then we move onto the sword. And after she knows how to wield it, we can try to unlock its divine ability."

"Shouldn't we start with the sword?" I asked. "I feel like knowing how to fight is the most important thing." The previous battles rang in my mind. The intensity. The adrenaline. The fear. I didn't want to be caught in another one of those without a sword in hand and the knowledge of how to use it.

"No!" Miss Stone yelled. "Your ability to defend yourself is far more important! If you can't protect yourself in battle, you're as good as dead! No matter how talented or skilled of a fighter you are!" She looked at me with a scolding glare that made me afraid to speak.

"She's right," Hercules said, sounding a little afraid himself.

"Okay," I agreed with caution. "Teach me."

"Hercules, as the Demigod of strength and heroics, has a similar ability to Amazons," Miss Stone said. "He's the perfect training dummy."

"Thanks," Hercules said with a fake smile.

"Are you stronger than us?" I asked.

"Wanna find out?" he asked, punching each fist downward before raising them playfully.

"Kinda," I answered, raising mine as well.

"He's not stronger than an Amazon," Miss Stone said, cutting through the joy in the air. "Near Amazon strength. But, unlike Amazons, he is invulnerable. Nothing can hurt him."

"Except for a divine weapon. Those things can kill just about anything." Hercules added. "So when you advance to sword training, be careful."

"But, aren't you also invincible?" I asked Miss Stone. "I saw you in that fight. You took a blow that should have done damage but didn't leave a scratch."

"That is what I'm going to teach you today," she told me. "While we are more durable than humans, we also can also deploy temporary invulnerability. Unlike Hercules, whose invulnerability is a constant, we have to activate ours."

"How do I do it?" I asked, straightening my body and preparing myself to absorb the lesson.

"We can send our strength to a specific part of our body," she said, beginning to pace around Hercules and me. "In doing so, we turn the skin into an impenetrable armor. It can come in handy but it has its drawbacks. While you are doing this, you likely won't be able to call on your strength at the same time."

"So I can only fight or block an attack," I said. "But I can't throw a punch and protect myself at the same time."

"That is correct."

"That sucks," I said. "It would be cool if I could just turn this armor thing on and walk around with it all the time, especially during a fight."

"Even if you could use it at the same moment as your strength," Miss Stone said. "It wouldn't work like that. It's localized protection. You can only use it on a specific point of your body."

"Which means," Hercules jumped in. "In order to use it, you have to know exactly where a blow is going to land."

"How am I supposed to know that?"

"It comes with practice," Miss Stone said. "As you train, you'll learn how to recognize where an attack is likely to hit you during a fight. Then you will only need to worry about surprise attacks."

"Right," I said, dreading all that I was hearing. It all sounded so out of my control. Like even with the powers I was given, there were complexities that still made it feel impossible to use. And if I couldn't use these powers properly, I could die. If I died, Miss Stone and all other Amazons locked away from their home might never be able to return. Or worse, if I fail, an entire race of people could die along with me.

"Hercules will hit you," Miss Stone said with ease. "You

will not hit him back. You will focus on blocking his punches."

"Oh damn," Hercules said, putting a hand on his chest. "So we are just jumping straight into it?"

He looked at Miss Stone for confirmation, but she simply stared back at him without a word. Hearing the message loud and clear, he and I faced each other. "Sorry about this," he said. "I'll try to pull my punches."

Before I could respond, he stepped forward. He shoved his fist outward, crashing it into my abdomen. A thundering pain erupted from the contact, stealing my breath and propelling me backward. I fell flat on my ass.

"Get up," Miss Stone said, looking down at me struggling to catch my breath. "Try again." She extended her hand. When I grabbed onto it, she swiftly tugged me to my feet. "You know the hit is coming. Focus your mind on that. Prepare yourself mentally. Your body will do the rest."

I positioned myself in front of Hercules and he swung immediately. His fist was heading straight for my shoulder. Instinct kicking in, I brought my hand up. My palm against his fingers, I redirected his fist, pushing it to the side. The momentum of the punch carried him forward, prompting him to stumble slightly to my left. I grabbed him by the arm before his stumble could turn into a fall.

"Quick thinking," Hercules said, finding his footing.

"No!" Miss Stone barked. "This is not a lesson on deflection and evasion. This is a lesson on protection and defense."

"I'm trying," I told her. "This is literally day one. Give me some time."

"You might not have that luxury," Miss Stone pointed out. "We don't have time for you to ignore the lessons I'm trying to impart. Do not run, do not deflect. Take the hit. Use your power to defend yourself from it."

"Let's go again," Hercules said, looking back and forth between us. I don't know why Miss Stone was being so tough on me. I hadn't expected this. She was always serious but never seemed this intense within her serious nature.

"Sure," I agreed, stepping back.

"Don't hold back," Miss Stone said coldly. Hercules looked at her, prepared to say something. She gave him a look that seemed to strike down his words before he could utter them.

He obediently raised his fists again. This time, barreling toward me much faster than before. I wanted to duck away, or swing my leg at his ankles, or grab his fist mid-punch. Options flooded my mind, but I pushed them out. Once silence fell in my brain, it felt like everything was moving slowly. No, not everything. Hercules. The fist coming for me was inching closer at a snail's pace. I could see it coming, soon to land on my forehead.

The space between my eyes began to burn as if a fire had ignited under my skin. I fought through the pain, braving the burn. I braced myself as knuckles connected to my skull. I felt his skin against mine, a soft tap, but there was no strong impact. His arm stiffened as his body jolted against the resistance of my body. His eyes widened and a pleasing smile burst on his face.

"Good, Bryn!" I heard Miss Stone cheer with the slightest hint of joy.

I grabbed Hercules by the wrist as the burning on my face dissipated. The pain melted into strength as I tossed him to the side. He fumbled into Miss Stone's arms. She pushed him off of her and clapped her hands together.

"I did it?" I asked, craving confirmation and praise.

"I've never hit an Amazon before. That durability is no joke," Hercules said, massaging his arm. "Is that what it feels like when people hit me?"

"I would imagine so," Miss Stone said.

"Does it always burn like that?" I asked, remembering the sensation that came with my invulnerable forehead.

"Unfortunately, yes," Miss Stone said. "It's just the bodily reaction to our armoring ability."

"That sucks," I said. "But I guess protection is worth it."

"Let's keep going," Miss Stone said. "You've had a successful attempt much sooner than I expected, but we need to ensure consistent successes. You need to get this down perfectly."

"I'm ready," I said, still high on the excitement of success. Enthusiasm building in my bones, I couldn't help but imagine what kind of person Miss Stone was turning me into. A warrior, yes, but how different was warrior Bryn from Bryn the person? I tried to imagine her, but no image was conjured in my brain. In the absence of a clear and imagined potential future, fear and anxiety found their way in. Instead of Warrior Bryn, the idea of death loomed. The thought of training gave way to battles too impossible to step into. Magic powers as a fact of life made me queasy.

Things were different now, and this new path was progressing with me chained in. No escape.

***

"Bryn met Hercules!" Macks called out in complete disbelief.

"And he's into her," Lucinda said with pride, reading the same group text.

"Do you know him?" Macks asked.

"No, I've never had the pleasure," she said. "But I've heard stories."

"I've never met a god before," Macks said. They were so wrapped up in their identity as a sorcerex, they didn't fully realize what these new revelations opened up. There were all of these mythological figures and creatures that were suddenly real and out there. And Macks was thrilled by the idea that they could come face to face with them.

"They aren't that great," Ceci said. She sat on their couch, examining her manicured nails. "People like to put them on a pedestal, and they *so* enjoy it. But they don't deserve it."

"Have you met gods?" Macks asked, teeming with jealousy. They were never one of those kids that was really into mythology, but now that mythology was fact, they were all in. It was thrilling.

"That's not what we are here to discuss." Ceci jumped

up. "This is magic 101. And I'm your professor, Ceci, with my TA Lucinda."

"I'm no one's assistant," Lucinda said. "You're in our house, by the way. If anyone is calling the shots here, it's not you."

"This is my area of expertise," she said, unbothered.

"She is doing a really nice thing, offering to help," Macks said, pulling Lucinda back from the edge of anger.

"If we want to learn nymph magic, you can take the lead. But I'm your gal for sorcery." Ceci wore black checkered pants and a deep purple shirt that hung off her shoulders slightly.

Lucinda groaned. She wore a long platinum-blonde wig that Macks had only ever seen her pull out if she was going to an event where she needed to impress white people.

"What's first?" Macks asked.

"The basics," Ceci said, gesturing to a vase of wilting brown flowers that she brought with her. "Think about what you want, what you yearn for, and visualize it." She looked at Lucinda with raised eyebrows.

Lucinda groaned again before raising a hand over the flowers. She took a deep breath and held it for a moment. As she exhaled, the flowers sprouted up, as if waking from slumber. The crinkled petals smoothed like silk. The brown color faded and turned to shades of pink and white.

"It's a lot like manifesting," Lucinda said, admiring the revitalized flowers.

"That's the basic building block of magic," Ceci said. "Be you a witch, a nymph, or a sorcerex." She reached down and grasped the head of a pink rose in her hand, ripping the petals from the stem. Lucinda winced as Ceci crumbled the flower in her fist. She threw her hand into the air, and when she released her fingers, a tiny bluebird took flight. It zipped through the room, making wide circles around the three of them before it escaped through an opened window.

"Did you just turn a flower into a bird?" Macks asked. Even though they saw it with their own eyes, they were struck with blunt disbelief.

"Transmogrification," Ceci said. "One of the many tools in our belt."

"So, I should be able to turn things into bugs?" Macks asked.

"And bugs into other things," Ceci said. "Would you like to try?"

"I don't really know how," Macks said. "You'll have to show me."

Lucinda put her arm around Macks' shoulder. "Start with a feeling. Magic is rooted in emotion."

"I thought it was rooted in manifestation," Macks said.

"It's both," Lucinda laughed. "Your emotions bring out the magic and then you use your intention to influence the result."

"You say it like it's so simple." Macks plucked a tiny white petal from one of the flowers. They pressed it between their palms and tightly shut their eyes.

Nothing.

"You need to rely on a strong emotion," Lucinda said. "When I'm revitalizing plants, I think of my nymph sisters and how happy they made me when we were together. Sometimes I think of you and Bryn."

"When I call forth an animal, I try to bring up the image of people who have wronged me, and the anger they caused," Ceci said. "I like to think with the power I have, no one would be able to mistreat me again."

"That's dark," Lucinda said. Macks didn't dare open their eyes, out of fear of losing the concentration they were chasing.

"That's real," Ceci said in a gotcha tone.

Macks tried to imagine the last thing that made them feel something particularly powerful. The only thing that came to mind was Bryn's coworker, London.

She had secured Macks a videographer job at Divinity Magazine. It was mostly filming and editing for their social media team. But it also meant working with journalists to make documentary-style videos for the FOAM feature. It was a big deal, a great job, and somehow London had convinced Miss Stone to make it happen. On top of the joy behind the exciting new job, there was also her smile. When Macks went to the office to sign the paperwork, London was there to greet them. From the moment Macks arrived to the moment they left, she was grinning. A smile that made Macks smile back. A smile that made it really easy for Macks to say yes when London asked if they'd be interested in a coffee date. A smile that made Macks' stomach flutter.

"It worked," Lucinda said with a gasp.

Macks' eyes shot open, and they immediately looked down at their hands. But the flower petal remained unchanged. Just as they were about to question Lucinda, they raised their eyes to see a dozen orange and yellow butterflies rising and falling in the space around them like shooting stars in the night.

"Conjuration," Ceci said. "Another tool you have as a sorcerex."

Chapter 19

"This just feels wrong," I said, examining myself in the mirror one last time. Just moments ago, Lucinda and Macks had helped with my hair and makeup so frantically that it made me anxious.

"Are you not interested?" Lucinda asked, gazing into the reflective surface with me. "I've heard nothing but good things about him, which is rare for gods. Even demigods."

"I'm interested," I told her, blood rushing to my cheeks. "It just feels like poor timing." I brushed my hands down my skirt.

"When would a better time be?" she asked.

"When there isn't a pissed-off demigod trying to kill me," I said, looking her reflection in the eyes.

"Bryn, when this is over, you have no idea what your life will look like," she told me. "There might never be the perfect time to date, to go watch a movie, to go get your nails done. So you take the opportunities when they come, and deal with Amazon shit when you need to. Right now, you're just training and waiting. This demigod hasn't shown his face since you got the sword. So, this is probably the perfect time."

"You sound like him," I scoffed.

"Great minds think like me," she joked.

I was wearing a sleeveless white crop top and an olive-colored plaid skirt with a pilgrim-esque buckle on the side. I thought it was cute. Simple but also makes a statement. The pop of color looked good against my brown skin.

Dressing for a date, especially a first date, was always a feat in and of itself. It was an opportunity to make an impression and show the person who you are, or at least, who you want them to see you as. The problem with this first date was he knew me already. Parts of me. He had been training me to fight. He knew the predetermined destiny that had been laid out for me long before I was born. He saw me as something I didn't even see myself as. He saw a princess and a warrior.

No matter what I wore, no matter what I did, he'd have that image of me. An image I didn't even know if I fit into. It was a lot of pressure. Usually, on a date, I'm worried about forging a connection. Now I was worried about matching his expectations. That's not something I ever worried about before. In the past, if I didn't match up with someone's idea or assumptions, I would just move on. Fuck them. But this time.

This guy.

There was a knock on the door.

Macks moved instantly while Lucinda and I looked at the source of the noise hesitantly. "I can't believe a famous person is coming to our apartment." They stopped before opening the door and turned to us. "Is 'person' appropriate?

For any of us?" A look of shock and horror was growing on their face.

"We aren't human but we are still people," Lucinda said, rushing over to them. "No need to spiral." She cradled their cheeks in her palms and tenderly tapped her forehead against theirs.

After taking a collective breath, they turned to the door. Lucinda pulled it open. She and Macks stood there, like a wall between me and the threshold.

"Uh, hello," his voice said, slightly stammering. "I'm here for Bryn."

"I'm Lucinda and this is Macks," Lucinda said. "We are the roommates."

"The nymph and the sorcerex!" I heard him say with excitement. "Bryn told me a lot about you."

"She's told us about you too," Macks said with excitement. "I've also heard your life story from books and stuff."

"Don't believe everything you read," he laughed. "A good chunk of our mythology is really just myth."

"True," said Lucinda. "There's so much about us that never made it into the stories, and there's just as much fiction that made it in too."

"As fascinating as this all is," I said, slightly louder than my resting volume. "We aren't here for a history lesson." Macks and Lucinda stepped to the side, parting like the Red Sea.

Hercules stood at my door, framed like a work of art. He wore tan pants and a form-fitting white shirt under a jacket made of white floral lace. He smiled at me like he did when he saw me for the first time. That smile, that first glance, was etched in my brain. The kind of smile that energizes you when you see it.

"Hi," I said.

"Hey," he said. He held up a collection of flowers. The petals were white with purple bleeding through from the edges. "These are for you."

"Thank you," I said as I came forward to take them.

"Flowers!" Lucinda said dramatically. "And they say chivalry is dead."

"Well, I am an old soul," he said with a wink.

"I'll get these into some water for you," Lucinda said, taking the flowers from my hands. "You two go have fun, and you'll tell us every sordid detail when you get home."

Macks and Lucinda practically pushed me out the door, waving goodbye like parents watching their child walk into her first day of school.

"They're cute," Hercules said with a chuckle.

"Yeah, that's why I keep them around." We headed outside of the building, and I allowed him to take the lead in the direction we were headed.

"How are they holding up with everything?" he asked.

"We're all adjusting," I said with a sigh. "Macks is taking it like a champ. I freaked when all this started, but they are embracing it. There is something comforting about it, if I'm being honest."

"Why is that?"

"We are kind of in the same boat," I told him. "I've

known about my strength most of my life, but am just now learning the whole truth. Macks has been normal their whole life, and now they suddenly aren't. The fact that it's happening around the same time, makes me feel less alone. And seeing them handle it, makes me feel like I can too."

"What about Lucinda?" The question lashed at me like a whip.

"She's always known about this and intentionally kept it from me," I said, biting my lip. "I still don't know how to feel about that." I wanted to forgive her. I was trying to. I know she didn't mean to hurt me. But the hurt was still there.

"Understandable," he said, quickly and with vigor. "We don't have to go there. Let's focus on the day ahead of us."

I laughed, gladly accepting the distraction. "Where are we going anyway?"

"I've got it all planned out." He took my hand in his and a warmth exploded around me, embracing me in heart stopping excitement as he led me down the street.

He took me to the Met. When he told me that was the plan, I wasn't entirely blown away at the thought of a museum I've visited many times already. Especially considering the number of tourists that swarm the place on any given day. But being there with him was a completely different experience than I imagined. Museums take on a whole new meaning when you visit with someone who lived through the history that is collected there. He pointed out his favorite paintings and sculptures before leaning in and whispering in my ear. He shared memories attached to each one. A protective secret between the two of us. Things that would confuse or baffle anyone who might overhear. He took great care as we went through the Greek and Roman art exhibits. A twinkle in his eyes, as if he were flipping through a treasured photo album.

He shared fond memories as we explored the Medieval Art exhibit. These years, for him, were a period of exuberant partying that I didn't know was possible for the time period. But also, one of the few times in his life where he felt powerless. Death and corruption were commonplace everywhere he went. Even the strongest man in the world can't defend people from a plague.

We strolled through the Arms and Armor exhibit, as he told me about the wars he's seen and the battles my people covertly took part in. I hadn't realized, but in almost every war and human conflict, there was a supernatural evil under the surface, either manipulating or taking advantage. The Amazons would covertly infiltrate these conflicts and eliminate the inhuman forces, leaving humans to conclude the battles on their own terms.

After the museum we walked through the park, bathed in sunlight. As we came to a quiet spot by the lake, someone was waiting for us. A woman in a blazer and tie stood in front of a picnic blanket sprawled out on the grass. A charcuterie board of crackers and fancy cheese sat at the center of the blanket with a tiny vase holding a single flower placed next to it. We sat on the blanket and the woman poured a bottle of champagne into two plastic flutes. She excused herself, putting enough distance between us to give us privacy but staying within eyesight in case we needed to flag her down.

"This is so nice." I couldn't think of anything else to say.

"Just trying to show you a good time," he said as we tapped our glasses together.

"I'm sure you do this for all the girls," I laughed.

"Actually, I haven't been on the dating scene lately." He took a sip of champagne. "I…I had gotten out of a pretty toxic relationship a while ago, and I only recently felt like I could put myself back out there."

"Well, thank you for getting back out there with me." I suddenly forgot to breathe. I sipped from my glass in an attempt to distract my body. The bubbles danced as they flowed down my throat. I glanced around the sun-soaked park. People in the distance walked the trails, took photos of the scenery, and sat laughing in the grass. Enjoying their day. The joyful energy was overflowing.

I looked down and our picnic flower caught my eye. It was the same spicy pink color as Lucinda's favorite party wig. The wig she wore whenever we went to an event together. Lucinda adorning her head with that color meant I would be having a night to remember. But I wasn't sure if I wanted to remember them anymore. My best friend had turned into a stain on my mind that I wanted to clean away. That I was trying to clean away. A stain I thought I was making progress on. No, I didn't want to remember. But I needed to. There was no room in my life for lies. I thought about how this flower, plucked from the ground for the sake of a pretty atmosphere, would soon wither away. Just like my friendship with Lucinda. How it had been plucked and was in danger of slipping into dust, all for the sake of false truths.

I couldn't let that happen.

"Is everything okay?" Hercules asked. I looked up to see his eyes glossy with concern. My brain faltered as I tried to find something to say in return. Over his shoulder, in the distance, I saw more people taking photos of nature on their phones. I felt bad because we must have been obstructing the view of whatever they found so moving. But as I continued to examine them, I realized their gaze was fixed on us.

I felt my face contort in disgust and Hercules turned immediately to pinpoint the offenders. "Oh yea," he said. "There are downsides to fame too."

"Strangers just take pictures of you?" I knew this was a thing that happened. Fans and paparazzi and journalists. But there was something about actually being the subject of the photos that made it all so real. Too real. Sickly discomfort started to creep in onto what has been a lovely outing. "It doesn't bother you?"

"You get used to it," he said, shrugging. "I've been doing this for a long time. Even before my last two personas. I was in the public eye."

"So you crave it?" I asked. "I'm not sure I do."

"I don't crave it. I was born into it. And then pushed into it...and then I guess I've been chasing it lately," he laughed. A silence fell for a moment. His smile melted slightly before he continued. "My mother. She was a princess."

"You're a prince and a demigod?" I asked. I took a swig of champagne, suddenly feeling even more inadequate.

"As far as the human world was concerned, I was the son of King Amphitryon and Princess Alcmene." His breath wavered slightly when he said her name. "And the supernatural world knew that Zeus was my real father. So I couldn't escape the spotlight in either world."

"Was it hard?" I asked.

"It was…intimidating," he answered. "I eventually went on to build a normal-ish life for myself. But, the gods had other plans for me."

"They forced you to become a hero?"

"In a way." He stopped making eye contact. "One of them forced my hand. So, I completed the twelve labors and solidified myself as the greatest hero or whatever. And after that, there's no coming back." He gestured to the amateur photographers in the distance.

"Sounds like we have something in common," I said. He looked up at me, eyebrows curled. "We had a normal life, despite the circumstances of our births. And then some greater purpose comes along and pushes us into heroism."

"Hey." He grabbed my hand. "I didn't mean… There's nothing wrong with how my life ended up. And I didn't mean to sound like I had lost something. I embrace it. I love it. And I think you can find things to love too."

"I loved my life before," I said, caressing my fingers across his.

"The idea of 'normal' came up earlier too. You said Macks had been normal their whole life. As if you weren't normal." His eyes struck mine like a blinding light. "But you are. You always have been. You might be different from the world around you, but you are exactly who and what you are supposed to be. And that's the most normal thing in the world. Just, try to remember that."

I didn't know what to say, which was a common occurrence lately. I needed to work on that.

He didn't say anything either. I thought he might be waiting for me to respond. And as words continued to escape me, he started to lean towards me. His tender lips pressed against mine.

And for a moment. Just a moment. I forgot about all of my woes. My fear, my anxiety, my anger, my insecurities. It all melted away for one glorious moment.

And I wish I could live in that moment forever.

Chapter 20

Miss Stone kicked me in the stomach with a stark scream. My body propelled away from her. I landed on my back, taking control of the momentum to roll backward and get myself back on my feet. I let the maneuver distract me, and I didn't even realize she was closing the distance between us until she was already swinging her circular blade at me.

It was a mistake, but one I could come back from.

I felt the intense burning over my entire forearm as I lifted it in front of my chest. Her weapon hit my arm and slid off in a rough collision.

It didn't hurt, and it didn't break the skin.

As the burning disappeared, I pulled my other arm back and shoved my open palm into her wrist. She dropped her weapon, and the blades separated as they clanged against the ground. I brought that same hand towards her face with as much force as I could manage. The back of my hand smashed against her cheek, and she flipped over, hitting the ground with her shoulder. Fast and hard.

"Oh shit!" I gasped. "I'm so sorry!" I extended my hand, and she grabbed it.

"Don't apologize," she said as I hoisted her up. "I

protected myself. I experienced the force, but not the pain of the blow. Or, at least, not most of it." She massaged the side of her face.

"That was a good one," Hercules said, leaning against a nearby wall. "Right? It looked good."

"It was executed well," Miss Stone said with a rare smile.

"Really?" I asked, trying not to sound too eager.

"Yes, we'll still need to work on it," Miss Stone said, walking towards Hercules. "But judging by the way you've held your own against me these past few weeks, I think your combat and defense skills are developing nicely."

It felt good to hear the hard work was paying off.

Hercules handed Miss Stone The Queen's Sword. The night black blade glistened slightly under the dimming sunlight. She handed it to me without a word.

We had been painstakingly practicing swordplay lately, folding it into training a little bit at a time, but holding it in my hand still felt strange.

Not only strange but frustrating. In learning how to hold, swing, and fight with the thing, I hadn't been able to activate its magic. The ability to make it transform.

The two of them were excellent teachers. Hercules was so confident and assuring, he made me feel like I could do anything. Miss Stone was so knowledgeable and determined, she made me feel prepared for the impossible. And there was something refreshing about being around people who were as strong as me. Knowing I didn't have to worry or hold back, sparring or not, was freeing.

I caught a glimpse of Hercules watching me when I looked up from the sword. There was a glimmer in his eyes that nearly made me forget what we were all here for. Memory of our kiss at the park flooded my mind, along with the many stolen moments where we shared other kisses.

"The first time you used the sword," Miss Stone said, pacing in front of me with both hands tucked behind her back. "You tapped into its power. Unlike most divine weapons, this sword's magic is only meant to work for a chosen few. Amazon Queens."

"That wasn't the transformation ability," I said.

"I know," she responded with a nod.

"And I still don't know how to activate anything on command," I added. "It was all an accident."

"It was instinct," Miss Stone said. "Warrior instincts."

"Right," I sighed. The truth was, even though I had accepted my warrior destiny, I was still terrified of it. And it was hard to embrace something so fully when it was surrounded by a shroud of fear.

Miss Stone stopped pacing when she reached the spot where her curved knives lay on the ground. She raised her hands, palms facing the floor, and the blades jumped into them. She looked at me with determination in her eyes.

My grip on the sword tightened.

I heard movement behind me. Quick hard steps. I ducked to my right just as Hercules' fist blew past my head. I turned while jumping back, placing both of them in front of me. I raised my sword, placing the tip of the blade just inches from his neck.

I hated myself instantly. "It's okay," he said, somehow seeing it in me. "I trust you."

The Queen's Sword was a divine weapon, capable of killing a god. So, even though Hercules was an invincible and immortal demigod, the weapon in my hand could act as his Achilles heel.

It was too dangerous to use in practice. In the past, Miss Stone had me stabbing it in the air or hitting projectiles the two of them tossed in my direction. But now, she was initiating a two-on-one sparring match.

"Focus on becoming one with the sword," Miss Stone said as she rushed forward. She jumped to Hercules' side and brought one of her blades into my sword. The two metals crashed against each other, forcing my hand away. "Let the warrior instinct tap into the sword's full potential."

She raised her leg to kick me, but I backed away, putting empty space between us. She threw both of her blades, and I swiped through the air with my sword, deflecting them. As the weapons left my view, Hercules was in front of me. He barreled towards me in a crouched position. His shoulder hit my abdomen before he wrapped his arms around me and lifted with his entire body.

As soon as I was in the air, he slammed me downward. I focused my energy on my back as I hit the ground, deflecting any pain from the crash. He lowered a fist towards me, I tossed the sword to the side and rolled in the opposite direction.

I heard the ground crack under his fist.

I got to my feet just in time to see Miss Stone's weapons magically find their way back into her hands.

I looked at my sword laying on the ground. Hercules was positioned between us. If I tried to make a play for it, he could easily interfere. And even if I did pass him, Miss Stone was just on the other side of it. She'd surely attack before I could lay my hands on it.

My mind raced trying to come up with an action plan. Any way I could get the sword in my hands.

Suddenly, I felt a humming in my bones as The Queen's Sword leaped into the air. It flew towards me, causing Hercules to duck in order to avoid being sliced through the neck. The sword's handle landed directly into my palm, and I wrapped my fingers around it.

"Nice!" Hercules cheered.

They both started to move towards me, not even taking a beat in response to my new trick. I knew what was coming. A full-on assault, from both of them at the same time. I felt it in my bones. I needed to think fast but they were moving faster than my mind could.

As they came closer and closer, I felt the sword vibrate in my hands. A low red light poured from the sword and flashed with a quick brightness. As the light disappeared, I was no longer holding the sword.

A long wooden staff sat in my hands. Leather strips were wrapped around its center, allowing my fingers to hold a tighter grip. Two spade shaped blades were fixed to both ends. The symbol of Ares was carved into the wood under each one. It was lightweight, and sturdy, but most importantly; it was long and double ended.

Hercules was on my right and Miss Stone was on my left, just steps away now. Instead of retreating, I stepped towards them, ducking down on my knees as I spun the staff in circles.

Miss Stone did an impressive backbend, dodging the swings. Hercules attempted to dodge to the side, but the reach was too wide. I felt a slight drag as the staff grazed his arm.

Miss Stone brought her blades into the air, sandwiching the staff between them. She twisted, forcing my arms and torso to the left, and swung her foot at my ankles. I fell to the right, as my weapon continued to the left. I hit the ground at Hercules' feet. The staff flashed red and turned back to its sword form before it hit the ground by Miss Stone.

"That was fantastic," Miss Stone said. Her words instantly canceled the faux hostile energy, ending the sparring match. Hercules extended his hand down. As he helped me to my feet, I noticed a trickle of blood traveling past his wrist.

"You're bleeding!" I exclaimed. "How?"

"You cut me with your weapon," he said, clearly confused by my question.

"But, not the sword," I said.

"The Queen's Sword is still a divine weapon, no matter what form it is in," Miss Stone said as her blades turned back into rings around her fingers. "She picked up the sword and handed it to me.

"That makes sense," I said, taking it. It was starting to feel like home in my hands.

"I'll be fine," he said with an overzealous smile. "I don't get hurt often, but when I do, I heal fast." I don't know why it didn't occur to me before. The sword didn't need to be in its true form. I could use it as any weapon in the world, and it would still be strong enough to kill a god. There was something equally comforting and terrifying about that.

"What were you thinking when it changed?" Miss Stone asked.

"Just that I needed a way to take care of two people at once."

"And then suddenly you had a quarterstaff," Hercules said.

"You stopped focusing on how to get it to change, and started focusing on why you needed it to change." Miss Stone put a hand on my shoulder. "The sword reacted to your needs. Your instincts melded as one."

"The sword has instincts?" I asked, trying my best not to scoff.

"Some believe divine weapons have some sort of sentience," she said.

"I've heard that," Hercules said. "But they are so rare that it's hard to prove."

"Weird," I said, under my breath. I looked down at the sword, trying to see if I could find a spark of life just by gazing at it. It didn't move, hum, or resonate psychically.

The long ebony metal just looked back at me. Perhaps it was trying to find something in me too.

I wanted to keep it with me. If it was supposed to be an extension of me… If it was my greatest defense against a looming threat… If it was intertwined with my destiny and *alive*, we shouldn't separate. If something happened and I needed it, I couldn't bank on the chance that Miss Stone was holding it for me nearby.

But I couldn't walk around with a sword on me. I would draw unwanted attention that I couldn't explain.

A red light blinked, illuminating the space around me. A thick pocketknife sat in my hand. The symbol of Ares was carved into its dark wooden handle. Its sleek black blade was partially curved and serrated. I folded the blade into the handle, securing its sharp edge. "Can I hold onto this?"

Miss Stone looked down at me with a clear sense of pride on her face. "It's yours. You don't have to ask."

Chapter 21

Flashes of white light bombarded us, cutting through the crisp darkness of night. Like stars exploding in the black sky. Bursting with intensity then disappearing, just to do it all over again.

"Mr. Nemean! Mr. Nemean!" One of the attackers called out. "How long has this been going on?"

"Hercules!" Another yelled, begging for attention. "Tell us her name! How did you two meet?"

"Is it serious?" The third asked. "You two have been seen together a lot. Seems serious! Who are your friends?"

Hercules and I had been walking down the street, along with London and Macks, after a lovely dinner. And just as a perfect night was about to end, we had been swarmed by cameras.

"This is insane!" I said, frustrated.

"Definitely not how I expected the double date to go," London laughed, shielding her eyes with her hands.

"I'm so sorry," Hercules apologized. "Someone must have seen us at the restaurant and tipped off the press."

"It's totally not your fault," London squealed. "Don't worry about it."

"Yeah," Macks chimed in, smiling for a few flashes. "It's kind of exciting."

The paparazzi were not our first surprise. That happened just a few days ago. Macks had been working at Divinity for about two weeks now. London, Macks, and I had been having lunch together whenever our work days aligned. At one of these lunches, I was talking about how Hercules had been invited to opening night at a new restaurant, given a whole table for a party of his choice. London jumped at the chance to make it a double date. I didn't even realize she and Macks had been an item until after I got the okay from Hercules.

So there we stood, on the street with a trio of paparazzi, after a night dining in the same room as celebrities and influencers. London and Macks had their fingers delicately intertwined. Hercules' arm rested comfortably around my shoulders. All four of us, captured and immortalized in tomorrow's tabloids.

"Hercules! According to the rumor mill, you're gay!" One of the paparazzi yelled. "With this new relationship, can we consider that rumor debunked?"

"My publicist will be pissed if I break another camera," Hercules said, turning to us with a forced, painfully fake, smile. I would have destroyed every camera in the world if it would ease his soul. But we only had three to deal with.

"I got this," London said, a proud smile rivaling his look of discomfort. She stepped forward. A few more camera flashes struck her, illuminating the pattern of daisies on her black sundress. "Hello. My name is London. I'm a journalist at Divinity Magazine. This is my partner, Macks, a brilliant documentary filmmaker."

"Partner?" Macks asked, leaning back and looking her up and down.

"Yeah," said London. "Right?"

"Yeah." I saw the corners of Macks' mouth inch upward and I felt overjoyed to witness the moment.

"We work with Bryn." London gestured to me. More camera flashes. I wanted to disappear. "You should know, this is all in its very early stages. And you're ruining the vibe."

"I doubt they care," I told her. She raised a hand, silencing me.

"Listen, I know you're trying to cash in on the gossip, but there is no story here. Trust me. Not yet." She was beguiling. "You are about to kill this story before it develops. And then what do you have. 'Famous model dates girl before local reporter fucked it up?' That's nothing. What you have now will buzz for a second and then fade away the second any other celebrity is photographed with a cake pop. But if you level with us, we might be able to come to an agreement. Let us finish our night in peace, I'll give you each my card. You reach out to me later, and I can guarantee you a feature article on the Divinity site. Whatever story you want to bring me, it doesn't matter. Your name on a Divinity story will be an instant career boost. Your respective presses will recognize your worth, outside presses will be clamoring to poach you. We get to finish our double date without having to evade prying eyes. Everyone wins here."

The flashes stopped. The paparazzi looked dumbfounded. Slow blinking at London, and then glancing amongst each other. It only took a few minutes for her to hand out her business cards and send them on their way.

"That was incredible," I said. "I really didn't think you'd be able to convince them."

"They are out here in the middle of the night desperately trying to get a scandalous pic of a pretty un-scandalous date," she laughed. "They are passionate about their careers and thirsty for anything to boost it. Once you know what someone wants, it's incredibly easy to influence them."

"They're probably still going to post those pictures," Hercules said. "I hope you're okay with that."

"Might give my film work some buzz," Macks said with a shrug.

"Nothing we can do about it now," I said, deciding to put the temporary setback aside. We continued our stroll, towards the subway station that would take us to our various homes.

"Thanks for letting us crash," London blurted out, clinging to Macks.

"It was nice to hang out outside of work," I said, trying to keep the invasive paparazzi out of my mind. "We should do it more."

"It's a shame Lucinda couldn't join," said Macks as we turned the corner on a quiet street.

"We can do it again," Hercules responded with a clap of his hands. "And force her to join." After the plans changed into a group, I invited Lucinda. It was part of my continued effort at forgiveness. Trying to rebuild our friendship.

"Oh no, my love!" She exclaimed. "Do your double date amongst the upper crusts. I wouldn't want to steal the moment. The spotlight just naturally follows me, you know. It wouldn't be fair for either of your budding romances."

I think she didn't want to be the odd one out.

As we strolled through darkness sandwiched between two apartment buildings, a figure turned the opposite corner, slowly walking towards us. We instinctively moved to make room for the man.

Before we passed each other, he spoke from across the way. "I hope you've had a fun night." His voice was deep and rough, like a crater. "Because it's over now."

Something about the voice sent a warning signal through my brain. Hercules tensed beside me. He stepped forward, placing an arm in front of me like a shield.

"Bryn…" Macks' voice sounded panicked, laced with caution.

As the man stepped closer, he became clearer in the night. He looked at us with burning eyes. His dark hair was slightly tussled. He wore a suit so black that he faded into the darkness.

Deimos.

"Shit," I said, reaching into my pocket. My fingers clutched my pocketknife, but I hesitated to pull it out.

"What's going on?" London asked, responding to the tension radiating from the rest of the group.

"You're with friends. How cute." Deimos looked at London with a devilish grin. His eyes danced across the rest of us. They lingered on Macks with a spark of recognition before moving to me. They narrowed with disdain. They moved to Hercules, and they softened immediately. The jagged expression on his face fell. His mouth dropped and his eyebrows raised. "Hercules…"

"Yeah," he said. I could hear something caught in his chest. More words that couldn't come.

"I didn't know you were involved in this." Deimos stood up straight, releasing his aggressive stance. The inky blackness slipped from his voice. "I didn't know you were involved with her."

"Yeah," he said. "I am. And it's good that I am. So I can talk you out of this before it goes too far. Before *you* go too far."

"There's no turning back from this," Deimos growled. "This is my path. My righteous journey. My destiny!"

"Can someone explain what's going on?" London hissed.

"You should go," I said. "This is too much to explain, but you shouldn't be mixed up in it." Once she was safe and he was taken care of, I'd think of a lie to tell her.

"I'm sorry you chose the wrong side," Deimos said, looking only at Hercules. "But I can't let anything, or anyone, get in my way." He pointed his fingertips to the ground and quickly raised his hands to the sky. Two spirals of dark red smoke materialized between him and our group. They collapsed into themselves, expanding in size before imploding.

As the smoke dissipated, something emerged. Long dark, canine-like claws attached to feminine bodies. They were tall and slender, with coal-black skin. They were wrinkled as if they were elderly, but beneath the weathered skin was clearly defined and spry muscle. Tattered brown cloth hung off their bodies in ribbons. Their massive feet rested firmly on their clawed toes, elevating their heels and making them stand even taller. Large leathery wings stretched from their arms and connected to the side of their torsos. Their faces had animalistic features, like a dog without fur.

"Oh dear god," Hercules sighed so quietly I almost didn't hear. "Not furies."

"What the fuck?" London said, coupled with a shriek that was all too familiar. Poor girl kept getting pulled into this fight. But there was no time to deal with that right now.

"What are these things?" I asked Hercules as I watched the monsters gaze upon us with their bloodshot eyes.

"They are agents of chaos," he answered. "With a compulsive need to enact judgment on others. They are cursed women usually used as attack dogs, sicced on criminals, by gods and sorcerers."

"Why are you guys talking like this is just a normal thing?" London asked. Panic was rising in her voice.

"Macks!" I yelled. They had been locked in a stance of awe.

Their body jolted as if awoken by a shock. They grabbed London by the elbows. "I should get you out of here."

"No!" She protested. "How are you not terrified right now?"

"Trust me, I am fighting the urge to shit myself!" Macks yelled. "But that's not going to be helpful. So, I'm pushing through it."

"Why aren't they attacking?" I asked Hercules, realizing that they could have easily reigned down some chaos in our panicked state.

"Because I haven't told them to yet," Deimos said with a chuckle. "I want to enjoy this."

"Don't do this, De," Hercules pleaded.

"You of all people should know that I have to," he shot back. "All that time we spent together. I've shared with you my desire to prove myself worthy in my father's eyes."

"And this is how you want to do it?" There was pain in Hercules' eyes, zeroed right into Deimos, whose face was full of betrayal.

"What does he mean?" I asked. "You've spent time together? I thought you didn't know him."

"We actually…dated." The reveal cut me in the gut. "On and off. For, like, a century."

How could he not tell us this? He had a relationship with the person trying to kill me. They *knew* each other. This felt like something he should have disclosed. The fact that he didn't, felt like a deception of the deepest kind. Did he have information on this man that could help us? Were there lingering feelings that might be a liability? There were so many new factors that were at play now.

And what about us? We were starting something. Could I trust someone who would lie about something like this? Could I be with someone who would date a man capable of the heinous acts Deimos committed and the atrocities he aspired to carry out?

"What? A century?" London asked, still fighting against Macks' efforts to pull her away.

"He never told you?" Deimos looked at me now. A satisfied smirk on his face. "I guess I'm still in there somewhere. You only keep secrets to protect the heart." A chattering noise rumbled in the furies' throats. "Come back to me. When this is all over, and I'm standing by my father's side as his equal, just as you do with yours, we can be together as gods."

"I'm not standing by his side," Hercules scoffed. "I don't even talk to him because he's gone. Like all of the gods. This thing you're chasing is pointless! And I'm not going to let you kill an entire group of women to obtain it."

"That's a shame." Deimos' voice fell flat, devoid of the emotion that was just resting in his plea. I pulled out my pocketknife, releasing the blade. He looked at it with a smile. "Cute. But you won't get a chance to use it. My little pets will see to that." He looked at Hercules again, putting a hand over his heart. "I'm sorry. I truly didn't know you would be with her."

The monsters lifted their muzzles to the sky and released a high-pitched warble. The sound sent bursts of flames racing across my entire body, directly under my skin. The memory of the spiller I killed played in my brain. A vivid memory that stabbed at my very soul. Like I was there all over again, only this time I was the one dying. These things were taking the black smudge on my conscience and turning it into a bitter poison.

I heard Hercules groan beside me as he dropped to his knees in agony. I could only imagine, with his long life as a warrior, how many lives he had taken. The amount of guilt weaponized against him must be unimaginable.

Unable to fight the pain, I dropped the knife and the second it released from my fingers it turned back into a sword. It clamored on the ground and Deimos was on the move.

He sprinted forward, hand outstretched towards the ground.

"No!" I heard Macks yell. The furies didn't affect them, and I was grateful for it. Macks jumped forward with their palms raised forward. Amongst the painful ringing in my ears, I heard a buzzing. Large oval-shaped bugs, each with rhino-like horns protruding from their heads, materialized as if pouring from Macks' hands. The swarm crashed into Deimos like a massive fist, sending him backward.

He found his footing after the stumble and growled. "Annoying," he said. The furies stopped their sonic assault, and I felt the pain melt away.

The furies were only discernible by the patchy gray hair on their heads.

The one with a long tangled mess of hair lunged

forward, flapping its wings and lifting upward. Its elongated feet clutched onto Macks' shoulders and took them soaring upwards.

"Oh my god!" London called out as Macks went further and further into the night sky, the swarm of beetles following closely behind.

The one with short tufts of hair pounced on top of Hercules, pinning him to the ground as he struggled. I put out my hand and my sword jumped up. As I grabbed it, Deimos was moving towards me again. Red sparks danced across his fingers.

"Go ahead," I spat, tightening my grip. "We saw how that went last time."

"You are a child, girl," he said, stone faced. "Your mother wanted to hide you away, thinking it would protect you, but in reality it only stunted you. Where a warrior should stand before me, there is only an infant playing pretend."

The red sparks flew. I swiped my sword upward, hitting the blast of energy and forcing it to be absorbed into the blade. Before I could throw it back at him, he was directly in front of me. So close I could feel the heat of his anger radiating from him. He placed his hands on my shoulders so gently that it was scary. His hands sparked again, and I felt sizzling pain crash against me. My chest grew tight, and my heart raced. I couldn't breathe. I was afraid I might suffocate or that the pain would stop my heart. I had to put an end to it.

I refused to let the sword go this time. In my hand, it

transformed into something else. A clunky black box with two prongs at its ends and the symbol of Ares at the center. I pushed it into him as red sparks bounced between the two tips.

As the taser struck him, he started to convulse. He released me and the pain and terror left my body, leaving only an echo. Flames of red energy danced across his body as he fell to his knees.

"How did this not kill you," I said. "This is a divine weapon!" I saw his body make stiff movement, as if he was trying to stand but couldn't.

"You didn't expect it to be that easy, did you?" Deimos said through his teeth. "Next time, conjure a lethal weapon." His body faded into a deep red smoke before disappearing. I cursed myself for letting him get away again. It was a nasty and annoying habit of his.

I looked over to see London staring straight up into the air. The furie that had taken Macks was slammed into the ground by a cloud of insects. Looking up, I saw Macks gently floating down, carried by the rest of the swarm. Once their feet were on the ground, they approached London.

I heard a groan come from Hercules. Turning my attention, I saw that he was still struggling with his attacker. It was on top of him, lashing and slashing with its claws. He squirmed underneath it, using his unpinned arm to deflect blows. If he wasn't freed yet, these things must be insanely strong.

The taser in my hand shifted to a black handle, embroidered with the symbol of Ares, attached to a ridiculously long braided strand of red leather. At the end of the braid was a single strand of leather that ended in a frayed flurry.

I didn't know how to do this. I let the weapon guide me. I raised my hand, hoisting the length of the leather, and flicked my arm. The whip lashed out with a crack and wrapped around the neck of the furie. Dark red blood dripped from underneath where the whip dug into its skin. I yanked with all my might, pulling it off of him. A trail of blood followed it through the air. It let out a pathetic cry as it tumbled on the ground. I pulled the whip back, prepared to hit it again. It attempted to stand but fell back down, its body crumbling to dust picked up by a gust of night air.

The other furie squealed at the sight, jumping up from where Macks' bugs had thrown it. It grabbed the closest body to it. Macks. It pressed them against the wall of a nearby building. Opening its long mouth to reveal wildly crooked teeth. It prepared to take a bite with Macks only staring in horror.

A brown fist collided with the side of the furie's face. It didn't budge, as if the punch had no force behind it. The furie turned its head towards London, who looked absolutely shocked at what she had done. It snarled, raising a clawed foot to strike her. I threw out my whip. It wrapped around the furie's ankle with startling speed. As I pulled, The furie fell backward. Macks fell to the ground as they were released. Blood poured from the monster's ankle as its foot separated from its body. The severed appendage disintegrated almost instantly.

Hercules ran towards London and Macks, checking to make sure they were okay. The furie lifted with a flap of its wings and glared at me. It staggered on its lopsided footing, glaring at me. The whip morphed back into a sword as it came towards me. It lowered its shoulder and bashed me with its wing, pushing me with incredible force that stung across my entire body. As it pulled back to hit me with another blow, I swung the sword.

It cut through the wing like paper, severing a slice from its lower region. It attempted to take flight, but the damage prevented it from catching air. It fell to the ground, holding itself on its one good foot. It lashed its muzzle at me as it grabbed onto my wrist with its claws.

It pinned my arms to my side, preventing me from fighting back. While I couldn't swing the sword, I refused to drop it. As it lifted me into the air, I kicked at its chest but it resisted my strength.

"Bryn!" I heard Hercules call from behind me.

"Please," I begged. "Get them out of here. I'll figure this out."

"We won't leave you!" Macks called out as I heard the buzzing of insects swell.

Over the monster's shoulder, past the lashing canine teeth and wild eyes, I saw movement in a nearby flowerbed. A rose was growing like a balloon being filled with air. It gained height and size in a matter of seconds, until its bulb was as big as a refrigerator. The bulb wilted down, as if weeping, and opened its petals.

Lucinda stepped onto the alley with rage in her eyes.

"Get your paws off of my friend!" she demanded as the overgrown flower petals broke apart into shards and flew through the air. They cut through the wings of the creature, leaving the leathery skin looking like swiss cheese oozing with blood.

It screeched, shaking me in the air but not letting go. The buzzing of the insects intensified as they blew by me in a zooming swarm. Hundreds of tiny bodies colliding with the furie like a barrage of bullets. It dropped me and I felt a collection of bugs press against my back, gently leading me to the ground.

I tried not to think about how gross that was.

While the bugs still attacked, I plunged my sword straight into the furie's chest. It cried out as it turned to dust and Macks bugs flew away in every direction.

"How did you know?" I asked Lucinda, not quite believing I was even seeing her.

"I texted her the second I realized the man in the alley was Deimos," Macks said, sounding exhausted.

"I'm glad you're okay. That looked like a close call," Lucinda said with a relieved sigh.

I wrapped my arms around her and hugged her tightly. I felt her body tense and then soften as she returned the hug. In this moment, my anger and resentment had dissipated, and I didn't feel the threat of it rising again. I was grateful for that. I was grateful for her.

"Can someone tell me what is happening?" London asked, pushing Hercules away from her.

We all looked at each other, and I knew what we were thinking.

Do we tell her the truth? Do we lie? Do we let Miss Stone's connections cover it up again?

"Okay," Macks began to speak.

"Wait," I said with caution.

"No, she deserves to know," Macks insisted before turning to her. "So, it's a long story but the short version is: magic is real. I have magic bug powers, Hercules is *the* Hercules, Bryn is an Amazon, and that man is a Demigod who wants to kill her entire race."

London just stared at them, her lip quivering.

"And I'm a tree nymph," Lucinda said in a cheery tone.

"And Miss Stone is an Amazon too," I added, regretfully.

Silence rested around us for a moment. The gears in her brain were visibly turning.

"Okay," she said, nodding her head but looking at something that was not there. "And the monster things were furies? Like, from mythology."

"Yes," I answered. "Not the first mythological monster you've seen actually."

"What?" she asked, confused.

"We were attacked by something after the protest. You just don't remember," I explained. "But we can revisit that later."

"How are you feeling?" Macks asked, stepping closer to her.

"Um…I don't know." London said. "I guess I'm not

terribly surprised. Like, this is New York. You see things and hear things all the time in this city that makes you think…that makes you know in the back of your mind that there is more out there. But it's a whole other thing to see it in action."

"I know it's a shock," Hercules said. "But I have to tell you, what you did was incredible. Most people would be too terrified to try and fight a monster with their bare hands, especially on a first encounter. And you squared up, without hesitation."

"Macks was in trouble," London said, as if her reaction was obviously her only option.

"That was very courageous," he said. "I commend you."

"We should get out of here," Lucinda said. "We can unpack this when we aren't out in the open."

"I'm not going anywhere with you people," London said.

"What do you mean?" Macks asked.

"I can wrap my mind about all of this being real," she said, backing away from us. "But I might need a minute to wrap my mind around the fact that my friend, new partner, and my boss are all not human."

"We can help you process," I offered. "It's easier with people. Trust me."

"No. I just need time and space," London insisted, looking at Macks. "I'm sorry. I'll…I'll let you know when I make it home." She turned and scurried off into the darkness.

Chapter 22

"It doesn't make any sense," Miss Stone said, leaning against her desk. "Furies are wild and unpredictable but one thing is for certain: they go after those who effectuate injustice."

"Exactly," Hercules said. "I've seen them on the battlefield but I've never known them to go along with someone's personal vendetta before."

"They tend to obey their makers," Lucinda added. She wore a black corset under an open pink blazer, with matching dress pants. Her hair, while also pink, was a much hotter pink than the deep color of her silky clothes.

It was the night of Divinity Magazine's bi-annual office party. Miss Stone, Macks, and myself were in attendance as part of the Divinity team, while Lucinda and Hercules were in attendance as a combination of plus one and subjects in the recent issue. We took the event as an opportunity and snuck away to discuss the other night.

"Which makes it even more strange," Miss Stone said. She wore a black jacket and pants with a white blouse that featured a statement collar so large that it extended past her shoulders. "That's the work of a god or a sorcerer's spell.

Deimos doesn't make furies. He makes these…" she looked at Macks, as if fishing for something she couldn't quite see.

"Spillers," they said with pride. They wore a button-up shirt and a black tie with pink flowers that intentionally matched Lucinda's fit.

"Yeah," said Hercules, who thought the party was casual, so he just wore jeans and a polo shirt. "I've never known him to be able to create any sort of beast. So that begs the question, where did he get them?"

"Is it possible that this is just something you didn't know about him?" I asked, raw emotion bubbling under the surface. "You know, you can't know everything about the person you're dating." I wore a hot pink paisley full-skirt dress.

"I guess it's possible," he said, avoiding eye contact with me.

"Besides, does it matter how he got them," I said to the group. "The fact of the matter is, he had them. He tried to kill us with them, and we beat him. But he's going to be back. He's not going to stop coming for me until I make him stop."

"With the way your training has been going, coupled with your natural warrior instinct," Miss Stone said. "You've proven that you can handle him."

"So, let's end it," Lucinda said, puffing up her chest. "With all of us beside you, he can't stand a chance."

"Now that he's seen us all in action," Hercules said with caution. "He's going to find a way to come at us much harder. He's cunning and adaptive and he hates losing."

"So, what do we do?" Macks asked.

"We don't give him the chance," I said. "He runs away, collects himself, and throws something new at us. It's his pattern. We have to take away his element of surprise."

"How would you suggest we do that?" Miss Stone asked. Her tone made me feel like she was testing me. I turned to Hercules.

"Do you know where he lives or hangs out?" I asked. "Considering how much time you've spent together, you have to know something that might help us find him and get the drop on him."

"I can do some digging," he sighed. "It's been a minute but I can reach out to mutual friends and see if they know where he is now."

"Okay. And once we have that information we will come up with a plan," Miss Stone said. "But for now, we should get back to the party before anyone questions what we're doing."

"Do we have to," Hercules groaned at me, placing his forehead on my shoulder. "I feel like everyone is staring at me."

"That's because the celebrities on the cover of the magazine don't really come to our office parties," a voice said from the doorway of Miss Stone's office.

A bright yellow sundress leaned against the threshold. Umber brown skin delicately peeking through.

"London," was all I could manage to say as a thousand apologies ran through my mind. "You came."

She hadn't been to work all week, not since the alley

incident. She had ignored my texts and dodged my calls. Even Miss Stone couldn't reach her, only getting a response from work related emails.

"Of course I came, I put a lot of work into this magazine. I'm not going to miss a chance to celebrate that." She approached Macks, linking her arm with theirs. "Also, I've been talking to Macks and unpacking things. I don't really understand all of this stuff. But I care about you guys, so I want to understand."

"I'm sorry you had to find out about this mess," Miss Stone said, standing up straight and towering over the room. "But if anyone was to learn the truth and take it with stride, it is most definitely you." A smile stretched across her face so wide, it squinted her eyes.

"I knew you were special since the day I met you," London told her. "This whole time you were just even more special than I had ever imagined."

"Well, now that you know the truth," she responded. "It just gets more expansive from here."

"Let's hope I can handle it." London squeezed Macks' shoulder.

"Macks and I also just found out about this stuff," I offered. "We can learn together."

"Okay!" Lucinda cheered, clapping her hands together to demand attention. "That's it. We are going to party! We are going to go off into the night, get out of our heads, and just be. We'll demystify this whole thing for our friend here." She raised her hands towards London as if revealing something no one has seen before.

"Okay, sure," London chuckled after realizing Lucinda was waiting for a response.

"We're literally at a party right now," I said.

"A work party," Lucinda said with a curled lip. "And we are talking about monsters, demigods, and other supernatural shit. We need fun. London needs to see us outside of the drama."

"What are you suggesting?" Macks asked.

"We could go to Ruthie's!" Hercules cheered.

"Ruthie's!" Lucinda echoed. "I haven't been there in ages."

"What's Ruthie's?" London asked, excitement peeking through her voice.

"Only the best queer bar around," Lucinda said, hugging herself.

"I've never heard of it," I said. I thought I knew most of the queer spaces in the city either through experience or word of mouth. "If it's the best, why haven't we been?"

"It's a queer bar specifically for supernaturals," Hercules added.

"You've never been in the know until now," Lucinda explained "I couldn't take you. But now we are all in the club. So we have to go! And you, Miss Elizabeth Stone, are coming too!"

Miss Stone was clearly caught off guard by the excitement suddenly directed at her. "Sure, if I must," she said with feigned reluctance. "But you all should really get back to the party we are currently at. I'll be there shortly.

Go. Mingle. Have fun." She motioned us out of her office, and we moved like puppets on a string.

"London!!" Minerva called out as we entered the photography studio that had been cleared out to make room for the office party. "Where have you been? Come here, there's so much tea you missed this week." Minerva grabbed London's hand, and almost by instinct, she grabbed Macks with her other hand. She led them away towards the drink table after giving a polite nod to those of us she was leaving behind.

Lucinda, Hercules, and I continued into the room. Large printouts of each magazine cover since the last party hung overhead. A man whom I had seen around the office but never met pointed at Hercules and then at the poster of him wearing a ball gown. Hercules smiled and waved.

"Girl," Lucinda said, placing a hand on my arm. "I have a surprise for you and it just came through the door."

"A surprise?" I asked, confused by the idea. What kind of gift would she give me at an office party of all places?

"In honor of our mending relationship, I wanted to orchestrate something to make you smile," she said, smiling enough for the both of us. She pointed to the other side of the room, and I turned towards the entrance.

A woman stood in the doorway looking around the room with a shy demeanor. She wore black dress pants and an orange blouse so bright that it demanded a spotlight. She wore ruby red glasses with a golden chain that stretched behind her ears. Her face was decorated with wrinkles, a mark of experience and laughter. As she looked around the room, her eyes found me. She sent warmth through my body with her grin.

"You invited my mom?" I turned to Lucinda, feeling both joy and panic.

"Your mom?" Hercules said, scanning the door to sneak a peek.

"I thought you'd be happy about that," Lucinda said, eyes wide.

"I am, I am," I told her as my mother began to cross the room. "I just haven't told her everything yet."

"You haven't told her!" Lucinda scolded, lightly smacking my shoulder. "You literally tell her everything. I would think solving your biggest life mystery would have come up."

"It's just tough telling her that cus it opens the whole birth mother can of worms. I don't want her to think I'm trying to replace her."

"Super valid," Lucinda said under her breath. My mother was closing in. "I guess we are pretending tonight." My mother inched even closer. "I hope you're ready," Lucinda said to Hercules.

"Parents love me," he said confidently, standing straight and clearing his throat.

"Mami!" I said with excitement as she wrapped her arms around me, providing a comfort I had forgotten I needed during my recent ordeals. "I didn't know you'd be here."

"Lucinda called and told us that this was happening. I wanted to come and celebrate you," she said, pulling away and cupping my face in her hands. "Your Papi stayed home with your brother. We didn't know if children were allowed, but he sends his love. All three of us will come into the city soon. We can celebrate you fully."

"Marcela!" Lucinda called out, giving my mother a hug.

"It's good to see you, my dear," my mom said before looking at Hercules. "And you must be the *famous* boyfriend I've heard so much about."

"Bryn talks about me?" he asked with a laugh. He gave my mom a sturdy handshake. "I've heard wonderful things about you as well. It's a pleasure to meet you."

I took my mother around the room, introducing her to everyone in the office and explaining all of the amazing things the magazine does and the cool things I was given the opportunity to learn. When she saw Macks, she couldn't help but gush and kiss their cheeks.

After a while of mingling, Miss Stone appeared clinking an office pen against a glass of wine. My mother turned away from Hercules, who had been schmoozing her for the past ten minutes, and asked me, "Is that her?"

I nodded as the room quieted and gave her all of the attention available.

"I don't normally do this, but lately I've felt very hopeful and proud of the work we do. I wanted to take a moment and acknowledge that," she said to the room. "I come from a very…let's just say 'ambitious' family. A long line of people who strive to do good. When I embarked on this journey and started my career, I got the questions: 'How does this further the cause? How does your work help people? I'll admit, I didn't know how to answer those questions then. But now, I can confidently answer. We make people feel visible. We make people feel heard. We are champions of self-expression. Little girls see our magazine and they are inspired to let themselves shine through their clothes. Queer people read our magazine and know that they are not alone and that they are celebrated. We create coverage on topics people care about, no matter how big or small. We provide a platform for those fighting to enact change. If those aren't acts of good, I don't know what is. I want to thank you all for being part of my dream, and showing me the good we can do here."

Her eyes connected with mine over the sea of people watching her. "Thank you for showing up and doing the work. I hope we continue to make great strides together." She raised her glass and every hand in the room followed suit like a field of blooming flowers greeting the sun.

As the toast concluded and applause rang through the crowd, Miss Stone made her way toward us. "Hello," she said, extending her hand to my mother. "I don't think we've had the pleasure."

"I am a big fan," my mom said, joining her in a handshake. "I'm Bryn's mom. I wanted to thank you for giving her this opportunity. She's worked so hard to get her foot in the door and it seems that you've thrown it wide open for her."

"Marcela," Miss Stone said happily. "It's lovely to meet you. I've heard such wonderful things." Miss Stone gave me a knowing glance before continuing. "You have raised a remarkable daughter. You should be proud of her tenacity and courage."

"That's so kind of you," my mom said, smiling at me.

"I hope you enjoy the party," Miss Stone said, looking at me again. "I should let you two continue catching up. I'm sure Bryn has lots to tell you." And with that, Miss Stone was absorbed into the crowd.

"Mom," I said, knowing what I had to do. "Can we talk for a minute, in private?"

"What's going on, mi vida?" she asked as we approached my desk in Miss Stone's private corner of the office. The sounds of the party trickled across the office like muffled thoughts.

"There is something you should know about my life here," I told her. Panic was building in my chest. Her eyes glistened in that special way that always told me she was listening to me, with her entire being, as a child. "Miss Stone is like me. She is strong. Supernaturally strong."

Her mouth dropped open to a wide toothless grin. "That's great news. Surprising, but great! You're not alone anymore." There was genuine joy in her voice. "Has she been able to shed more light on where it comes from, how you both are the way you are?"

"We are Amazons," I said plainly. "Like, in mythology."

"Oh my," she responded. And I could tell she was exploring her memory of history and literature trying to piece things together.

"Warrior women who come from the god of war to

fight supernatural battles and defend innocents," I explained.

Her expression went sour. "So you are expected to fight in wars?"

"I'm already fighting in one," I told her. There was a pain in my heart like I was disappointing her. "There's a demigod out there who wants to kill my entire race as some sort of twisted vendetta. He set his sight on me because my birth mother is Queen and if he can wipe out her bloodline, there's no one left to lead the Amazons."

"Your birth mother..." Her entire body went still. "Have you met her?"

"No!" I said quickly. "She locked herself away in the place we come from. That's how I ended up with you. She sent me away at birth, to protect me. And Miss Stone was supposed to train me once my strength came in. But we didn't find each other until now."

"This has all been decided for you since birth?" She placed a hand on her chest and stepped back slightly as if taking it all in. "Why the delay? Why did she not find you until now?"

"It actually wasn't Miss Stone's job to find me," I said, bracing myself. "It was Lucinda's job to bring me to her. She's not human, older than she looks, and kinda employed by a god to look after me since birth and deliver me to Miss Stone once I became an Amazon."

"But she didn't?"

"She developed an attachment to me and didn't want to uproot my childhood like that. So she held it off and befriended me as an adult, and tried to keep me far from this life for as long as she could."

At this point, the color had drained from my mother's face. She looked at me like I was one of her art pieces, finally finished, and she was gazing at the work fully realized in front of her.

"My daughter is a princess," she said, her voice fluttering. "Princess Bryn, bringer of light. Everything you saw yourself as ever since you were a little girl, manifested to who you are now." She smiled and wrapped her arms around me. "Oh, mi cielo! Thank you for telling me this. I'm so glad you finally have the answers you've been searching for." Her grip around me tightened. "And I'm so sorry the answers come at the cost of such a heavy burden." As comfort built in my gut and the weight of a secret fell from my shoulders, there was movement coming from the direction of the party.

Lucinda stopped in her tracks when she saw the embrace. My mother peeled away from me and turned to see her.

"Hercules said you were having a talk," Lucinda spoke softly. "I thought maybe I could help clear the air."

My mother walked to her without saying a word. Once she was face to face with Lucinda, she spoke slowly, "You knew about my daughter's destiny her whole life and said nothing?"

Lucinda looked flabbergasted. She nodded her head, as if afraid to speak.

"Thank you," my mother said, taking Lucinda's hands

in hers. "Thank you for protecting my child, and letting her have a life. You've done her a favor we didn't even know she needed. I don't know how I can repay you."

"You don't repay me," Lucinda said with a smile as a tear came down her cheek. "I love her and your family. Knowing that forsaking my duty has given you a little brightness, is payment enough."

My mother turned back to me and beckoned me forward. As I joined the two of them, my mother wrapped Lucinda and me in a healing embrace. Standing there, Lucinda and I in my mother's arms, enveloped by truth and gratitude, I finally felt free for the first time in a long time. And it felt good.

Chapter 23

We gathered in the dead of night, dressed to impress and inhibitions lowered. Hercules guided us through a city of darkness. London, ever so anxious about the world she would be introduced to, clung to Macks' hand. Lucinda was brimming with excitement that steadily intensified since these plans were made.

Hercules stopped walking, prompting us all to bring our journey to an end. He stood there with a smile on his face, gesturing to nothing. An inconspicuous building in Hell's Kitchen. Tall and shrouded in the darkness. No discernible signage. The entrance to the building was quietly inactive.

"This is it?" London asked with a curled lip. Her peach-colored cocktail dress had a slit running up her left leg.

"You don't see it," Hercules said with an ear-to-ear grin. "That's the point. That's the cool thing! Everyone but me and Lucinda won't be able to see it at first. It's actually going to be harder for you, being human." He approached London, placing his hands on her shoulders and positioning her body towards whatever he was looking at.

"Are you saying it's magically hidden?" Macks asked.

They wore a patchwork suit of different plaid patterns. Large red and white ceramic mushrooms hung from their ears.

"By a cloaking spell designed to make your mind ignore it," Lucinda said. "The spell works less on people exposed to magic, even less on people with magic, and doesn't work at all on people who know what to look for."

"How do we see through it if it's our first time?" I asked, trying to focus on the building's entrance.

"Stop trying to find what's not there," Hercules said.

"Accept that it's there, even though you can't see it." Lucinda's words clung to the night breeze. Lucinda wore a long black gown, cinched up on her left thigh revealing white stockings and garters. Black lace gloves stretched up her arms, nearly reaching her shoulders. Silver pearls were draped around her neck, resting on her propped-up cleavage.

"I mean, we all know it's here," I told her. "You both wouldn't lie to us."

"But the spell is going to push against your perception," Hercules said, ever so softly. "Push back."

Suddenly, as if noticing something immediately after glancing over it, my eyes were torn away from the building's entrance. A few feet away, another door was embedded in the building's facade. A single red door, riddled with graffiti. A tall man with ebony skin and a long trench coat stood in front of it.

"Woah!" London said, looking at the newly formed door.

"You're seeing it now too?" Macks asked.

"I think we all are," I said.

"Perfect!" Lucinda cheered. "Now we can enter!"

The man in front of the door nodded and stepped aside without a word. The red door swung open without being touched. Hercules took my hand, and we walked through together. The second we were off the street, we were enveloped by a cool sweet air running through a dark corridor. The impression of noise wiggled around us. The hall didn't end with a door or a wall, but it just ended. As if a curtain of nothing lifted to reveal something.

Suddenly we were standing in a massive ballroom under a crystal chandelier the size of Texas. Orbs of light, illuminating the space, bobbed in the air like boats on the water. Circular tables sat in bunches on the right and left sides of the ballroom. A long sleek black bar sat on the far end of the room, a wall of liquor bottles towering behind it. Two staircases sat on either end of the bar, leading to a mezzanine that wrapped around the entire circular room. Music pumped into space but there were no visible speakers. Across from the bar sat a stage. A single performer stood there.

Her hair was layered with blonde and brown. She was tall and wore a tight black dress. Rings sat on every finger, and multiple bracelets on each wrist. Silver chains hung from her neck and waist. Her deep raspy voice flooded out over the crowd.

Amongst the dance floor were a few elevated platforms. On top of them, go-go dancers strutted their stuff as people watched. A woman in a skirt and nipple pasties threw her hands up as part of her performance and fireworks shot from her fingers. Those watching her cheered as they clamored to stick dollar bills in the waistline of her skirt. The other performer, a muscular man with dark skin wearing only a colorful jockstrap, seemed to glow a light blue color. The blue light covered his body and when it disappeared, he was no longer dancing on the platform. That same light flashed somewhere on the upper level near a group of people watching the show below. The dancer was there now. He was swarmed by his viewers. Many ran their hands across his body, in absolute thrill, while others shoved money at him. After a moment he flashed blue again and disappeared, reappearing on his dance platform.

A man at the tail end of the dancefloor talked to a group of three or four people as they moved to the music. He waited for each of them to respond, taking great care to hear their answers. After they each have spoken, his body shifted like a mirage in the heat. There were suddenly two exact copies of him. His duplicate walked to the bar and lists off a drink order to a bartender. The duplicate drops some cash on the bar top and points to his group before walking back. The duplicate merged back with the original, who was dancing with his friends, and he didn't miss a beat as he became whole again.

Behind the bar, glasses and bottles lifted into the air, pouring, and mixing drinks on their own. A remarkably tall cocktail waiter with six arms took each drink in a different hand and swiftly delivered them to the duplicating man's friend group.

"Oh my…" London's words lost her as she and the rest of us entered the ballroom.

"Everyone is really just, free to be themselves, out in the open here," I remarked.

"A great place to come to embrace your queer supernatural self," Hercules said, placing his arm around me.

"And a great place to be if you want to see the joy of the supernatural world," Lucinda said to London. "Welcome to Ruthie's!"

"Hercules?" A voice called out from the mezzanine, dragging his name like a song. A woman began to descend the staircase, slowly as if soaking up the moment. And I swear it was almost like a spotlight was on her.

She approached us, giving Hercules a large hug before pulling away and looking at us all. "It is lovely to see you!"

"Everyone, meet Ruthie," he announced. "The icon herself, creator and owner of this historic safe haven."

"Awe," she gushed. "Don't ever stop saying nice things about me." She had donned a see-through red ball gown, revealing matching red lingerie underneath. Her eyelashes were long and decorated with jewels. Her colorful makeup swept across her face and seemed to light up the room around her. "Who are our friends?"

"This is my girlfriend, Bryn," Hercules said.

"You're gorgeous, Doll," Ruthie said, grasping my hands. I wore a light-blue single-shouldered gown with a thigh-high slit. Originally a boring two shouldered and slit-less slip dress, I bought it at a thrift store and altered it to be flowy and skin forward.

"Thank you," I blushed. "And this is our friend Lucinda."

"I've seen you around, but not for a while," Ruthie said, hugging her like an old friend.

"I had to lay low for a little while, but I'm glad to be back," Lucinda said.

"It's great to officially meet you," Ruthie said with a smile.

"This is Macks and London," Hercules said, gesturing to the pair. "London is human, while Macks and Bryn are just coming into their identities. So we are introducing them to our world."

"And you came to my bar to do it," Ruthie said. "Good choice."

"So, what kind of supernatural person are you?" London asked. Ruthie looked at her with an innocent smile but didn't answer the question. "Oh. Should I not ask that?" London looked at us for help.

"No, Doll," Ruthie exclaimed with a forgiving smile. "You can ask, but I don't have to answer." She winked with a pop of her ankle.

"What Ruthie is, is a great mystery amongst supernatural circles," Lucinda said, placing a comforting hand on London's shoulders. "There are a lot of old and rare things out there that are not common knowledge."

"Unique? Yes, but not old!" Ruthie called out, placing

a hand on her chest. "I've been around for centuries but *old* will never describe me."

Lucinda laughed. "While we don't know what she is, we know she can do incredible things. She used her power to create this place."

"Ruthie's exists in multiple cities around the world, at the same time," Hercules said.

"It's part of my mission to create a safe space," Ruthie added. "I have to make it accessible for as many of us as possible. So you have entrances that connect to New York, San Francisco, L.A., Tokyo, Paris, Dallas, and more." She lifted her shoulders, forming a pedestal for the proud expression on her face.

"That's incredible," I said, taking it all in.

"Oh sweetie, I know I am," she laughed. "Now, Hercules called ahead. I've set up a private area for your party. Elizabeth Stone arrived a few moments ago, she's waiting for you there. I'll have someone escort you." She raised her hands and clapped them together. A cocktail waitress appeared as if stepping out of nowhere. "I would join you but I would never forgive myself if I stole all the attention from your big night out." She kissed Hercules on the cheeks and beckoned us to follow the waitress.

She took us up the stairs, past the people looking over the railing towards the dance floor. The second level was massive. It extended far past the walls of the ballroom, which wasn't possible considering that the building looked perfectly uniform from the outside. It was as if the second floor belonged to a much bigger building than the first floor, but somehow, they stood on top of each other with an exterior smaller than the interior.

There was another bar and another area for dancing. There were also a number of areas marked off by velvet ropes. Booth seating, private rooms behind closed doors, and even private dance platforms. The waitress took us to one of those booths. The velvet rope opened like a gate as we approached. Miss Stone stood to greet us.

She was radiant in a long silver halter neck dress. Her afro sat like a crown on top of her head. She gave us a reserved smile.

"You made it!" Lucinda cheered.

"I must admit," Miss Stone said. "I almost declined your invitation. Going to the club with your mentee and her friends is quite…unorthodox."

"I'm glad you changed your mind," I told her. "It might do us some good to see each other outside of the office and training."

"When was the last time you let yourself have fun?" London asked her. "I used to be your assistant, I know how you schedule yourself."

"You've been so focused on what's coming, they're right, you should just live in the now. At least for one night," Hercules added.

"Well, I should also admit that I had ulterior motives for accepting the invitation." She looked at me, the right corner of her mouth curling upwards. "Can I steal you away for a moment?"

I wasn't sure what she had in store for me but I followed

without a second thought. She took me through crowds and down a hallway in silence. I didn't feel an awkward or tense air around her. I felt a low vibration, like deep thought.

"I have some friends who have a private room here on permanent retainer," she said as we came to a stop. "Some women I think you should meet." We stood in front of a door marked "VIP." She pushed it open and led me through the threshold.

It was a small room with plush chairs and a fancy table embedded into the wall. Red light danced above our heads. Two occupants sat at the table with five empty martini glasses sprawled out in front of them. They looked up at us with smiles.

The first was a strawberry blonde draped in a silk shawl. Her skin was plump and rosy. She held wisdom in her eyes. The folds on her neck and around her eyes suggested years well lived. There was a familiarity about her as if I had seen her before.

"You must be Bryn," she said. "My name is Bebe, she/her. It's a pleasure to meet you." She stood up, pressing her hands together and bringing them to her lips, as if in prayer.

"I'm Karmen, they/them," the other said. "Thank you for taking time out of your night to meet us." They were completely unfamiliar to me. There was a sense of maturity about them, coupled with flawless skin, it was impossible to tell if they were fifty or thirty. Nonetheless, they were a striking beauty. Their skin was burnt umber. They wore a bright orange skin-tight dress. The wispy dark curls on their head didn't pass their ears.

"Um, no problem." I wasn't sure what to make of this meeting.

"I thought it was time you met other Amazons," Miss Stone said, hugging her associates before she sat down.

"Oh my god," I said, rushing to join them at the table. I felt a flutter in my chest. I didn't quite know what to say. "It's great to meet more of us."

"Oh Elizabeth," Bebe chuckled, turning to me. "Not just Amazons. Trans Amazons!"

"She thought it would be beneficial to know there are more of us," Karmen said, sipping their cocktail. "To actually be in a room of people who walk your path fully."

"To be Amazon is one thing," Miss Stone said.

"To be trans is another," said Karmen.

"And to be both is just fucking cosmic," Bebe finished.

Chapter 24

"So, future Queen," Karmen said, leaning back to look at me. We exchanged pleasantries and introductions. Karmen was living solely on the island the Amazons call home. They were a spy, sent out into the human world to work cloak-and-dagger missions for the Queen. My birth mother would send them and a select few to investigate and end supernatural corruption and influence. "We kinda met once before. Last time I saw your mother, she was about ready to pop."

Karmen was sent out on a mission shortly before my mother gave birth and sent me away, closing off the island from the outside world. They had no idea it was coming and only planned on being away from home for a few months, not a few decades. They were forced to adjust to living in a world they had only ever visited.

"I've never met anyone in the royal family," said Bebe with a long sigh. Bebe was born in the human world and sent to the island to train when she came into her strength. When she turned eighteen, she returned to the human world and became a political activist by day and monster hunter by night. Her Amazonian purpose was to better the world on two fronts. This is where I recognized her from. For forty years she had been at the forefront of countless social justice movements. I had seen her face in old protest photography, documentaries, the news, and at pride parades. I realized she was even a keynote speaker at a queer and trans conference I went to in college.

"So what does a Queen do?" I asked them, careful not to ask about my mother but the title she holds. The title that I might hold one day.

"She oversees armies and makes decisions for our people," Miss Stone answered. "Handling operations all over this world, ensuring we keep true to our purpose. And we, as Amazons, follow that position of power with our last breath."

"I don't know how you all do this," I said. "Knowing since birth that you'd be going down this path, dedicating your life to it. It's terrifying."

"I actually think being born into it makes things easier," Karmen said. "Knowing I had a greater purpose from a young age made me feel special."

"Yes!" Bebe squealed. "And it never once felt strange or overwhelming, it was just normal. I'm sorry you didn't have the same experience."

"That's not even the worst of it," Karmen said, putting a hand on my arm. "You didn't have the groundwork to prepare you for your purpose, but you were also missing your sisterhood."

"There is a school of thought, by some supernatural

theorists," Miss Stone said, "that an Amazon's strength is increased through her connection to the community."

"Which makes sense," Karmen said, sounding like they were ready to debate. "We are children of Ares, god of war. What is an army but a type of community? What is a community if not an army of people who share a heart? Is it so crazy to think that Ares created an army, a sisterhood, that is strengthened through their connection to each other?"

"And that could be why every Queen has always been the strongest of her time," Bebe said with a shrug. "Our numbers grow with every generation."

"Or that's because they are descended from the first Amazon," Miss Stone laughed. "Who was the strongest Amazon in history."

"We won't know for sure," Bebe laughed with her. "But I have to agree with Karmen, that sounds like a plausible theory."

"So, what's been happening lately," I said. "Being locked from your home, separated from your sisters, and scattered in the wind. Do you think it weakens you?"

"Perhaps," Bebe said, looking at the ceiling. "It's been so long, it's hard to remember what my heart felt like before."

"But that will all be over soon," Karmen said. "You've identified the threat against us and you're making moves to end it."

"Yeah, all I have to do is stop a demigod," I scoffed.

"Which you will do," Miss Stone said firmly.

"He wants to end your line, and permanently end the mantle of Queen," Karmen said. "If our community is our heart, the Queen is our head. We need both if we are going to survive."

"So, can I expect you two to be fighting beside us?" I asked. "I would feel better with more Amazons there."

"Bryn." Miss Stone's voice sounded grim. Like she dreaded what was coming out of her mouth. "A demigod is far beyond anything the Amazons have ever faced before. You're the only one of us with a god-killing weapon. We don't even know if anyone other than you *can* stop him."

What she said made perfect sense. I hated that. I wanted things to be easier. I wanted people more capable than me to be there with me. I wanted people to lean on because I didn't know if I could stand on my own.

"That being said," Bebe said. "We will support you in any way that we can."

"While it's true, the more Amazons put in the demigod's line of fire, the closer we are to extinction," Karmen said. "We discussed with Elizabeth how we can assist in other ways."

"We know he has the power to create his own army," Miss Stone told me, straightening her back. "He will likely try to use that against us. He will launch a full-on assault. And while you take the fight to him, there will be as many of us that we can gather to deal with his army."

My anxiety flustered for a moment. "You're right," I said, even though I hated to admit it. "It has to be me. This is what we've been training for."

"The mark of a true Queen is standing up, even when she is too afraid to do so," Bebe said with a soothing tone.

"You are strong enough to do this," Miss Stone said.

"And you have us and your friends to lean on," Karmen added.

"Just remember," Bebe began. "There is a power; strength and magic, that comes with your identity and community. And you have multiple dancing around in your heart. Every part of you comes together to make something incredible."

Chapter 25

After returning to my friends, I tried my best to do what we set out to do. Put the stress of my situation out of my mind, for just one night. We drank. We talked, getting to know each other better. We danced. Miss Stone watched us dance, like a mother watching her children play.

There was something incredibly freeing about being somewhere where nothing was a secret. For most of my life, I had to work to keep my strength hidden. It was a continuous effort that weighed on my mind. I didn't realize how heavy that weight had been until I was at a place where it no longer mattered. Almost everyone inside this bar had a secret like mine, and within these walls, the secrets didn't matter.

"So how long have you been coming here?" London asked Hercules.

"Since it opened," he said, pouring himself a glass from the free margarita pitcher Ruthie had sent over. "This place opened in…" he scrunched his face, trying to remember. "96'! But I've known Ruthie for fifty or sixty years. We always managed to cross each other's paths. When that happens enough, you tend to stay on each other's radar."

"It's still so crazy to me that you've been around for thousands of years," London laughed.

"Having a terrible father has some perks," he said, raising his glass.

"So, demigods live forever but Amazons don't?" London asked. "But the Amazons come from a god too."

"Ares created us to be something different entirely," Miss Stone explained. "Our history books tell us that the first Amazon was a demigod, but she was merely a template for what Ares was trying to achieve. He rewrote the rules of his own lineage, so his sons would be demigods but his daughters would be something new."

"That makes sense," said Macks, who was lapping up the supernatural knowledge.

"It's probably better that way," London said. "A long life sounds tough. Especially when you live amongst humans. I can't imagine how seeing the world change around you while you stay stagnant. It sounds lonely."

"A couple thousand years," he said, staring into his glass. "Nothing in this world is the same as when I came into it."

"A life full of goodbyes," Lucinda said, sinking into the booth. I had almost forgotten Lucinda also had a long life. Maybe that's why she was so hesitant to watch me fulfill my destiny. I know she had a sisterhood of nymphs she had to walk away from in order to look after me. When we became friends and the time came for her to push me into something greater, something that could take me away from her, potentially away from life itself, maybe the thought of another goodbye was too much.

"A life full of goodbyes is also a life full of hellos," Hercules said, resting his hand on my thigh. "Every time I start my life over, I get to forge a new sense of self, discover new places, and let new people in."

"With your recent method of pretending to be your own descendants," Miss Stone said. "I imagine you're able to hold onto some aspects of the life you built."

"Exactly," he said. "Even if it is a little convoluted."

"What about a real family?" London asked. "Have you ever done that?"

"He has a whole heavenly family tree," Macks said.

"Zeus didn't act fatherly enough for me to consider him family. But I had my mother and her husband," he answered, sucking in his lips. "And..." he stopped talking before his next thought could be fully realized. His mouth opened as if the words were there, invisible in the air.

"Is everything okay," I asked quietly, leaning into him.

"Yeah," he said as if he was lacking breath.

"But what about starting a family of your own?" Macks asked. "In all these years, have you ever laid down those roots?"

"Macks," Miss Stone said. A warning disguised as a name.

"That was a long time ago," he said, physically recoiling from the thought.

"We don't have to talk about this," Lucinda said curtly.

"Oh." Macks' eyes grew wide as the tension leveled. "I'm so sorry. This is verging into heavy territory, huh?"

"It was before I ever became this…hero." He spat out the word like it was bitter. "At the beginning of my life. They were my first goodbye."

"I can't even imagine," London gasped.

"Hazards of a long life, I guess," Hercules said with a half laugh. He sat for a moment before standing. "Excuse me."

He turned from us and began to sink into the crowded club.

"Oh no," London said with a hand to her heart. "I didn't mean to…"

"Should we apologize?" Macks asked, moving to get up.

"No, no," I said, standing instead. "I'll go. He just needs some space."

As I left the table, Miss Stone's hand touched my elbow, prompting me to stop for just a moment. "There are some wounds that refuse to heal, no matter how old they are," she said so softly that I almost didn't hear her over the music. "Sometimes, we can't help heal them, but we can bear witness."

I followed his trail, nearly losing him. I saw him leave through a set of double doors. After pushing through the sea of people, I opened those doors and found myself outside on a massive balcony where the music inside was barely a whisper. I scanned the people peering over the edge, taking in the views, until I finally found him. He stood, leaning forward on the railing, looking far ahead into the distance.

As I approached him, I noticed the buildings around us were not nearly as tall as they had been when we entered. We were level with many, even looking over some. Which was impossible on only the second or third floor of the building. The darkness in the sky felt different too. We were no longer in the deep dark of night, but the dim darkness with a hint of light, like the morning darkness gearing for the arrival of the sun.

These differences didn't truly hit me until I reached for him. As my hand touched him, my eyes went over his shoulder. There, in the distance, drenched in glittering lights was a tall monument. Four legs stretch upward and come together to form an elongated point. A curvy pyramid under a new sky.

"Is that what I think it is?"

"Welcome to Paris," he said without turning to face me. "Different balconies exist in different cities. This one was always my favorite."

Are you okay?" I asked, joining him by his side, gazing at his view.

He turned away from me slightly. His head slumped forward, and I could hear soft sobs escape his lips.

"I'm okay," he sniffled. "Really, go back inside."

"You can talk to me," I told him. I placed my hand on his shoulder and his body flinched. I fought the urge to pull away. I knew, despite his instincts to fight it, what he needed was someone who would be there to listen.

"I was married before." He kept his head down.

"To a human," I said.

"To one of the great loves of my life," he said.

"One of?" I asked.

He lifted his head. Soft tears decorated his face with sparkles in the night. "When you live as long as I do, you end up having multiple great love stories." He wiped his tears away and forced a smile. "Each one just as magnificent and painful as the last."

"She was your first?"

"My first love." His smile shifted slightly as if something real was breaking through. "The only human love."

"What happened to her?" I asked, taking his hand in mine.

"She didn't grow old like she was supposed to," he said. "I came into this world when Zeus possessed a King and conceived a child with his wife while allowing her to believe he was the real king, not some fucked up god taking advantage of her."

"That's awful," I said. The mere thought of this violation made me feel ill.

"He's trash," Hercules said, clenching his grip on my hand. "And that disgusting act that created me had continued repercussions that keep falling on me. My mother and her husband had a child that looked like him but there was something extra in me they couldn't deny. They both had been victims of his actions, in different but equally traumatizing ways and I was a reminder of that."

"Did they treat you badly because of it?"

"They tried not to. My mother was an angel, despite what happened. She gave me more love than I knew what to do with. She never showed it on the outside, but every so often I would see something in her eyes. Like a worry or a fear that he might come for me, or come back for her. Sometimes I wondered if she was worried that I would grow up to be like my godly father instead of my human one." He took a deep breath and held it for a moment. "He found it harder to hide his feelings. I don't blame him. It's a confusing situation. I was only partly his kid, whereas I was fully my mother's. He had to share the idea of fatherhood with some cosmic being that hijacked his body and violated his wife. When he'd get angry, he'd tell me I wasn't really his. He'd call me a monster's spawn. There were times he'd look at me and I swear he couldn't even see me."

"That's awful," I told him. "To have all of that on you as a child."

"I didn't even understand where all of it was coming from as a child," he said. "I had to put these pieces together later in life."

That's even worse. Feeling these tensions growing up but not knowing where they were coming from sounds like torture."

"And that's not the only torturous fallout left by Zeus," he said. "I grew up, adjusting to the idea of what I was to the best of my ability, and I got married. My wife and I had a daughter." There was a smile on his face, cutting through the tears like a dim light in the fog. "Another god took offense to Zeus' actions. Hera was always threatened by me. She thought Zeus was making some sort of power play against her or something." He scoffed. "I don't actually know what she was thinking, or why she waited to take it out on me. But when I finally had control of my life, when I was happy and surrounded by love, she enacted her twisted revenge."

"She killed your family?"

"She cursed me." A sob broke free from him, cutting off his words for a moment. "She made me kill them. My girls. She got into my head and twisted my thoughts. She made it so I *wanted* to hurt them. To this day, I can still remember the bloodthirsty rage I felt towards them. I know it was fabricated by her, but it felt so real in the moment. The memory of what I did… It will never leave me."

My heart sank deep into my chest, finding a dark chasm I didn't know existed. "Why would she… How does that hurt Zeus?"

"The gods are known for cruelty, not logic," he said, looking away from me. "She didn't like that Zeus created me, so she made me suffer for existing."

"You don't deserve that," I told him. "Your family didn't deserve that."

"I know. But it still happened."

"And it's not your fault," I insisted. "You know you didn't have control."

"It took me a long time to accept that," he said. "That's the reason I became a legend. I needed to prove to myself that I wasn't a monster. So I set out on a journey to complete my heroic trials, twelve nearly impossible feats, and solidify myself as a force of good."

"And you dedicated your eternal life to continue doing good," I said.

"Every time I save someone, every time I help someone, I prevent the pain I feel from finding someone else."

"Thank you for sharing this with me," I told him. "I'm sorry you lost them. But you're doing so much more than preventing pain. If your heroic deeds are done in their name, you're keeping them alive in a way."

"That's the least I could do." He pushed away from the balcony railing and leaned his head back. Face towards the sky, he closed his eyes, trapping the tears inside. "When you've lost someone you love, you hold them with you for everything you do after that."

"Do you carry Deimos with you?" I tried not to sound accusing. I felt something in the back of my mind. When we first mentioned Deimos to Hercules, when they came face to face in the alley, when Hercules told us about their history, even when he kept their history a secret, there was something unsaid but painfully loud. I couldn't put my finger on it at first, or maybe I just didn't want to admit it. They had been in love.

"I was mad at the gods for so long," Hercules said. "So much hatred and resentment was inside my body, that I stopped realizing it was even there. And then I met Deimos, and he was feeling all of these same things, and we bonded over that. And then eventually, us spending time together chipped away at those negative feelings and replaced them with a tenderness for each other."

"I can't imagine someone like him being capable of love," I said, trying my best to hear him with an open mind.

"He wasn't always like he is now. The Deimos I knew was a different man entirely. He was always disappointed that the gods didn't give us enough recognition. He has always wanted to win the pride of Ares, and that need for approval eventually turned into a twisted rage. But even then, I never imagined that rage would come this far."

"What was he like when you were together," I asked.

"Caring. Passionate. Fearless." Hercules opened his eyes, and no more tears fell. He looked at me. "He was driven by the idea of strength and power but simultaneously had the softest touch. He never talked about hurting people to get what he wanted. He's in a bad place right now, but I know it's not the real him."

"Real him or not," I said. "He's still doing these horrible things. He's killing people."

"But if the man I know is still in there." His voice fell and rose like the waves of the ocean. "Maybe I can convince him to put all of this behind him. I could avoid a fight. I can protect you."

Chapter 26

"You haven't heard from him at all?" Lucinda asked, rubbing sleep from her eyes.

"No," I told her. "He was supposed to let me know when he made it home."

After our night of partying, Hercules decided not to come home with the rest of us. His normal spark of joy hadn't returned after our conversation on the balcony, and he thought it best if he ended the night on his own. I wouldn't be worried if things hadn't been so heavy.

"He said something about confronting Deimos," I said. The gravity of the situation was building in my chest.

"You don't think he actually would, do you?" Macks asked.

"I don't know but we have to find him," I said. "I should tell Miss Stone."

"I'm heading into the office," London said, putting on the pair of wedged heels that seem to stay at our apartment. "I'll fill her in. You guys focus on tracking him down."

"Thank you," I told her. She gave me a hug and I didn't know if it was a goodbye hug or an everything-will-be-okay hug. After kissing Macks on the cheek, she headed to the door and pulled it open.

"Oh!" she chirped in surprise.

Ceci stood on the other side of the door, leaning against the threshold. Her long dark hair was pulled into a braid. She wore jean shorts and a glowing white top. "Hello," she said. "I'm looking for Macks."

London turned, giving Macks an inquisitive look.

"Magic tutor," they said.

"Oh right!" London turned back to her. "I've heard a lot about you. Come on in." They squeezed past each other without saying another word. Ceci closed the door behind her.

"Why the long faces?" she asked, looking at the three of us with a look that nearly read as disappointment.

"My boyfriend."

"The demigod," Ceci interrupted.

"Yes," I confirmed. "He's missing and I'm concerned something might have happened to him. Maybe something at the hands of the other demigod we are dealing with."

"We just don't know how to find him," Lucinda said.

"Well it's a good thing I'm here," Ceci said with a burst of energy. "I know what today's lesson will be." She looked at Macks with determined eyes.

"Me?" Macks asked. "How am I supposed to find him?"

"This boy," Ceci said to me. "He gives you butterflies in your stomach?"

I hadn't thought about it before. I knew I was into him. How could I not be? He was beautiful, a literal god. And even beyond that, he has shown me the breath and kindness of his soul at every turn. He made me feel confident. He's shown me vulnerability. Every time I'm with him, even the first time we met, there was something there. A simmering in my core.

"Yeah, I guess he does," I said, unsure how this revelation was supposed to be helpful.

"Butterflies are bugs," Ceci said, confidently.

"But that's just a metaphor," Macks said.

"You are a sorcerex. You bring metaphor to life. There is no reason you can't conjure up a little love bug to lead your friend to her man."

"Could you really do that?" I asked Macks. Hope flashed like fireworks in the back of my mind. "Do you think it could work?"

"You kind of did something similar before," Lucinda said with a shrug.

Macks said with uncertainty, "I can...I can definitely try."

"How do we do it?" I asked.

"Let the magic guide you," Ceci told Macks. "Remember all that I've taught you these past few weeks."

"Wait!" I yelped. A spark of paranoia fueled inspiration burned through me. I ran to my room and grabbed The Queen's Sword. The second it was in my hands, I felt an eerie sense of calm. As if holding it meant that any complications in front of me would soon be slayed.

When I returned, Macks joined me in the center of the room. Lucinda and Ceci took generous steps backwards that made me nervous. "Give me your hand," Macks said, holding their hand up as if offering me something. I followed instructions and placed my fingers in their palm. "Now, think about him, I guess."

"More confident!" Ceci demanded. "You command the magic, you make the rules. There is no room to question yourself."

"Okay, right," Macks said, shaking their head and wiggling their body. They straightened their back, and I was surprised with how tall they seemed at this moment, despite their small stature. They took my hand again, this time raising their free hand to cradle the side of my head. "Picture him in your mind."

A kind heart. Wavy brown curls. Unwavering confidence, verging on cockiness. Glimmering green eyes. Heroic spirit. Silky tan skin. A delicate nature. A breathtaking smile. An intense belief in me.

That was him. If anything bad happened to him, if I lost him, I'm not sure how I could come back from that.

Macks pulled their hand away from my head. Dancing across their fingers was a small butterfly with bright purple wings adorned with splotches of red and pink. It crawled onto their index finger and looked at me. I'm not sure if you can make eye contact with a butterfly, but we experienced the closest thing to that.

As it looked at me, I was mesmerized. It was like this tiny insect was reaching into me and pulling something out. With every passing second another identical butterfly would appear, one by one, as if melting into existence.

"Um, Macks," Lucinda said with concern. They stepped forward as the air filled with the swarm. "This is a lot."

"I know," they said. They pulled away from me as the butterfly in their hand joined the fluttering swarm. They raised a hand, signaling Lucinda not to interfere. As the butterflies circled me, I felt a wisping wind embrace my body. "Bring him home."

For a moment, my view was flooded by the swirl of color and rapid dance of tiny wings. In the next instant, the tiny bodies dispersed, separating and disappearing into the air.

I was no longer in my living room, looking at Macks, Lucinda, and Ceci. I was in a small room, a liminal space. White walls sandwiched between a silver elevator and large black doors with an abstract shaped mirror sweeping through the center. I examined my surroundings, not sure if I should enter the elevator or pass through the doors. A window was off to the side, and I approached, peering outside into the morning light. Judging by the distinctive skyline, I was in Manhattan. High up in Manhattan. This had to be the penthouse of an apartment or hotel. If Macks' love bugs delivered me here, the clear direction was through the doors. I pushed through them, making eye contact with my reflection as the doors parted.

I was greeted by a wide open space with deep red walls, and velvet red sofas around a glass coffee table. The far wall was one giant window with long black curtains framing the view of the city on the other side. A crystal chandelier hung from the ceiling, nearly blinding me with shimmering light. A chrome red piano sat on an elevated platform to the left of the sitting room, to the left, a sleek black kitchen.

There were no signs of life.

Just past the piano a black staircase reached into the ceiling. I made my way to the second floor. Decked out in even more red, was a hallway that held three dark wooden doors. Sickening silence hung in the air, dripping on my skin. The door on the far end was the only one left ajar. I decided to look there first.

It was a room with dark walls. Blackout curtains cut out any hope of daylight. A large bed draped with red sheets with black filigree sat against the wall like a throne. In the bed, under the blankets, was a head of curly brown hair connected to a tanned and muscular torso, a pale arm firmly wrapped around him.

"Oh my god." I couldn't believe what I was seeing. Hercules, embraced by the very same man that was trying to kill me, my family, my entire race. Laying there, sleeping with a look of bliss on his gentle face. The face I missed. The face I was worried about. I staggered on my feet, unsure of what my next move should be. My heart tore in two, forcing violent gasps to be ripped from my chest.

Hercules' eyes shot open suddenly. A look of fear instantly stretched across his face as he jumped from the bed, rushing to grab the pants we wore last night and pull them over his bare legs. A necklace I had never seen before dangled from his neck. A silver chain with a curved ivory horn shaped charm hung above his chiseled chest. "Bryn, this wasn't…"

"No!" I didn't want to hear him try to explain.

Deimos Rose from the bed, rubbing sleep from his eyes. When he finally opened them and saw me standing there, a look of satisfaction bloomed.

"Hello," he sang. He crawled out of the bed and covered his naked body with a flowing silk robe. "Sorry you had to find out like this."

There wasn't an ounce of sympathy in his voice.

"Shut up," Hercules spat. Deimos looked at him with uncertainty. "Bryn, please."

I turned and walked out of the room. I ran down the stairs, the only thought in my mind was to remove myself from the situation. I couldn't be there.

"Wait!" Hercules called out, following close behind me. I nearly reached the exit when his hand grabbed my wrist. In his grip, I couldn't move. Not only because he wouldn't let me, but because his touch still felt magnetic to me.

"I thought something bad happened," I told him. "I was freaking out! I was coming to save you! And it turns out you were perfectly fine. Sleeping with the enemy."

"We love each other, girl," Deimos called in a defensive tone as he came down the stairwell.

"We loved each other once," Hercules corrected. "I loved him once. And I really did come here trying to convince him to give all of this up. I came here to do the right thing." Tears collected in the corners of his eyes, but they refused to fall. "But we were talking, and all of these old feelings came rushing back. I got swept up in those feelings. We have a long history, those feelings… They are intoxicating. Things got out of hand, and before I knew it we…"

"I know," I said. "I saw."

"It was a mistake."

"A mistake?" Deimos asked. He stopped at the foot of the stairs. I recognized something in his voice. A kind of hurt. The same hurt I was feeling. "No, no. You can't say that. We had something beautiful. We were finally going to be *us* again."

"There is no us anymore, Deimos!" Hercules yelled with intense anger. He turned to him, stepping away from me. "We don't work! We tried so many times but something always gets in our way. You know this. And now, with this crusade you're on, how do you expect me to go along with that?"

"I only want my birthright!" he whined back. "I deserve to stand in my father's legacy with the man I love by my side."

"The man you love gets to choose where he stands!" Hercules shot back. "And I've made that choice. I can't get behind what you're doing. I can't let you do it. And I can't be with you. I'm with Bryn now." he looked at me with puppy-dog eyes. As if he were a victim in this. "Or at least, I hope I still can be."

"How can you even ask me that two seconds after I just caught you in bed with him?" I couldn't even begin to process the implications of that right now.

"No!" Deimos cried out. Tears ran down his face. He disappeared in a puff of blood-red smoke, reappearing directly in front of me. It all happened so fast, I had no time to react. His meaty palm wrapped around my neck, quickly and tightly, cutting off my air mid-breath. He slammed me into the wall, sending a painful vibration through my body. The collision forced the Queen's Sword to slip from my fingers. "Why does everyone I love leave me for these women? You. My father. Why am I not good enough? You saw how well we got together. How easily we fall back into each other's arms. We can have that. We can be together as long as there are no distractions."

He looked at me with a cold emptiness as he spoke. His dark eyes looked atrophied, as if he was long gone from reality itself. As I looked into the void he contained, his grip tightened. Ice cold pin pricks scattered across my entire body. "That's why Bryn has to die. And the same for all of the Amazons. My father will finally see me once they are out of the way. He'll realize the strength I have. He'll come back to me. You both will."

His face devoid of life morphed to blazing disdain so quickly that I almost didn't even recognize the shift. Grimacing teeth on top of a tight jaw, furrowed brow, veins pulsing from his forehead. Yet his eyes told a different story entirely. One of sadness. A violent stillness nestled under glossy hurt. His eyes narrowed, taking on a more menacing look but they still screamed of pain rather than anger.

One hand on his wrist and the other against his chest, I pushed against Deimos, but he would not budge, despite my strength. I struggled to pull in tiny gasps of air. "Stop this!" Hercules called out. "You want me to love you, but I can't love someone who does things like this! If you hurt her, I will never forgive you. Any love I have for you will be gone. I can promise you that."

Deimos' face softened for just a second. In that second his grip loosened slightly. I took in a deep breath and lowered my hand. The Queen's Sword jumped up and I gripped it tightly. It instantly bursted into a red light, leaving behind a small canister with the symbol of Ares embossed onto its side. I raised the canister and pressed the button on top. A red spray spritzed from the canister, falling directly into Deimos' sad eyes. As the liquid hit him, he screamed, releasing me and backing away. I heard the sizzle of his skin as he fell to his knees and desperately tried to cover his eyes with his hands.

The canister transformed into a long knife, not quite as long or heavy as a sword. I pointed the blade directly at the cowering demigod. He growled before standing again. The skin around his eyes was brown and blistering. His pupils were bloodshot. He was pissed.

I was prepared to shove my blade through his chest, but he didn't move towards me. Just as I considered making the move myself, he stepped back. He raised a hand and the doors to his penthouse opened behind us.

"Leave!" He commanded. I didn't know what to make of this sudden change of heart.

"Does this mean you're calling it all off?" Hercules asked, coming up to stand next to me.

"No," Deimos spat. "I'm just done playing games. It's over now. The final battle is upon us and this is not the right battleground. If I'm to gain the respect of my father, we need a proper fight."

"Are you saying we schedule a fight?" I asked. "You can't be serious."

"Tomorrow, at dawn," he said, completely serious. "You pick the place. You bring your army, I'll bring mine."

"D," Hercules pleaded.

"I must do this," Deimos said, his voice breaking slightly. "When this is over, you'll come around. And if you don't, at least I'll have my father."

"Fine," I agreed. I was ready to put an end to this. I had no idea if my fighting skills were at the level they needed to be, but at this moment, I didn't care. "Prospect Park. There's a field there. It should be relatively free of innocent bystanders." It was a large park broken up into sections by paths and thick trees. Macks, Lucinda, and I would picnic there a lot because it was so close to our apartment. Some parts of the park had a lot of foot traffic, and others would only experience high volumes of people when there were events being held there. It was the first place that came to mind for something like this.

Deimos scoffed. "Taking lesser beings into such consideration. You really are an Amazon." He turned away from us and began walking up the stairs. "The next time we see each other, one of us dies," he said without looking at us, as he disappeared at the top of the staircase.

I turned the Queen's Sword back into a pocketknife

and slipped it into my pocket. I quickly turned and walked to the elevator. I heard Hercules following quickly behind.

"Can we talk about this, please?" he begged as the elevator doors slid open. We both entered but I refused to engage in his request.

"I came here to try to end things peacefully, and things got out of hand," he said, in response to my silence. "I know it was wrong, and I have no excuse. It was a moment of weakness. But as far as I'm concerned, that was a final goodbye. I know now that he can't change. Trying to make him was a wasted effort."

"And all you had to do was sleep with him to figure that out," I jabbed, pushing the button to send the elevator to the lobby.

"I'm sorry," he said after a long pause. He touched the necklace around his neck. "When I came to him, he started to hear me out at first. He told me how much he missed me and he gave this to me. I thought it was a sign of change. But now, after everything I've seen, I'll keep it as a reminder that he's too far gone."

I was in no mood to accept his apology. I didn't know if I ever could. I just wanted to focus on what lies ahead. I didn't even want to comment on how strange it seemed to keep a gift from a deranged and murderous ex. If he needed a memento to remind him of the darkness in that man's heart, so be it.

"Fine," I said.

Chapter 27

"So this is it?" Lucinda asked, her voice low and grim to an extent I didn't know was possible for her. "This is truly *the* moment."

"Bryn's destiny," Miss Stone said.

"Which could very well be her execution," Lucinda snapped back.

"That doesn't really matter," I interjected.

"To hell it doesn't!" Lucinda yelled. "This is exactly what I've been trying to avoid!"

"How many times do we have to go over this," Miss Stone said, bringing a fist to her lips. "This isn't something you can stop! That should be painfully apparent by now. Fate demands it. My people's future depends on it. The safety of both the natural and supernatural world may very well hang in the balance."

"Enough you two!" I screamed, feeling a headache creeping forward. "This is not the time to have this argument, *again*. We are in this situation. It's happening right now, all around us. We don't have time to do this. We need to focus on how we are going to get through this."

"Spoken like a true leader," Miss Stone said with a small smirk.

"So, what *is* the plan?" Macks asked. They sat on the couch in our living room with Lucinda. I stood in front of them with Miss Stone, who looked out of place in my quaint living space, by my side. Hercules silently leaned against the back wall.

"His ultimate goal is to wipe out the Queen's bloodline, so no more Queens can be born," I said. "So our ultimate goal is to make sure he doesn't get the sword."

"Shouldn't our goal be to keep you alive?" Hercules asked, sounding offended by my suggested plan.

"No, that's goal number two," I answered. "The sword is a key to the Amazon homeland. If he gets it, he can go there and kill the Queen. As long as she's locked away there, there is still a chance the bloodline can continue even if I'm dead."

"Bryn," Lucinda said, her voice breaking.

"No," I told her. "This is the plan. I have a sister out there somewhere, and we have no idea if he's gotten to her or not. My birth mother is the only one we know for sure is safe."

"Okay," Hercules said softly. "If that's what you need the plan to be, I'll follow you."

"Oh, first you're cheating on her, now you're cosigning her death warrant," Lucinda scoffed. "How honorable."

"Stop," I demanded. I wasn't trying to be bogged down by anything extra. I needed to drop all of the insignificant bullshit. I let silence rest for a moment before continuing.

"I need you all to know. I have to do this, but none of you are required to fight this fight."

"What? No," Macks said, crossing their arms. "We are in this together. We're family. Not even the family you're born with, we are the family you choose. That means your fights are our fights."

"There is absolutely no way I'm going to let you face your potential death alone," Lucinda said. "I love you too much to not help you through this."

"I owe it to you, and myself, to see this through," Hercules said with a single nod. His support brought a smile to my face. I caught myself and pulled the smile back.

"As your mentor, and a woman loyal to the crown, I'll follow you into battle," Miss Stone announced. "And other Amazons will as well."

I wanted to fight against their support. I didn't want their lives to be threatened because of the cards I had been dealt. I wanted to protect them, but I knew they were all doing this for the same reason. To protect me. As much as I hated the idea of them being in danger, at the same time, my heart was full.

"He'll have an army," I said.

"That's where the Amazons come in," Miss Stone said. We'll organize. Your foot soldiers will do damage control against his own. You'll go after him directly, while all of us here run support."

"His biggest asset is his spillers," Hercules said. "But you have a demigod, Amazons, a nymph, and a sorcerex.

The unique variety at your disposal will give you the upper hand. His army can't match that."

"How are we going to keep humans out of harm's way?" Macks asked.

"Hopefully it will be early enough that we won't have to worry about people being around," I said.

"We can't bank on that. Some people go on early morning runs. Couldn't be me, but I know these people exist," Lucinda said. "And it's not just people being hurt that we should be worried about. We also need to be sure there are no witnesses in general. People seeing a magical battle of this magnitude would expose the supernatural world."

"I might know someone who can help with that," Hercules said with a flutter of excitement. He pulled out his phone and began typing a message. After a second, he placed his phone back into his pocket. He looked up at us, looking satisfied but saying nothing.

"Who?" I asked after it became clear he was not going to explain on his own.

"Me!" A bright voice exploded out of nowhere, causing me to jump slightly.

"Where did you come from?" Macks asked, clutching their chest.

Ruthie stood in our living room, where she had not been before. She wore a lime green denim dress that stopped at her upper thigh. The deep and wide V-neck cut extended all the way down to her bellybutton. A strap with a large decorative belt buckle covered her breasts. Her voluminous blonde hair neatly hung over one shoulder.

"From my house," she answered with a bubbly tone. "I heard you needed me, so I decided to pop on over."

"We are gearing up for a fight against the demigod Deimos," I told her.

"He wants to wage war against the Amazonian throne," Miss Stone added.

"Oh," Ruthie said, dragging out the word. "I'm a pacifist. My whole thing is creating safe spaces. Taking up arms to harm others is in direct opposition to my mission."

"We aren't asking you to fight," Hercules said, coming forward from his secluded corner of the room. "We need to keep the fight isolated, so no innocents get hurt."

"Ah! Keeping people safe," Ruthie squealed. "That is something I can help with."

"What are you offering?" I asked her.

"I can create pocket dimensions," she said with a grin.

"You can?"

"Of course! When you're as fabulous as me, you have sway over everything, including the universe," she said, flipping her hair. "How do you think my bar exists in multiple cities at the same time?"

"And you really expect us not to ask what kind of supernatural being you are?" Macks asked. "That sounds insanely powerful."

"Look at me, honey. Did you expect anything else?" She breezed past the question. "The thing is, like I said earlier, I don't fight. I'll help you but I'm no warrior. I will make a copy of your battleground that exists..." She struggled to find the next words before settling on what direction to go. "…somewhere else. No randoms would wander into the fight. Once the battle is over, I'll dismantle it and bring you back to real New York."

"Couldn't you just make a pocket dimension and leave him trapped there? Avoid a fight all together?" I asked her.

"I absolutely could, but he's a demigod. As a species their power varies. There's no telling if he's strong enough to escape a prison of that magnitude or not."

"If you can do this, it would be a great help." I told her.

"Of course, Doll" she said with a flutter of her long eyelashes. "The death of the Amazons spells trouble for everyone."

"We can't let some man-child with daddy issues throw the world into peril," I said.

"There's enough of that in the human world," she responded. "You just let me know when and where and I'll do what I can."

"Tomorrow at dawn," Miss Stone said.

"Sounds so dramatic," Ruthie said, shaking her head. "Then I will see you all tomorrow." She turned to me. "May the fate of the world rest firmly on your competent shoulders." She winked, disappearing into thin air as her eye closed.

"Seriously," Macks called out. "What *is* she?"

"We should get to work," Miss Stone said to me as she pulled out her phone. "I'll start reaching out to the local Amazon network. We all need to make sure our skills are honed. And we should go over every potential scenario we can imagine, and make plans to counter them."

"Right," Hercules said. "Like studying the night before the big exam."

As Miss Stone began to make calls, the rest of us gathered around our dining table. We had been brainstorming for two hours when there was a knock on our door. We knew exactly who it was. I had called them, and after hearing what was happening they insisted on coming by. I was thankful for that.

I went to the door and pulled it open. Before me, the door frame acting as a picture frame, was a living portrait of my family.

My mother was beside my father, her eyes soft and her lips smiling, but I could tell she was fighting back tears. My father, with deep brown skin and a balding head, gave me a toothy grin. My little brother stood centered in front of them, with my father's hand on his shoulder as if to keep him from slipping away, despite the fact that his attention was completely absorbed into his handheld gaming system.

"Oh, Muñequita," my father exhaled. Releasing my brother, he came to me like rainfall. He wrapped his arms around me, and I returned the gesture without a word, embracing the comfort of my father's presence. My mother joined in, encasing me in a paternal cocoon.

"You guys act like you're never going to see her again," my brother said. I could practically hear his eyes rolling.

"Mateus!" Lucinda sang from the table.

"What's up, little man?" Macks tacked on. He ran into the apartment, straight to my housemates, excitedly telling Macks about the movie he watched last night.

He didn't know about my strength. It was a secret we all kept from him, originally because he was too young to trust with it. We always imagined telling him one day, but the day never came. When you've kept a secret for so long, sometimes you get too comfortable.

To him, this was an ordinary visit to his big sister. He had no idea this was a potential goodbye.

***

"There's this guy in my class," Mateus said with his head lying on my shoulder.

"Yeah?" I asked. My mother had made an industrial-sized pot of pozole, and we all had feasted. Even Miss Stone indulged in a meal and conversation. Now we all sat in a food haze. Lucinda, Mateus, and I sat on the couch, Macks on the floor next to us, and Hercules in the nearby sofa chair. Miss Stone and my parents sat at our dinner table, having their own conversation.

"Yeah. I never really talked to him before but we have been going to school together for years," he continued. "Well, this year, he came to school as a boy instead of a girl. And all of the girls he used to hang out with suddenly stopped talking to him."

"Oh," I said, physically recoiling. "I didn't know kids still did that."

"Aren't you guys supposed to be super progressive?" Lucinda asked.

"Not these girls, apparently," he sighed. "So anyway, I started hanging out with him. And now we're like best buds. I guess I'm kind of like his Macks."

"That's beautiful," Macks said with a beaming smile.

"I'm proud of you Bud," I said, bringing my hand up to pat his cheek. He reluctantly accepted the display of affection.

"You sound like a good kid," Hercules said. Mateus was the best kid. Only ten years old and wise beyond his years. Not only was he killing it in school, but he had a genuine thirst for knowledge outside of his required learning. You could talk to him about anything, and he'd hold his own, no matter how obscure the subject.

He had a kind heart. So many people I knew growing up were constantly at odds with their siblings. Our relationship never seemed to waver. Our mom used to say I was his favorite person. "He wasn't a mommy's boy or a daddy's boy. From the second he was born, he was just Bryn's baby brother."

I was always thankful I came out around the same time he was born. He has only ever known me as me. As Bryn. As his sister. He had such a big heart. If I never came out all those years ago and came out tomorrow, I'm sure he'd accept me as a sister with his entire being. The thought of what was coming was especially hard to imagine because if it went wrong, he'd lose me. Without warning and in the dark. I'd lose him. I'd lose everyone. All of the people who hold a piece of my heart.

Mateus sat up and squinted at Hercules. "Kids at my school didn't believe me when I said my sister was dating a celebrity," he said, sounding accusatory.

Hercules just laughed. I decided not to burden my little

brother with our complicated relationship status. Even if I wanted to, I didn't know what I would say because I didn't even know where we stood. So, I would just let him think we were together. Maybe because that's what I wanted.

"Why are you telling kids about who I'm dating?" I jabbed him with my elbow.

"Do you know how many girls have *him* as their cellphone wallpaper?" he said dramatically. "I wasn't going to pass up on that kind of credibility." Lucinda and Macks started cackling.

"Well, how about we take a selfie?" Hercules offered. "That way you have proof."

"Can we?" Mateus asked, jumping up and sitting on the arm of his chair. He pulled out his phone and gave it to Hercules. The two of them began to pose for all sorts of photos, smiling and silly-faced, as Miss Stone stood up from the table.

"Thank you so much for the meal," she said to my mother. "I should probably be going. Lots to prepare." She turned to me. "Enjoy your time with your family. I'll see you tomorrow morning."

I nodded. My parents said their goodbyes and she showed herself out. I stood up from the couch and made my way to the table. As I sat, my mother's hand reached for mine. I placed my fingers in her grasp, and my father asked, "How are you holding up?" His voice was soft but sturdy.

"I'm terrified," I told them. Saying the word out loud gave me permission to feel and brought a rush shooting from my core up into my chest. "I have no idea what tomorrow will bring. And I really don't want to…" I couldn't bring myself to finish the sentence.

"You won't," my mother said with confidence.

"You haven't seen what he's capable of," I told her, fighting back tears. "He's a demigod. You can't even imagine."

"That doesn't matter," my dad said, shaking his head. "You are strong. I believe in you, without a doubt."

"My strength might not be enough," I said. I appreciated his unwavering fatherly sensibilities, but at this moment it felt delusional. "It wasn't enough to save other Amazons in the past."

"Not your physical strength," my mom said, tightening her grip on my hand. "You are the bravest girl I've ever met. You have the strength to chase your dreams, to live your truth, to accept the impossible and still find a way to thrive, to do what's right even when it's hard. I could see it in you from the very beginning. When I looked at that little baby and suddenly felt I could do anything with her in my life, I knew she had to be mine. And every day, that feeling persists. Knowing you, there is no doubt in our minds. Your courage will carry you through."

I hoped to God my parent's vision of me would reign true tomorrow. I had no reason to doubt their belief. No one in this world knew me better, knew me more fully, than the man and woman who raised me. If they looked at me and saw a woman of courage and strength, then that is exactly who I was. And I would walk into battle holding their confidence in my heart.

Chapter 28

I looked at the stained-glass windows of the outdoor subway platform. The hint of light that signaled the coming of dawn clung to the mosaic shards. Macks, Lucinda, Hercules, and I stood in silence as the train approached to carry us towards danger. We sat in the empty seats, minds absorbed in the unknown.

"Riding the subway into battle was not on my bingo card," Lucinda said, breaking the silence.

"I don't know," Hercules sighed. "Better than the horse-drawn chariots from the old days. Less horse shit."

And with that, tensions broke. For just a moment the three of us were laughing. Hercules and Lucinda went back and forth comparing life today with their many years throughout history. After a few stories and subway stops, we had arrived. We walked as morning darkness became daylight, and the sidewalk was met by lush greenery. Deep into the park, we arrived at a wide circular clearing, surrounded by a ring of trees arranged like the walls of an arena. One single tree in the rounded perimeter had bright red leaves, looking out of place with its green leafed companions. I hoped to god, or perhaps *the* gods, that it wasn't some sort of omen.

In the center of the field, Ruthie stood in a blue dress that flowed in the breeze. Miss Stone waited with her, wearing black pants and a dark shirt with a leather trench coat. She looked bad ass.

"Ready, Doll?" Ruthie asked as we approached.

"I don't think I can ever be ready for this," I sighed.

"You're ready," Miss Stone said. "And you have us with you."

"Remember your training," Hercules said in my ear. Feeling the warmth of his breath on my neck made me long for him and the way we were just two days ago. When I could turn and kiss him without hesitation. When I didn't have the image of his betrayal in my mind.

"Does everyone know their role to play?" Miss Stone asked.

"Thankfully, Bryn picked a park," Lucinda said. "I'm surrounded by nature, in my element."

"Lucinda and I will focus on his foot soldiers," Macks added.

"You and I will protect Bryn," Hercules said to Miss Stone. He wore a long gray plaid trench coat over a top that gave the impression of chain mail, and I wondered if it was practical or aesthetic.

"And that will hopefully give me enough opportunity to land a killing blow," I said.

"And we have some of our Amazons that are in the

NYPD patrolling the park, keeping people away from this area," Miss Stone said.

"And I'll do my thang," Ruthie said with enthusiasm. "Closing off the fighters in a private cosmic space, just to be extra safe."

"And what about the Amazons that are supposed to fight with us?" I asked.

"We are here," I heard a voice say behind me.

I turned to see Karmen and Bebe walking towards us. They looked like they just stepped out of a history book. Metal chest plates sat over tunic-like dresses. Boots with protective plating ran up their legs, while the same plating sat on their forearms.

"We've gathered as many as we could under short notice," Bebe said. She held a large oblong shield with an intricate design of lines and curves.

"We hope it will be helpful to you," Karmen said. They had a long pointed spear strapped to their back. Behind them, in the distance, multiple figures entered the clearing. A few dozen women and fems, some adorned in armor, some draped in their own tunics, and others in jeans and T-shirts. All carrying various weaponry.

The air vibrated as we all stood together. There was an energy present, and I felt it wash over me. A feeling of comfort and unwavering strength. With every breath I took, it was like sunshine was racing through my veins. Was this what it truly meant to be an Amazon?

"Now that everyone is here," Ruthie said. "I'll prepare myself." She bowed her head and stepped off to the side.

Raising her hands slightly in front of her, she closed her eyes and began to concentrate. I could hear her muttering under her breath, just quiet enough to not make out any words. Or perhaps the words weren't in a language my mind was able to register.

"Macks, Lucinda. Please come with me," Miss Stone said before addressing me. "I know this is probably overwhelming. I'll brief your fighters on what to expect, you just focus on your victory." She walked towards the small army, joined by Karmen and Bebe, with Macks and Lucinda close behind.

I didn't know how to focus on victory. All I could focus on was how real and final everything felt. The fact that my friends were willing to go to battle for me sizzled in my mind. The sight of soldiers ready to march behind me was hard to ignore. Images of my family waiting for me, with fear for the worst in their hearts, ran through my mind. I needed to win for them.

As my brain spiraled, thinking of my purpose, Hercules pulled me to the side. He said, "This isn't the first time I've fought alongside the Amazons."

"I know," I said, sounding more cold than I intended.

"But did you know the Amazons I was connected to were your family?" he asked. "Your direct ancestors."

"No, I didn't know," I said.

"I knew Hippolyta; the second Queen, daughter of the first; Otrera," he told me. "One of my labors was to help rescue her sister. The two of us rode into battle together, side by side, just like you and I are today."

"Why are you telling me this?" There was something interesting about him knowing my ancestor, but I didn't know how immortal fun facts were supposed to help us now.

"You remind me a lot of her," he said with a smile. "She was nervous about her position and upholding her mother's legacy. But she cared so deeply for her people and her family, just like you care for your friends and a whole race of people you barely know. And she let that carry her through battle. And I think if she could see you now, she'd be proud. All of your ancestors, and even your mother, would be so proud of what you're doing today."

A warmth bubbled in my chest. "Thank you. That means a lot." I wasn't afraid to admit that I didn't know what I was doing. I didn't know if I had what it took to be Queen. Hell, I didn't know if I even wanted to be Queen. But I understood the importance of it all. I knew it was the right thing. I knew that every woman before me was full of righteous purpose, and if they looked at me and saw someone who was also worthy of that, I'd do my best to live up to their legacy.

"When this is over," Hercules said before stopping, choking on his words. "We...can we...we should try again. Let me earn back your trust."

I reached for the necklace that sat above his chest. My fingers grazed the smooth surface of the jewelry, feeling the hard muscles underneath. If this trinket could pose as a reminder of Deimos' inability to change, it could also stand as a symbol of Hercules' dedication to making things right.

I didn't know if it was possible, but I wanted it to be, so I was willing to try.

His hand raised, meeting mine at his chest. He took my fingers into his palm, replacing my grasp on the necklace with an embrace of our fingers. He leaned closer. His supple lips parted my own. His tongue danced in my mouth, and I fell into him. His free arm wrapped around my waist. I felt a moment of peace, a break from the chaos. I allowed myself to be lost in him for just a moment. And I forgot about the perils that surrounded me.

"Excuse me." Miss Stone's voice pulled me back into reality. Hercules and I separated, looking at each other.

"Now you have to survive this," he whispered to me. He turned and joined the army that had formed.

"Any moment now," Miss Stone said. "I wanted to check in on you. How are you feeling?"

"I'm trying to be confident. There's a lot of people who believe in me, and that helps," I said. "But I don't know if it's enough. I know that as a daughter of Ares, I should be ready for war. But I don't know if I am."

Miss Stone laughed, which shook me more than anything I could have anticipated. "Ares is not just the god of war," she said with a bright smile. "He's also the god of courage. And you have embodied that virtue tenfold."

"My parents said something similar last night," I told her.

"Because the people close to you see what you bring to the table," she said, placing her hands on my shoulders. "And that's not all you bring. The Amazons are descended from Ares but we follow two other gods as well. Athena, goddess of wisdom, and Artemis goddess of purity. Their virtues are also tools we bring with us into battle. As long as you're courageous in spirit, of wise mind, and pure of heart, you embody what it means to be an Amazon."

"Do you remember how nymphs act in service of a god?" I heard Lucinda ask as she stepped forward. "Artemis is the goddess I serve. She is the one who sent me to look after you."

"And the oracle that foresaw your destiny, and advised I take the sword to train you, spoke on behalf of Athena," Miss Stone added. "Ares created you, Athena guides you, and Artemis protects you."

Knowing that these powerful forces have been working behind the scenes, with faith in me, ensuring that I would be ready for this moment, was surreal. That coupled with the people who stood by me without a second thought, and the family who loved me so fully, made me feel like I could do anything. This has been brewing for so long. Every step I've ever taken was always bringing me here. I was ready. I had to be.

I looked at all of the faces that stood before me. I searched for the words to express my newfound sense of being. Before I could address this newly formed army, there was movement on the other side of the field. I didn't see it, but I felt the encroaching darkness. And I saw the faces of Amazons harden. I saw Lucinda and Macks' faces contort with worry. I saw Hercules stiffen as if to protect himself from an invisible attack.

I turned to see Deimos walking across the field, a mob of countless bodies twisting and contorting behind him. They were still, not following. Just lying in wait.

"Looks like no monsters," Macks gulped. "Just spillers."

"I'd rather monsters," I said, pulling out my pocketknife. With a flash of red light, it grew and transformed into a sword in my hands.

Ruthie lifted her head, ending her meditation. "It's now or never." She brought her hands together and twirling ribbons of colorless light materialized, weaving in between each of her fingers. "Good luck, and I'll see you on the other side." She raised her hands, guiding the light upward as if releasing a bird. The mystical energy erupted into the sky, raining down in a domed shape, stretching past the bordering trees. The dome of energy quickly began to move inward, imploding on itself. It blew past the mob of spillers, flowed through the army of Amazons, and swept by Deimos and myself. Moving in all directions, it came together at a single point. The light collided with Ruthie in a bright flash, and in a second, she was gone.

Nothing felt different. I didn't feel like I had been moved. And the area around me was still a clearing in the park. Although the more I examined the surrounding area, the more it became clear that whatever she did had worked.

Just past the ring of trees, where more trees and bicycle paths should sit, there was nothing. Just an emptiness, like the haze in your eyes as you fall asleep. I looked at the sky above us and instead of a morning blue with emerging sunshine, there was a midnight-purple expanse. Swirling balls of gaseous fire in a rainbow of colors decorated the new sky. Planetary bodies with swirling rings floated in the distance, with shooting stars flying in all directions.

I wanted to marvel at the sight, but there was no time. The enemy approached.

Deimos, dressed in a knight black three-piece suit, moved like a shadow across the greenery. The only color on him was a blood-red tie. He stopped just a few feet away, glaring directly into my eyes. Anger swirled across his face. I took a deep breath, embracing what was to come.

Lucinda and Macks stood on either side of me, While Hercules joined Macks on my left and Miss Stone joined Lucinda on my right.

"No matter what happens," Macks began.

"We are with you to the very end," Lucinda finished.

"Is this your vanguard," Deimos scoffed. He looked over my shoulder, eyes narrowing at the Amazons behind me. "And your tiny army."

"The size of an army doesn't matter," I said. "We're stopping you, no matter how big or small."

His eyes lowered to the sword in my hands. "I tire of you. Today you take your last breath and I take *my* birthright. And with the key in my hand, I will walk into the land of the Amazons and run the Queen through with her own sword."

Rolling murmurs of discontent could be heard behind me but no one moved.

"This is your last chance to stop this," I said. "No one

needs to die here." It felt right to offer him the chance, even though I knew in my bones he wouldn't take it.

"You can be so much more than a grudge-fueled genocide," Hercules said.

Deimos snapped his head to the side, looking at Hercules with disdain. "My eternal life is full of emptiness!" he screamed. "You of all people should know what it is like to have to go through a life in the shadow of a god that turned his back on you after creating you!"

"I do!" Hercules snapped back. "And I'm better for it! I would never kill because of it."

"You don't understand my vision," Deimos whined. "I deserve more, I deserve my father's recognition! If I were to walk away from that, what do I have?" He was practically foaming at the mouth. "No..." His voice grew quiet and hauntingly still. "This must be done."

He raised a hand, looking at me with empty eyes. He spoke one single word, softly as he closed his fingers into a fist. "Attack."

The mob in the distance lurched forward. Screaming vessels of anger and fear ran forward, warbling as black sludge spilled from their faces. Some of them had the signs of being too far gone, the ghost-white hair and dark red veins stretching across their entire bodies. Others retained their normal hair color and their corrupted veins only on their faces.

"Remember, we save those who we can," I called out to my allies. "And those who are too far gone, end it quickly and mercifully."

"Forward! With the guidance of Athena, the blessing of Artemis, and the might of Ares," Miss Stone called out.

The crowd of Amazons behind her echoed, "With the might of Ares!" And with that, they ran forward, passing my friends and me to meet the enemy on the field. Waves of bodies clashed together in battle like a storming sea.

Deimos stood before us, as the chaos unfolded behind him. His stillness etched fear into my heart. Two white-haired spillers lunged forth, breaking through the battle ahead. Lucinda raised a hand, and two tendrils shot up from the ground, wrapping them tightly until they produced an audible crack. The vines dropped the lifeless bodies to the ground.

Deimos reached for the Queen's Sword, but I jumped backward. Hercules slid forward, punching him square in the jaw. Deimos tumbled as three more spillers came forward. Miss Stone summoned her circular blades and sliced through two of them with ease.

The straggler was swept up by a buzzing yellow swarm and thrown to the side. The swarm of bees shifted life a flower blowing in the wind.

"I've been reading up on bugs since discovering what I am. I've learned some useful stuff," Macks said to Deimos as he found his footing. "Did you know when a hornet invades a beehive, the bees band together to roast it alive with their body heat? I wonder what happens when you apply sorcerex magic to that defense tactic." The swarm of bees morphed their shape, flying in a spiral formation all around us. They flew close to the ground, spinning until the blades of grass sparked with flame. They rose upward, creating a wall of fire around the six of us. The sounds of wails and battle cries poured through the flames along with heat.

"Smart," Deimos spat. "But your little magic tricks won't save your friend."

"But It'll help keep some of your soldiers away," Macks said.

Suddenly, Hercules wrapped his arms around Deimos, pinning his hands to his side. "Do it now!" he commanded.

I raised my sword and lunged forward. As the tip approached Deimos' chest, he let out a cry and his body exploded with red lightning. The energy barreled off of him, pushing us all in various directions. I fell back, nearly landing in the flames behind me. We were all on the ground in the ring of fire, with Deimos left as the only one standing, free of Hercules' grasp. He ran forward and I pushed myself from the ground as quickly as I could. He lashed out his arm straight at my head. I called my strength to collect at my forehead, feeling the burn of protection. His fist collided with me without pain, stopping him in his tracks.

The buzzing bees, raging fire, and fighting on the other side of the flames filled the air with sound. The sword in my hand turned to a shorter, slightly curved blade. I pulled it upward, slicing at his arm. He jumped back, wincing in pain as blood spilled through his ripped sleeve. Within seconds, Hercules was on his feet too. Rapid-fire fists fell onto Deimos. He blocked the punches with his good arm.

Lucinda pulled more roots from the ground. They

began whipping at Deimos, tearing his clothes to ribbons. Miss Stone threw her circular blades, and they glided towards his head. Just before impact, he was swept away by a puff of maroon-colored smoke, sending her blades through the surrounding fire.

"Damn it," I groaned.

"It's okay," Hercules said, panting from exhaustion. He must have been putting all of his strength into those punches. "He couldn't have gotten far."

"We are in a pocket dimension that consists of just this field," Miss Stone said. Macks twirled their fingers, and the buzzing bees scattered, disappearing into the sky as the towering flames fizzled out.

As the flames died down, I saw the Amazons scattered around the field over vanquished spillers. The pillar of smoke zipped through the air, circling like a vulture. It swooped down into the center of the field. Deimos stood there, wide eyed and brandished teeth. He threw out his hands in various directions, releasing bolts of red lightning. Pairs of Amazon warriors were struck with each blast, each seemingly too quick to dodge. He turned his focus on Macks and Lucinda. Before I knew it, he had fired. There was no time for me to get in front of them.

My sword took its normal shape, and I pointed it forward. The blast of lightning took a sharp turn, finding my blade's magnetic lure. The lightning clung to the metal and sunk into it like water to a sponge.

"Thanks," Lucinda gasped, clinging to Macks.

Miss Stone's twin blades flew through the air and

found their way into her hands. "You two, check on the others. Hercules and I will keep him busy and give Bryn time to find her opening." Without a word, Macks and Lucinda began running to the Amazons that sprawled across the grass, one by one.

Deimos ran forward, disappearing in red smoke and reappearing behind me. Before I had time to react, he grabbed my wrist. His grip was like fire against my skin. He tried to jerk the sword from my fingers. Miss Stone swung a blade at his head, but he ducked and weaved. Hercules kicked him in the gut. He grunted and doubled over but his grip remained strong. I yelled and attempted to pull away from him. As I yanked, the sword released the stored energy, throwing Deimos onto his back. He looked up at me with a growl. I raised the sword and brought it down, just for him to roll out of the way.

The sword plunged into the earth and suddenly he tackled me. We both tumbled to the ground, leaving the sword sticking out of the dirt. He was on top of me. He raised a fist, sparking with his crimson energy, and brought it down into my face. Flaming pain splintered across my entire body. He raised it again. This time, before he could land the next blow, I punched him in his throat. He gagged and choked for air. I slammed the palm of my hand into his chest with a thunderous clap, sending him flying backward.

"You bitch!" he screamed, still laying on the ground. He rose to his feet as if lifted by a sudden gust of wind. He clenched his fists closed and strings of red lighting fell from his hands. Not energy blasts this time. It was like he held physical objects. Ropes of fear energy in his hand. He threw each hand out before I could reach my sword. Miss Stone and Hercules were each wrapped up by the coiling energy. I heard groans of pain as they struggled to keep standing. "This isn't how my story ends."

As he spoke the words, the perimeter of the clearing began to move with life. More white-haired spillers came from behind the trees. They walked slowly, as if they lacked full control of their bodies, but after they came fully into view they broke out into full sprints. They were coming in fast from all directions. Deimos let out a deep bellowing chuckle that seemed to echo in the air.

I ran to my sword, freeing it from the ground. spillers jumped on Hercules and Miss Stone, still bound by their mystical chains. Four of them clawed at Macks as they dodged the swipes. Two had managed to grab Lucinda by the arms while a third wrapped its hands around her neck. Other spillers launched themselves onto the downed Amazons from Deimos' previous attack. With them too weak to defend themselves, the spillers began tearing into them.

And with the frenzy around me, I held my sword, ready to swing. But to my surprise, nothing was coming for me. Deimos stood, hunched over slightly, watching me as one single spiller approached me. It walked slowly instead of running.

Red lines stretched and splintered across brown skin. Black blood dripped from a gaping mouth. Ghostly white curls stretched in every direction. Blacked out eyes stared lifelessly at me.

"No!" Macks screamed as spillers piled on top of them, pulling them to the ground. But they weren't screaming about their attackers, they were upset by the spiller in front of me.

My friend stood before me, so far corrupted by anger and fear that there was no life left. A vessel of corruption. An incurable tool in a demigod's war. I tried to call out to her, as if my voice could cure the infection, but my voice broke into a whisper. "London..."

Chapter 29

"This can't be happening," Macks cried, struggling under violent bodies.

"No," I heard Miss Stone gasp as she took in the scene. "The only way through corruption this far gone is death. He wants to torment us, make us do something we can't come back from."

My mind was in mayhem. I hated myself at that moment. London was targeted to hurt me. She was a pawn in his twisted game because I let her get too close. Now she was gone, and I had to do something unthinkable. Was this what it truly meant to be an Amazon? War and loss and impossible choices?

"We are *not* doing this!" Macks yelled, kicking a spiller off of them and wiggling out from the others. "Bryn, you need to find a way to save her, I swear to god." There was a rigidness to Macks I had never seen before. Anger and determination poured off of them.

They put their arms to their side, palms facing forward. The skin of each palm suddenly ripped open. From the bloody void, large gray bugs flew into the air. A single bug flew to each and every spiller, except for London. As each insect burrowed into their target, the spillers immediately went stiff. They made jagged convulsions before dropping to the ground, paralyzed.

As if activated by the recent development, London began sprinting directly at me. She screamed a bloodcurdling wail that turned my bones to ice. I tightened the grip of my sword, unsure of what move to make.

Lucinda, now freed, came up beside me. She scooped her hand forward and nature responded. Blades of grass grew instantly into a patch of tall greenery between us and London. As she passed through the tall grass, the blades wrapped around her like the bandages. She was cocooned from the neck down, unable to move or break free. "This should buy us some time," she said.

Deimos limped forward, stopping by London's side. He looked at us all with twisted joy. "You're weak. I turn one person into my soldier and you're hesitating. This is why you people are undeserving of my father. He needs someone who will stop at nothing to act in his name! That is what I can offer him. I am his son! His blood runs through my veins! His power is embedded in my bones. The same power that allows me to do this." He caressed London's face. She twitched at his touch, releasing a growling purr as black blood poured from her lips. She looked nothing like herself. She was absent. Alien. A shell of the girl I knew. "And what do you have Bryn Gonzales-Ortiz? Human attachment. A distant relation to a god you don't deserve. None of his power, just a sword you use to steal it."

He was right. I was far removed from Ares. I had no

claim to the same amount of power that Deimos did. I only siphon it. But he was also wrong. These truths weren't a hindrance. These truths can be used against him. I had a weapon that absorbed Ares' power, the same power Deimos had. The power he used to corrupt innocent people with fear to create his soldiers.

"Give me the sword." He held out his hand with a devilish smile. "Accept the fact that you cannot win."

I didn't know how to do this, I didn't know if it would even work, but I knew I had to at least try. I raised the sword towards his outstretched hand. As he softened in anticipation, I quickly raised it higher in the air. It transformed into an ax, and I brought it down with all my might. He screamed in pain as he jumped backwards, and half of his forearm fell straight to the ground. He looked back and forth from me to the blood pouring from the space where his hand should be. He brought his remaining hand to the wound and his fingers sparked with his lightning. He groaned through his teeth as his flesh burned, stopping the bleeding.

My sword turned back into its original form, and I raised it above my head. I took all of my focus, all of my strength, out of my body and lent it to the sword. I felt her hum in my hand, like an engine coming to life. Red sparks started to form on London's skin, as well as the bodies of all the incapacitated spillers. The binds that held Hercules and Miss Stone began to writhe. With the sword and I thinking as one, I gave the mental command. Streams of red light pulled off of every spiller, Hercules, and Miss Stone.

As the corrupted energy filled the sword, the color came back to London's hair. The black slime falling from her face slowly turned red. The veins that engrossed her body began to recede. Black eyes faded as she lost consciousness. She fell limp, gently released by Lucinda's grassy grasp. Macks dropped to their knees, grabbing London in their arms. She was herself again.

One by one, each white-haired spiller around us regained themselves before passing out. Miss Stone and Hercules were released from their confinement, the ropes being sucked into my blade. After all of the energy was pulled, I lowered the sword. Its black blade was glowing as red as molten rock.

"What did you just do?" Hercules asked with amazement.

"The impossible," Miss Stone answered, without hesitation.

Deimos looked around with heavy and panicked breaths. Without a word, he looked at me and raised his hand. His palm glowed bright, almost blinding, and he released a continuous stream of dark red energy. The Queen's Sword released its own bolt of energy. My stream of fiery red lightning collided against his. We held each other at a stalemate, our energy beams pushing against each other. Stray sparks bounced around us in all directions. I could feel it like a physical strain on my body. I wondered if I'd run out of the energy I had just collected before I could put an end to him.

Worry crept across my body as I searched my mind for

any ounce of strength I could find. Miss Stone attempted to throw her blades at Deimos, but a branch of energy bounced her weapons back into her hands.

I thought about the strength the Amazons had, the strength of all of the Amazons who fought alongside us, the strength we all shared. A strength that was part of me.

I felt hands bracing my body, holding me steady. Lucinda and Macks were with me, giving an extra boost. They were making sure I stood tall, something they do spiritually as well as physically. The two of them would never let me fall. They were the embodiment of the support you can only get from friends and community. For as long as I've known them, I thought our community was as People of Color, as trans people, as queer people. But we were that and so much more now.

Feeling everyone with me, by my side, I funneled our collective strength into one final burst. I let out a cathartic scream, expelling all of my mental energy. The glowing red energy between Deimos and I flashed bright, lighting up the dark. Deep pink energy flooded from the Queen's Sword, completely devouring Deimos' red energy, stretching closer and closer, until it collided with him.

Pink flames engulfed his body, throwing him backwards. As the energy cleared, he laid on the ground, covered in burns and scars. His suit had burned off and nearly melted into his skin. The left side of his face was torn and blackened.

I could feel the sword's power level lowering back to its

normal rate. I had expelled everything I had stolen from him, plus my own generated energy.

"It's over," I said, looking at the broken man sprawled out on his back.

"You've done it," Miss Stone said. I could hear the smile in her voice. "Our people don't have to hide anymore. We can go home."

"What's going to happen to him?" Hercules asked, looking down at Deimos as he let out a groaning whimper.

"I suppose we'll have him imprisoned," Miss Stone said. "In his weakened state, it shouldn't be hard to contain him."

"Good," Macks said. They were on the ground by London's side, cradling her in their arms. "The bastard deserves it."

Suddenly, Lucinda's arms were around me in a tight embrace that took the wind out of me. I dropped my sword and returned the hug, overcome with an astonishing feeling of peace.

"I'm so glad you survived," she said in tears.

"Did you doubt me?" I asked with a chuckle.

"No, never." She sobbed more joyous tears. "I doubted him."

"We should check on the rest of the Amazons and rescued spillers and tend to the survivors," Hercules said. Lucinda pulled away from me and wiped the tears from her face. She went to examine the fallen, and Hercules came to me. "I've never seen anything like that before."

"I didn't even know I could do it," I told him.

"What did you do exactly?" he asked.

"I think I called on the sisterhood of the Amazons," I said. "But also…" I struggled to find the words. "Not just the Amazons."

"You took the sense of community the Amazons derive strength from," Miss Stone said, looking up into the purple sky. "And you expanded on it, made it your own. Your found family made you much stronger than he could have ever anticipated."

"Has anyone ever done that before?" I asked.

"Not that I'm aware of," Miss Stone said with pride.

"That's why you were chosen," Hercules said. "You're special, Bryn. That heart of yours is a big part of that."

"A pure heart," Miss Stone said. "A wise mind, and a courageous spirit. I knew you—"

Miss Stone's face suddenly grew grim, like the flip of a switch, the light was drained from her. Crimson light piercing her torso began to fade as she fell to her knees. Hercules caught her, pulling her close before laying her gently on the ground. Blood began leaking from her chest and pooling from the corners of her mouth. Deimos still laid on his back, his remaining hand extended towards us, glowing red.

"No," I breathed. My body collapsed. I fell on my hands and knees. Miss Stone gasped, struggling to bring in air. The deep brown color of her skin was beginning to dull. She looked up at me, trying to speak. "You have to do something," I pleaded to Hercules.

"I don't know what to do," he said in a panic. His hand pressed against her wound, her blood staining his skin.

There was movement behind me. Just as I turned, I saw Deimos' mangled body standing, his face straining as he moved, and his fingers wrapped around the handle of the Queen's Sword. He smiled, and even that looked painful for him.

"This is why you can't win!" He screamed, pointing the sword at me. I let my guard down before the conflict had been purely resolved. A stupid mistake. Now he had the sword. And Miss Stone… "You think your love gives you strength but it makes you weak."

"You son of a—" Hercules spoke but was cut off by Deimos.

"I love him, but it would never stop me from what must be done." He stumbled on his feet. The sword wobbled through the air as he moved. "I'm going to enjoy watching him mourn you." He stumbled forward, thrusting the tip of the sword at my throat. I ducked down, causing him to miss and continue stumbling forward.

I raised my fist, punching him in the gut. He fumbled backwards slightly, hanging on tightly to the sword. My body filled with red hot anger. So much that it physically hurt. I brought myself to my feet and swung. My fist hit his chest, forcing a grunt of pain from him.

Macks and Lucinda were suddenly next to me.

Lucinda raised a hand, pointing at him. Leaves fell from the surrounding trees, flying over in the wind. They circled him in a tight whirlwind formation. As they swung by him, they sliced him like knives. Macks raised both hands and a brigade of spiders seemed to materialize out of nowhere. Each tiny creature spun a string of web, weaving together to create a thick rope. The silky rope wrapped around his wrist, tethering his sword armed hand, making him incapable of swinging.

Lucinda's leaves cleared and I approached without a second thought. I placed one hand on his damaged shoulder and the other on the elbow of his intact arm. I pushed on his shoulder while pulling on the bend of his arm, until I heard the splintering crack of bone. He screamed as his fingers released the sword. Before it landed on the grass it flew upward, and I released Deimos and allowed it to find its way into my hands. I raised the sword, ready to plunge it into him.

"Wait!" he called out. "I surrender! Please, I will give it all up. I can accept defeat, just let me live. I can't go out like this, I would be a stain on my father's name to be slain in battle by an inferior enemy."

"Even pleading for your life, you're still an ass!" I spat. But looking at him, I noticed something haunting. He wasn't trying to be disparaging. He was genuinely afraid for his life. I didn't know the demigod of fear was capable of the emotion himself. He looked fragile and weak. Both emotionally and physically. He genuinely had no fight left in him.

I looked over to Miss Stone, still resting in Hercules' arms while he worked to minimize blood loss. Looking at her and back at Deimos, I was reminded of something Miss Stone said.

"Murder is an unnecessary act that comes from anger, not duty for the greater good."

I gazed upon this man; beaten, bound, and surrendered. I knew what Miss Stone would want me to do. But I also knew Miss Stone would never want anything again. I knew that I had barely gotten a chance to know her. And even though I hadn't learned much about her, I also knew she wanted to go home more than anything in this world. I knew that was no longer possible for her. And I couldn't let that go unpunished.

I drove my sword through Deimos' chest. I felt it pierce his flesh and slide through his innards. The crack of his ribs vibrated on my blade. His eyes widened in shock before falling dim and empty. The sword ripped through his back and stuck into the dirt, impaling him, propping his lifeless body like a lawn decoration.

I left him and the sword there and returned to my fallen mentor.

"Elizabeth," I called to her. She looked up at me weakly. She reached for my hand. As we touched, I couldn't help but notice that she was bone cold.

"You didn't have to do that," she wheezed. "He surrendered."

"There was no guarantee that he'd stay true to that," I told her. "And he... He hurt you. He didn't deserve a second chance."

"Bryn," she said softly, breathing slowly. "If you're to be Queen, you need to do better."

"I'm getting justice for you," I tried to explain.

"Promise me," she coughed. "Promise me you'll be better. Be the Queen I know you can be."

"I can be," tears fell from my face. I felt more bodies move to surround us. Lucinda and Macks. Bebe and Karmen, too weak to walk on their own, assisting each other. Along with five Amazons I couldn't name. "Please, someone," I sobbed. "Someone has to help her! There has to be something we can do."

"There is something I can do," a voice said. A new onlooker joined the crowd. Ceci stood above me, draped in a thin black gown.

"What are you doing here?" I asked, surprised to see her.

"I've been here, watching the whole time," she said with a soft smile. She reached down and brushed a single tear from my wet face. "I've been a bird in these trees since you arrived here."

I didn't bother to suggest that she should have helped us fight. That wasn't important now. "Can you help her?"

Without a word, Ceci walked to Deimos' body and pulled the sword free. What was left of him fell to the ground with a soft thud. She produced a small glass vial from a pocket in her gown. She held up the sword, tip facing downward and held the vial underneath. Blood fell from the blade, collecting in the glass receptacle. She then walked back to Elizabeth. Hercules stood up, offering her space to work, but I stayed. I refused to leave her.

Elizabeth tried to speak through labored breaths, but no words would form. "No, no," Ceci said with a nurturing tone. She held the vial of blood just under Elizabeth's face. "It's okay, just breathe. Breathe and let go."

After Elizabeth pulled in one last short breath, she exhaled a silver mist that seemed to float on the memory of her. Her hand fell away from mine, leaving her two silver rings in my palm. And with that, she was gone. Any semblance of Elizabeth Stone no longer rested in the body I grasped. The mist sat in the air between us for a short moment before gliding into Ceci's vial. She quickly closed the bottle with a fastened lid connected to a leather chord.

"How does this help her?" I asked, a sense of worry clawing at my ankles.

"It doesn't," Ceci said with a laugh as she put on the vial like a necklace. "I said I could do something, not help her."

"What do you mean?" I asked, anger and panic building around me.

"Ceci, what's going on?" Macks asked.

Still holding the sword, she says, "the blood of Ares, which is only potent enough if from him or his child, and the last breath of an Amazon, which I thought I'd collect from Bryn. But I'm not one to complain about a change of plan."

"What are you talking about," Lucinda asked with venom in her voice.

"Those sounded like ingredients," Bebe said, limping forward.

"Now, now," Ceci warned, holding up the sword. Bebe stopped in her tracks. "Let's not do anything stupid, lady. Especially in your weakened state."

"What are the ingredients for Ceci?" I asked sternly.

She looked at me, dark eyes lighting up like fireworks. "Ingredients to make the sword think I'm part of the Queen's bloodline."

"Why the hell would you want that?" I asked, standing, leaving Elizabeth.

"I've waited so long for this." She looked at the sword in her hands like it was made of diamonds.

"Give it back," I demanded, holding out my hand and calling to the sword in my mind. It did not come.

"Guess my little spell worked," Ceci laughed.

"Why are you doing this?" I asked her.

"I thought you were on our side," Macks said.

"I don't think she ever was," Lucinda said with realization.

"What is this?" Hercules said in anger. "After Bryn just defeated Deimos, you're going to co-opt his plan and steal the sword for your own gain?"

"This was never his crusade," Ceci said with a vicious tone. "This whole time he thought I was an ally helping him. But in reality, he was just a tool that I was happy to utilize." Something suddenly made sense. Deimos could create and control his spillers, but how did he have access to monsters? He had a sorceress of animals by his side.

"How could you possibly use a demigod as a tool?" Lucinda asked.

"The thing about men is, they are emotional. They lack the ability to think logically and instead they are prone to act without much thought," she answered. "So I whispered in his ear. Validated all of those fears and hurt feelings he already had, and pointed him in the right direction for his aimless revenge to get me exactly what I needed."

"So, does that mean you've been after the sword all this time, before we even met?" I asked.

"The only reason we met is because I wanted the sword," she said with a wide grin. "Us living in the same building, sending you on an errand so you can hear about the magazine job where you met your Amazon mentor. I gave fate a helping hand. Your little friend having magic was a fun surprise that I used to get even closer to you."

"It was all fake," Macks said softly.

"But why?" I asked, reaching for the sword in one quick and swift motion. Ceci evaded me with ease, spinning like a ballerina.

"Stupid girl! I expected you to figure me out long before now. This world's mythology is full of half truths about our history. It would benefit you to brush up on it. I am Circe, Sorceress of Animalistic Transformation, Queen of Beasts, and future ruler of the Amazons."

Gasps ran through the small audience. I kicked myself for not knowing enough about Greek mythology to figure this out sooner. I felt responsible. Whatever she had planned, was brought on by me and my own lack of preparedness.

"What are you going to do with the sword," I asked glaringly.

"I'm tired of being a second-class citizen when in reality I'm far superior," she grinned. "In this world, men walk all over us. In our society, the gods torment us. All while the Amazons sit on their little island with the power to change the tides but too afraid to use it. With the right leader, the Amazons can take over the world of men and decimate the gods."

"You're going to rage war on the gods?" Karmen asked with shock.

"That's what you people are made for, right?" Circe began to take steps backwards.

"Our people would never follow you," Bebe shot back.

"We'll see about that," she laughed, holding up the sword. "This will give me a lot of power, I just need some of your sisters to recognize the power I now hold. Every storm starts with a few drops of rain." Circe sliced through the air, separating the light and nothingness, ripping a hole in the universe itself. The Amazons gasped behind me. "If I walk through that portal with the sword in my hand, They'll be forced by tradition to recognize me as their leader."

"You crazy bitch," Lucinda said through her teeth.

"Sometimes…that's exactly what you have to be in order to get shit done," Circe said, tilting her head. "The Amazons dedicate their entire identity to a mission laid out for them centuries ago by a god who is no longer around. If I'm crazy for seeing their potential, so be it."

"We won't let you," Hercules said, inching forward.

"She has a divine weapon" I said, grabbing his arm. "We need to be smart about this."

"She's opened a damn portal," Hercules said. "If she walks through there, into the Amazon homeland, with the intention to be Queen, you know what she's going to do, right? She's going to have to take out the person currently on the throne."

"The mommy that abandoned you," Circe said with a fake pout. "That's exactly right. You don't mind, right? It's not like you owe her any loyalty."

"You're twisted," I said, releasing Hercules. We both stepped forward and within seconds Circe was swinging the sword. We ducked away in opposite directions, flanking her. She faced me, while Hercules faced her back. I kicked her in the chest, sending her towards Hercules.

He wrapped an arm around her, pinning her free hand down and grabbed the wrist of her sword wielding hand. "Drop it," he said, shaking her.

She laughed, seemingly unfazed by her capture. "Did you really think I wouldn't have a contingency plan?"

"Doesn't matter," I said, grasping the sword. Her grip wouldn't loosen.

She leaned her head forward so her lips practically grazed my ear. "I was the brains behind Deimos. Remind me, where did your boyfriend get his newest accessory?"

In that very instant, a feeling, like all of the air in my

lungs suddenly became toxic, came over me. Hercules' eyes widened, with pain or surprise, I couldn't tell. The chain around his neck tightened, like a choker rather than a necklace. He released Circe and she pulled the sword from my distracted grip.

I heard the cracking and grinding of bones as Hercules arched his back like he had just taken a blow to the spine. He groaned in pain as his body shifted. Legs snapping to take new shape. Muscles growing, splitting opened his clothes. Eyes changing color to a solid and milky gray. Nose and mouth elongating. Height extending to at least eight feet. Two horns broke through the skin of his forehead, curving inward halfway. Brown fur erupted over every inch of him.

"Oh my god," I gasped.

"Every Queen needs a general," Circe said, proudly looking up at her monstrosity.

"Hercules," I called to him. The beast looked down at me, but I could find no recognition in its soulless eyes. My knees faltered, no longer able to keep me upright. I felt Lucinda grab hold of me, keeping me from falling.

"Your boy toy is gone, only my pet remains," Circe said. "So here's what will happen. I'm going to walk through that gateway to your private island." She pointed with the sword like it was an extension of her finger. "And he's going to come with me. You will stay. I can't have both you and your mommy fighting me for the throne. If you follow these very easy instructions, your boyfriend stays alive. Maybe I'll even turn him back one day. But if you follow me, he dies like this."

I looked at the thing that used to be Hercules, standing there, lowing like an animal. I was desperate to find something, anything, that would show me he was there somewhere. The thought of him, trapped and transformed made me feel ill. I was paralyzed by the mere thought of it.

"The nymph and sorcerex stay too," Circe continued. "But if your Amazon pals want to join the new order, They are welcome." She didn't even wait for a response. She turned to the shimmering tear in the air and began to walk towards it. I couldn't let her get away.

My legs began moving before I even realized I regained feeling in them. I was heading straight toward Circe. I lunged at her, propelling myself in the air. A massive hand caught me by the neck. Rough fur scratched against my skin as the grip tightened. I knew enough about mythology to recognize the creature she had turned Hercules into.

The minotaur pulled me close. It roared, sending foul and steamy mist into my face. I thought it would snap my neck, ending me right there. I focused my strength to collect under the touch of its monstrous hands. As it tightened, my body wouldn't break. It groaned with an annoyance that still came through even on an animalistic face. It wound up its arm and tossed me away. I fell into Macks and Lucinda, sending the three of us tumbling into the grass as a twisted web of limbs.

I looked up, to see Circe looking over her shoulder, silhouetted by the golden light of the portal. "Try not to feel too bad," she said. "The game has been rigged against you from the beginning. It's nothing personal. Sometimes, a girl just has to take control of her destiny, and when things reach that point, it doesn't matter who she crosses along the way."

She stepped into the golden light and it engulfed her like a rising sea. The minotaur looked down at me with a lingering glance. With a huff, it turned and followed, kneeling down before diving into the light and disappearing.

"Bryn," Karmen said, wincing and holding their ribs. "We'll go."

"What?" I asked, struggling to stand with the echoing pain of the day racing through my body.

"She invited us to follow her," Bebe said, going towards the light. "We'll go but instead of joining her, we'll build a resistance on the island. Everyone there has no idea what happened here today, we can't let her go there alone and spin the truth however she sees fit. They won't follow her if they know the full story."

"Let me come with you," I told them, getting to my feet.

"No," Karmen insisted. "If you follow immediately, she'll be on the offensive. Who knows what she'll do. This requires a covert approach."

"Find another way there," Bebe said, "Join us in secret, and then we'll stop her together."

I didn't know how I was supposed to find a way there without the sword. This moment was the only sure-fire way to get there. I didn't want to miss a guaranteed path. But they were right. If I walked through that portal, Circe might kill Hercules. She might destroy countless lives trying to kill me. She might let half the island burn just because I didn't follow her instructions. I didn't know how unhinged she was. All I knew is that she was determined, powerful, and vengeful.

I nodded to them, agreeing reluctantly. "I'll be there. I'll find you."

"We expect nothing less," Bebe said, as she stepped through the light with Karmen by her side. The handful of Amazons that were left followed quickly behind. A small army that would hopefully act as a seed to a mighty resistance to a looming conquest.

The golden light pulsed and fell into itself, shrinking until there was nothing left. Once it was gone, a piercing pain struck my chest.

"Now what?" Macks said, as Lucinda helped them to their feet.

"We go home," I said. "But we don't give up."

Chapter 30

I laid on my couch, head nestled in my mother's lap and face wet with tears. No more tears came though. I had run dry. It felt like my heart was no longer beating. Like it was no longer in my body, and with every breath, I felt the absence more and more.

My mother brushed her fingers through my hair. She was a welcomed addition to everything I was feeling. Her sympathy was like a healing balm on my wound. After the fight, we came back to my apartment and filled in my parents about everything that went down.

"So, you're like an actual superhero," my brother said, leaning over the couch looking at me.

"I don't feel like one right now," I told him. After everything that had happened, keeping the secret from him seemed pointless. He accepted everything with stride. I think hearing it from everyone made it easier to swallow somehow.

"You saved an entire race of people," he shot back immediately. "And now you're going to save the world next."

He wasn't wrong, that was the plan. But I needed a minute to wallow in my grief beforehand.

"The media has already got wind of the bodies in the park," London sniffled. "They are setting up interviews with people in the office. So far, no police have come sniffing around. The story so far is a random tragic massacre that Elizabeth wound up in. The least I could do is keep guiding them in that direction." London, after regaining consciousness, simultaneously mourned her mentor with us and went to work maintaining appearances for the office and public eye.

After Ruthie disassembled her pocket dimension and brought us back to the real world, there were suddenly dozens of bodies sprawled across Prospect Park. We had no idea how to handle it. The few Amazon policewomen Miss Stone had called were thankfully there upon arrival. They told us to leave and they'd do their best, as women on the inside, to craft a cover story and make the rest of the law enforcement believe it.

"Are you sure you don't want to take some time?" Macks asked her. The two of them shared the sofa chair in our living room. "You've been through a lot."

"We all have, but you guys are going to keep on going, right?" London responded. "This is how I pull my weight. And besides…" She looked at me. "You saved me. When the only option was to put me out of my misery, you found another way. I owe you…I owe you everything."

"I was just doing my job," I said. Images of Elizabeth's body flashed in my mind. "I'm glad you're okay."

"What will you do now?" My dad asked. He and Lucinda sat at our dining table, out of view from my current position, drinking cups of Lucinda's homemade tea.

"I don't really know," I said, sitting upright to make eye contact.

"You don't have to know," my mother insisted. Hercules' transformation echoed as if it were happening again right in front of me.

"But the longer I take to figure it out, the more danger everyone is in," I told her.

"That's so badass," my brother commented. My mother immediately warned him about his word choice.

"It's just impossible to know," I explained. "The only known way there is with that sword. It's a divine weapon, literally made from a god. The same god that made the Amazons."

"Well, he's not the only god right?" Macks said softly. "They follow two others, right?"

"Artemis and Athena," Lucinda said, standing up from the table and quickly stepping over to us. "And they both have divine weapons. They're lost, but what if we found them?"

"Would that work?" I asked, afraid of getting too hopeful.

"In theory, they are connected to the Amazon belief system, so their divine weapons might be connected to the sword," she explained. "We spoke to Ruthie after she pulled us back from her pocket dimension. I didn't want to say anything until I knew for sure. The Amazon homeland is a pocket dimension too, and that's her bread and butter. She might be able to use the other weapons as a tether to the sword's physical location."

"And use that connection to crack the doorway open again," Macks added.

"And once it's cracked," I said. "We bust our way through."

"First things first, how do you find two long lost divine weapons?" London asked us.

"I have no idea," I said. My fingers crept up, grabbing hold of the string around my neck, massaging the two silver rings that hung from it. "But we'll figure it out. We have to."

Acknowledgements

Thank you to Caro De Robertis, and my peers from their "Kinship and Community" class, where the seeds that blossomed life into this project were sown through our exploration of Queer literature.

About TreVaughn Malik Roach-Carter

TreVaughn Malik Roach-Carter is a Queer Black writer born in Modesto, California. He holds a MFA in creative writing from San Francisco State University. His work has been featured in Ramblr Magazine, Tayo Magazine's special issue: SOFT, Transfer, BAD EGG Magazine, Borderless, The Ana, Stellium Magazine, and Querencia Press. He is a recipient of the Leo Litwalk Literature Award, a Browning Society Award, and a finalist for the Next Generation Indie Book Awards. He is the author of the Young Adult novel *The Aziza Chronicles: Awakening*, and the autofiction short story collection *Her Daughters*.

Books by TreVaughn Malik Roach-Carter

The Aziza Chronicles: Awakening
Bryn's Virtues: Courage

More From Deep Hearts YA

The Aziza Chronicles: Awakening
TreVaughn Malik Roach-Carter

Discovering her descent from mythological African warriors called the Aziza was just the beginning of Justice Montgomery's troubles. For not only has she been chosen to be their champion against supernatural evils—a demon is on the loose seeking to manipulate her into misusing her newfound powers.

Determined to do what's right and live up to her heritage, Justice trains and forms a band of allies, both human and supernatural. Yet the demon is determined to lead her astray, in the hope that her power might be used to enact an ancient prophecy.

Should she succeed, Justice might become one of the most legendary Aziza to ever live. But should she fail, she might resurrect a goddess of Hell, and doom the world.

More From Dreamsphere Books

Pillars of Cloud
Connor Irving

In the celestial high courts, the Seraphic Council has spoken: It's time for a new era.

The Arcadian Laws have been decreed, a cryptic code of control clamping down on the Alium—the clandestine community of the supernatural.

Lilith, the formidable Queen of Hell, shrouded in demonic legacy, amasses a mighty army. She is led by her four dangerous children: Astaroth, the ruthless, Estrie, the cunning, Loukas, the darkly charming, and Mania, the unpredictable.

As the shadow of war looms, Lilith takes arms to rebel against the celestial shackles imposed upon her and her people. Ancient entities grapple with contemporary chaos, and layers of secrets peel away with every tick of time.

The world shakes with the violence of battle, and one question remains: Would you sell your soul to save your people?